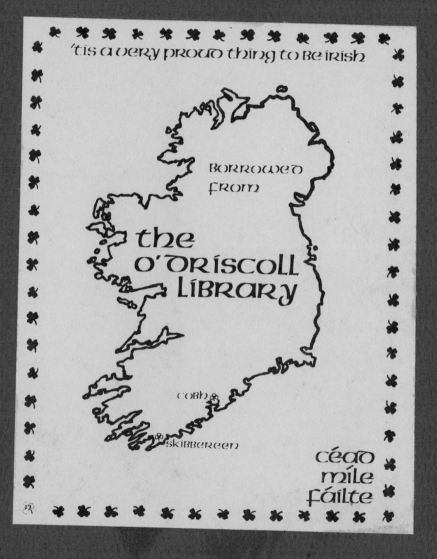

'tis a very proud thing to be irish

BORROWED
FROM

the
O'DRISCOLL
LIBRARY

COBH

SKIBBEREEN

céad
míle
fáilte

The Prisoner's Wife

Also by Jack Holland

Too Long a Sacrifice:
Life and Death in Northern Ireland
Since 1969

The Prisoner's Wife

Jack Holland

DODD, MEAD & COMPANY
New York

Library of Congress Cataloging in Publication Data

Holland, Jack, 1947–
  The prisoner's wife.

  I. Title.
PR6058.04437P7 1981   823'.914   81–3208
ISBN 0–396–07988–1   AACR2

For Mary,
ma compagne

How with this rage shall beauty hold a plea
Whose action is no stronger than a flower?

William Shakespeare

The
Prisoner's
Wife

1

*W*ord spread quickly through the ghetto. Crowds gathered at the corner of Farset Street and Wilson Street, the very heart of the maze of narrow streets and little red-brick houses known as the Falls, the largest working-class Catholic area in Belfast. Women in head scarves with arms folded, swarms of children in orbit around them, teenage boys in bulky black jackets with dirty jeans and heavy boots, teenage girls in long, thick, black skirts and thick platform shoes assembled at the corners or near the top of Wilson Street where Annie Neill lived. They talked and shook their heads; a few older men stood near them looking intently up and down Farset Street. There were no British army patrols in sight, not even the sound of a helicopter. They waited for the Provisional Irish Republican Army's punishment squad to arrive. Annie, twenty years old, married, husband in jail for membership of an illegal organization, waited also, sobbing uncontrollably as she lay on her bed in the front upstairs bedroom of her small house.

It was a windy summer's day, very cool, and the smoke from the chimneys of the houses trailed across the black slate rooftops. A tatter of white clouds blew over the bare green mass of the Divis Mountain that loomed above the jumble of streets, factories and chapels of the Falls. It was an area sealed off from the forces of law and order by the hatred and hostility of the people more securely than by any barricades. Inside the ghetto, the Provisionals administered their own justice, and it was that which the people had gathered to witness.

Those who had broken the law of the ghetto were to be punished by the law of the ghetto. Annie was one. She lay crumpled in her bed crying, her long red hair in a pool spreading its curls over the wet pillow. She heard the chatter of the crowds outside, though she tried not to. Above her bed hung a picture of the Sacred Heart; on the top of her little dresser there was a wedding picture. That was taken two years ago; since her husband's arrest she had been seen with other men, including, it was rumored, a British soldier in a downtown bar. She had been warned. Now there would be no more warnings. She had nowhere to go, no authority to appeal to; this was the Falls, where the only authority was the guerrillas.

Suddenly she noticed the crowd had stopped talking. There was silence. A man had stepped from among the women and children, followed by two teenage girls carrying a large can. The crowd had parted to let them through. The can oozed thick black tar. The man was carrying a piece of cardboard and a string, as well as some rope. The girls left the can at the door and waited as the man went into the little hallway and up the narrow staircase that led off it to the bedrooms. Annie heard the heavy tread on the creaking stairs. She lay still and quiet now. She had stopped crying. As the door of her bedroom jerked open she felt in a moment of panic that she might squeal. But who would hear her? And even if there were British soldiers nearby, she knew it would be better if they did not hear her. There was really no one to help her, nothing to be done.

"Whore!" the man spat at her. "Get up." He took her by the shoulder roughly and pulled her by the blouse. She staggered to her feet, stooping for a second to fix her shoes. Her face was peaked, pale and washed-out with crying. He pushed her through the door and down the dark stairway toward the waiting, silent crowds. The silence of the crowd was more unbearable than their previous chatter, more frightening. As she came to the door, the two teenage girls pulled her roughly; one gripped her around the neck with her arm, jerking her head backward; the other, wrenching two barrettes from Annie's thick red hair, so that all of it fell in a cascade down her back, took a fistful of hair tightly in one hand. She gripped it in a bunch near Annie's scalp and then, with her free hand, pulled out a big pair of steel scissors. The man came down the stairs and walked to the front of Annie to watch. He looked at the blouse stained with sweat under her armpits and the zone of her skin exposed around her waist. The girl squeezed the scissors hard, chopping crudely through the hair, which fell in swathes onto the pavement. The crowd watched quietly. The women, with their arms folded, shook their heads. The children stared. The teenage girls smirked nervously.

They hacked at her hair until it stood on her head like stubble in a wheat field after harvest. Annie hung limply now, half-kneeling. The man said, "Okay." Then he stepped forward with a razor and Annie pulled back. But the two girls pinned her arms behind her back and one put her arms around her naked waist and held her. The man gripped her around the neck with one arm; her head was thrust forward, held tightly in the grip of his arm, and she stopped struggling. He ran the razor over her head in quick, backward sweeps. She winced and groaned as it cut her scalp. One of the women standing near the front of the little circle that the crowd had formed turned away when she heard the edge of the razor scrape the scalp. When he finished, the razor was a mess of matted hair and blood. Annie was sobbing again. He let go of her head and stood back. He nodded in the direction of the lamp post at the top of the street. The two girls forced her to her feet and hustled her to the top of the street. The man came behind them carrying the can and board. One shoe came off and then the other, as she stumbled up the street. They pushed her against the cold green iron post, pinning her arms back. The man tied her hands roughly with the rope; when he let go she slid down the post, around which she used to swing as a little girl. Annie slumped forward, her face bent toward the pavement. The girls lifted the can of tar and poured it over her raw bald skull. The hot viscous substance rolled languidly over her head and face, coating her cheeks, drooping over her eyes like a black curtain. She closed her mouth and tried to hold her breath, but it bubbled in her nostrils, stuck in her mouth around her lips. She coughed, choked, spluttered. The man came up to her and spat on her, then hung the cardboard around her neck. Someone had written on it in a large jagged scrawl: "Whore. Brit Lover." A girl flung a handful of feathers at her in a perfunctory gesture. They blew away down the street.

The crowd watched silently, except for some of the teenage girls who giggled nervously at the sign. After a few minutes they dispersed. The man had vanished suddenly, as had his two teenage accomplices, merging imperceptibly into the watching crowd. The cardboard sign flapped as a strong gust of wind blew down from the bare, bleak slopes of the mountain, visible from the street, where it rose over the roofs and smoking chimneys of the ghetto.

Outside Annie's door the wind swirled her fallen hair, scattering it along the street, until there was nothing left on the pavement where she had been shorn except a few spots of blood and a ring of tar where the can had rested. She hung like a scorched corpse from the lamp post at the top of the street, motionless, dumb, and alone, until a cautious patrol of British soldiers edged its way down Farset Street toward her. They radioed an ambulance, and before long the corner was surrounded by soldiers and the blinking red light of the ambulance came racing down the street. They cut her loose.

Nora Costello saw what was happening from a distance. She was on her way to her old home to pick up some ornaments and kitchenware she'd left behind in a move she and her husband Johnny had recently made to a new house. It was in one of the new working-class developments on the outskirts of the city, built to replace the old Victorian slums like the Falls.

She was tall, dark-haired, and with large, deep, brown eyes that had a surprised, eager look in them, as if always apprehending something new. Her hair was long and hung freely down her back. Dressed in jeans and a T-shirt, she did not look much like other local women, but more like a university student. Yet her face was strong, high cheekboned and handsome in the way characteristic of the women of the area.

She had paused to watch, at first not certain of what was going on —there was always some kind of paramilitary activity in the area. She had asked one of the women standing in her doorway in Farset Street what was happening.

"Annie Neill's gettin' tarred and feathered," she replied. "They say she was running 'round with other men. Some say Brits. I don't know."

"Oh," Nora said, and walked on, rather sickened. She had seen several such scenes since 1969 and the start of the "troubles." A woman who was unfaithful to her husband in the Falls was already an outcast; if her husband was in prison for fighting the British, her unfaithfulness became treasonous. The morality of the Provisionals was the morality of the ghetto, which punished its own savagely, a privilege it would not accord to the state. The guerrillas could justify it by saying they were protecting the morale of their imprisoned members. John had often said as much to Nora. But she found the whole procedure disgusting and disturbing. It repulsed her to see women humiliated so effectively. She glanced to the side as she passed the crowd, noticing how beautiful the woman's thick red hair was. It made her shudder to see it hacked off.

She tried to dismiss the scene from her mind, but she thought about it on her way back to her new home. It was a war situation; brutalities were inevitable. After all, men were being killed for their beliefs and the British were the enemy. They were committing far worse atrocities.

Her home was at the top of a steep street that seemed to run to the very slopes of the nearby mountains. She was carrying a bag laden with odds and ends for her new house and felt rather tired, reluctant to face the climb. She looked up ahead of her. There were soldiers everywhere. A convoy of army jeeps along with a saracen was parked at the top of the street near her house. As she drew closer she saw her garden was swarming with soldiers. Two stood at the gate. Others were lining the street, watchful.

It was a raid. The Costellos had been raided before. The British army and police suspected her husband Johnny of being a leading member of the Belfast guerrillas. So far he had eluded them. Nora walked slowly up the street. Some of her neighbors came to the door. She felt this time there was something seriously wrong, that it was not just another raid.

One of the women came to her gate as Nora passed. She leaned over and said in a low voice, "Johnny's been arrested, love."

Nora did not stop, but glancing at her briefly, walked straight to her own house. Two soldiers barred her way.

"This is my house," she snapped at the soldier who told her to halt. His rifle was held across his chest, and when she tried to get past him he thrust it out, pushing her backward. The sergeant came to her door, which had obviously been busted open.

"Easy on, there, Blackwell," he shouted to the soldier. "Let the little lady in." Such rough tactics could provoke a riot.

The soldier stood aside. Nora walked up the steps to her front door.

"Where's Johnny?"

" 'E's where 'e belongs," the sergeant said. He was a stocky, middle-aged man.

"Is he hurt?"

"I knows not, nor cares," the sergeant replied, ushering her into the hallway. Two soldiers were lifting up her carpet. Others were yanking open the drawers in the kitchen. The oven doors were wide open and the racks lying on the kitchen floor. The cabinets in the front room had been gutted and their contents strewn everywhere. Nora looked around her in a kind of dream. No one spoke to her. She could hear the heavy tread of boots in the bedrooms above. A soldier came down the stairs with her wedding picture under his arm.

"Give me that," she scowled at him.

The sergeant came over and said, "Sorry, luv, we need it for identification." He nodded to the soldier, who threw the picture in a cardboard box that she hadn't noticed before. She looked in the box; it was full of newspapers and pictures; there was a plastic bag full of sheets.

Nora pulled at the sheets. Again the sergeant intervened.

"Testing," he said. "You never know what rubs off on the old sheet, do you, darling?" he sneered. "Maybe a touch of lead or—who knows what, eh? Now just you sit down and relax."

Nora sat down on the bottom step of the staircase, pale, angry, but almost numb with anxiety. The sergeant ignored her questions about John.

Suddenly, there was someone standing behind her on the stairs.

"Johnny's in trouble . . . ," a voice said rather hesitatingly with a strong Belfast accent.

"He's not hurt?" she replied anxiously, turning and looking up. A short, stocky man wearing a cloth cap was above her on the stairs near the landing. Detective Constable Roger Mackal of the Criminal Investigation Department had earlier that day arrested and charged her husband after a bank robbery. He had spent the last few minutes searching the upstairs rooms of the house: there was a question of missing money—some fifty thousand pounds or so. But all Mackal found were clothes and art books from Nora Costello's student days.

"He's in one piece, Missus Costello, but no thanks to himself." He came down the stairs and sat down near her.

"I'm sorry about all this," he said quietly, "but your husband was caught robbing a bank. A couple of his friends got away. Now it would help if you could . . . ," he hesitated, "if you could give us any—"

"I don't know anything!" she snapped. Mackal regarded the young woman sadly, but with resignation. It was the reaction he'd grown to expect. He stood up and took a form out of his pocket. It had marked on it all the items that were carted away for tests, to help the investigation. He asked her to sign it. But Nora didn't hear him.

Though she had prepared herself for this since the very beginning, it all seemed unreal to her. She looked over to the bag of ornaments and kitchenware she'd carried back with her from her old home. It was standing by the broken door.

"Anything you know and you want to tell us would look good, Missus Costello," the detective said routinely, without conviction. But Nora just shook her head scornfully.

A soldier outside shouted, "Sarge, there's a crowd coming up the street." The sergeant called to the men in the house to get ready to go. He picked up the box of her possessions and left.

"You'll get these back later, but first I must ask you to come along to the station."

Nora was told later that night that her husband, Johnny Costello, one of the most wanted Provisional IRA men in the city, was to be charged with attempted murder, robbery, illegal possession of a dangerous weapon with intent to cause serious injury, membership in an illegal organization and much else. He would probably be in jail for the rest of his life.

2

*t*he burnt skeleton of a bus lay on the roadway in the bright sunshine of an August morning like the remains of some prehistoric beast surrounded by the black pools of its own strange blood. Nora Costello, looking overdressed for that time of day in her narrow slit skirt and high platform shoes, glanced at it casually as she hurried by. It was a victim of last night's riots, which had left the Falls Road covered with broken bricks, smashed bottles and torn-up chunks of paving stone. The long twilights of the summer evenings were a favorite time for rioting in the ghetto; schools were closed, the weather was fair and the presence of British troops on the streets always provocative. Though the guerrillas were on ceasefire with the army, the children and the youths were generally uncontrollable and continued to attack state authority, as had been their custom for the last six years of "troubles." Nora had seen the aftermath of too many such confrontations to pay much attention to the desolation through which she made her way.

Two streets ahead of her stood the little cluster of women and children she was going to join. They were waiting for the early morning trip to Long Kesh Prison Camp to visit their imprisoned husbands, fathers, sons and brothers—members of the Provisional Irish Republican Army. The political wing of the IRA, Sinn Fein, laid on a minibus that regularly took the relatives to the camp.

The women and children were waiting outside an old pub that had been converted by Sinn Fein into a political office, apparently with the agreement of the British as part of the truce deal. Its walls were plastered with posters; new ones proclaimed: "TRUST US—IGNORE RUMORS. WE WON'T BETRAY YOU!" They were papered over some older posters and had already begun to peel off, revealing one which read: "1974—YEAR OF VICTORY." It was tattered and torn and a year out of date, put up when the building still housed a bar. Another poster showed the grotesquely swollen and bloodied face of an IRA prisoner in Long Kesh, his eyes reduced to narrow slits of puffed red skin. The slogan read: "REMEMBER THIS: END THE TORTURE NOW!" As Nora walked toward the little group she met the gaze of the distorted face; it was familiar to her, having appeared on nearly every gable wall in the Catholic areas of Belfast. But now they were being covered with the new "Trust Us" posters.

She'd heard rumors about ceasefire negotiations going on behind closed doors; it was not the first time the guerrillas had come to such arrangements with the British. Three years before, in 1972, a truce between them lasted for nearly a month; shortly after it collapsed her husband Johnny was arrested. She hoped that this time it would be more permanent, for if it was there was a chance that there might be an amnesty.

The other women turned toward her and a few nodded as she approached. Nora's husband was a local legend, already part of the folklore of the Falls, which, though it had no generals, presidents or prime ministers to celebrate, had found the stuff of mythology among its bankrobbers, gunmen, guerrilla leaders and bomb experts—of which it had plenty. Johnny Costello, reputed to be the leader of the notorious "moneybags" battalion of the IRA—the one that supplied the funds that bought the guns—had gone out with guns blazing, captured during a bank robbery, but only after he held off the security forces long enough for two of the gang to escape. It was said they got away with the money, though one of the escapees was killed shortly afterward at an army road check. No trace of the money was ever found. So Nora Costello was a hero's wife and something of a symbol. It was a role she was unhappy playing. The three years of her husband's absence had taken their toll; she was always straining under tension, her walk was rigid, her shoulders sloped forward in an almost self-conscious way that made her bosom seem sunken and hidden, and her face was drawn.

Only her deep brown eyes had not lost their softness, nor her thick dark hair its sheen.

She said hello to the women whom she saw, whom she had seen for the last three years or more, waiting one morning of every week in sunlight or in the dark mornings of wet winter drizzle, or in the fogs of autumn. They were always there with their children, whom she watched grow over the years.

At eight o'clock in the morning Nora did not feel like the wife of a legend, merely winded, tired, still sleepy and a bit self-conscious about her clothes. The other women, most of them in their late thirties, were normally dressed, in loose synthetic knit slacks; they had head scarves, and their children clung to them or leaned against them still half-asleep. But Nora always dressed up. Johnny liked to see her looking good. The other women seemed to have given up on their appearance; they had stopped trying to be wives for their imprisoned husbands and reverted to the role they felt happier in—that of mother, provider, soother, supporter. But Nora Costello was different. Though anxious and often depressed, she was glad to dress up—even if she didn't particularly like her husband's taste in women's clothes—to look desirable, though the man who desired her was inaccessible. To feel that he desired her was something—she tried to convince herself it was enough. It wasn't, but it was all she had, and the strain was beginning to tell in her walk, her posture, her face.

The minibus had not yet arrived. She rested against the wall of the old pub and placed the brown paper package she was carrying down at her feet. Each woman had one, marked with the name and compound of the man it was going to. As political prisoners, IRA members were allowed one such parcel a week. They were surrendered to the wardens, inspected and then distributed. This week Johnny had asked for some short pieces of wood and some screws and string; he was making a model harp as a present.

Apart from nodding and saying hello Nora did not communicate with the others. She did not feel up to it. As the years went by she tried increasingly to distance herself from her weekly routine journey to the huge prison camp. And that led to a certain isolation, for the camp dominated the lives of everyone in that little group and the lives of countless others in Belfast. It loomed over them, the children, the mothers, the wives, the sisters, as surely as it did over the prisoners themselves.

She was waiting there five minutes before Sean McGreary, a big, bulky ex-bricklayer, pulled the van up at the corner. He stuck his head, round and covered in short, stubbly ginger hair, out of the window and shouted, "Okay, ladies, pile in." There was a moment of chaos as the children broke loose, scrambling in through the door on the side of the van, eager to get a window seat. The women, whose lives were spent trying to keep order in the mayhem of over-crowding, followed behind them carrying the parcels and began to sort out their offspring and arrange seating. A few rambunctious boys got swatted, but the children, though rough and rowdy and contemptuous of the authority of the state, still showed ingrained respect for family elders and obeyed. Nora came last, as usual, and took off her platform shoes before she got in to make it easier to navigate the narrow aisle from the door to the back seat where she sat. It was a wobbly stool placed near the rear door, which was broken so never opened. When she had adjusted herself McGreary warned everyone to hold tight and started up the motor. The van moved off.

She was wobbly for the first few seconds before readjusting her stool. Then she settled down, leaning against the window at her right, and gazed outside. The minibus sped along the Falls Road, avoiding litter from the last riot with an ease that came from much practice. The Falls—which means *hedgerows* in Irish—runs south out of Belfast toward the motorway. The present road follows roughly an old route that dated from Elizabethan times, used by the native Irish to get to the hills and away from the English colonists, then ensconced behind a wall protecting the early settlement of Belfast. Elizabethan law did not permit the natives to enter the city; they did their trading outside the gates, and gradually over the years an Irish settlement grew up there around the spine of the Falls. Nineteen seventy-five found the natives —now working-class Catholics—still gathered in the Victorian slum sandwiched between the chapels and mills, outside the tight ring of security gates thrown up around the center of Belfast by the British. The Irish did not carry spears but gelignite bombs and armalite rifles and AK-47s. And they looked at the security gates with the same hostility as their long-haired ancestors regarded the walls of the colonists.

After about a mile the minibus left the road where it turned off west to the mountains and headed onto the motorway. From there it was a clean, swift run for about ten miles before they would leave it for the back roads and laneways that would lead them circuitously to the camp. Nora watched the bare green slopes of the Divis and Black mountains to the west getting farther away as the minibus went south toward the low, rolling drumlin hills of County Down—Protestant land: good, thick soil, sheltered, subdued landscape. She always found it relaxing. The scramble of new housing developments where many Catholics now lived and where she herself had a home was getting smaller in the distance, until it looked like a red rash on the green skin of the mountains. The minibus turned off the motorway and into the back lanes between the hedgerows thick with summer blossoms. The windows were beginning to fog up with breath. The bus was full of smoke. The women were talking with an intensity felt only by people who have never experienced leisure. The lush suburbs of south Belfast merged imperceptibly into the quiet hills. The talk in the van soon turned to death. There had been a body found that morning on the outskirts of the Falls area. It was of a man shot once in the head slumped in the front seat of a car parked near a lonely crossroads. The women were speculating as usual as to who he was, how he died and why.

"Tout," said the driver authoritatively. "Tout" was the local word for an informer—the most despised being in the ghetto. "That area's full of touts." The women shook their heads and clacked their tongues. "Shooting's too good for the likes," he said with disgust.

"Still, Sean," one woman piped up above the noise of the motor, "he was some mother's son." The women all nodded.

"Right enough, Eileen, right enough. It's terrible times we live in," another added. They were full of tenderness for the dead man and fell silent for a moment. Brutality accompanied their daily lives, and perhaps as a result the women had a poignant awareness of the fragility and vulnerability of life, saddening them. Only the very hardest of them would withhold sympathy from even the enemy, a young soldier shot dead on their street, or an informer "executed" and dumped on a wasteground.

When Nora heard the conversation turn to speculation about the status of the current ceasefire, she became attentive. McGreary led off, stating confidently that there were big moves going on behind closed doors. He liked to give the impression he was in the know—and he might have been, for the Provisionals were a Byzantine organization, complicated, devious, mysterious—so the women listened.

"The Brits are going to pull out—it's in the cards," he explained.

"Will they open the Kesh?" someone asked.

"Sure, that's part of the deal. The internees will get out before

Christmas and there'll be a general amnesty for the sentenced prisoners. The plans are being worked out."

One of the women said the British government was denying it was
talking to the guerrillas, but Sean dismissed it with a knowing smile.
Nora had heard such talk before, all the women had; it was part of their
common existence, always full of rumors of great changes, changes that
generally didn't come. The prisoners were the same; every week there
was another spate of stories about what the British were going to do.
It kept the prisoners and their loved ones going, from week to week,
year to year. It wore Nora down to a nervous tatter. Her life had
become a series of expectations never fulfilled. The other women gener-
ated their own expectations among themselves. Five minutes or so after
McGreary had made his remarks they had almost convinced themselves that their men would all be out by Christmas. But when the
minibus came within sight of Long Kesh, looming suddenly over the
hedgerows, its high watchtowers seemingly stalking them like ugly stick
insects, they became quiet. One of the little girls burst into tears, as
she did every visit when they came in sight of the camp. Her mother
hushed her. "You're going to see your da," she whispered into the
child's ear. The little girl continued to sob. The women had stopped
talking about the imminent release of their men and just looked with
resignation out the windows at the mass of wire, the watchtowers, the
huge gates, which were getting closer. Nora, too, became depressed at
this point, depressed at how permanent the place looked. One of the
children near the front banged his head against the window as the
minibus made a sharp turn. A little girl fell backward off balance and
scraped her hand on the tattered seat, bumping her baby sister as she
did so. There was a chorus of wails. "Who's riding shotgun, Sean?" one
of the women shouted in the midst of the pandemonium as the vehicle
lurched around a tight corner with the instability of an old stagecoach
on a dirt road. The crying broke the tension as the bus rode over the
yellow ramp with a bump and came to a halt at the first gate.

Nora put on her shoes, adjusted her tights, checked her face in her
pocket mirror; her eyes seemed tired and shallow, as if she had been
crying a lot. Hastily she fumbled for a little eye shadow. When finished,
she snapped the pocket mirror shut, picked up her parcel and made her
way gingerly down the aisle to the exit, where Sean waited for her,
holding out his hand. The others were already lined up waiting to begin
the long security procedure that had to be gone through before getting
into the visiting area. The women were all chatting again, nervously,

and the children were staring bemusedly at the wire fence in front of them and the high watchtowers behind it. They too were nervous and baffled by it all. Nora took her place in the line.

Half an hour later, the multiple searches and checks at an end, she sat in one of the little wooden cubicles where the visits took place. Her knees were squeezed under the mean little table that squatted between her and where her husband would be sitting—a final, petty, absurdly small barrier between them, which she hated almost more than the walls and watchtowers.

There were rows of cubicles on both sides of the big Nissen hut reserved for the visitors. Already most of them were occupied by waiting women and children. The prisoners had to come from some distance away, traveling in prison vans from the compounds where they were held. Long Kesh resembled a prisoner-of-war camp more than it did a conventional prison, the men being kept in long corrugated iron huts grouped in compounds. Johnny Costello was in Compound 5. Nora sat with her back to the cubicle entrance, listening to the nervous noise of children behind her. They had reached a pitch now and were hard to control. The early rise, the jarring journey, the cramped bus, the tension of the camp, all began to tell on the children and on the women who tried to keep them in at least a loose orbit around them until male authority could arrive and calm things.

Nora thought she might do her face up a little bit and instinctively reached down under the table for her bag; there was nothing there. She remembered, of course, all bags, purses, pens, makeup utensils, anything loose in one's pocket, however innocuous it seemed, was taken from the visitors before they were allowed to enter the precincts of the camp. After three years she still forgot that!

A warder came in through the prisoners' entrance and called out, "Costello, cubicle twelve." Nora sat upright, listening for the sound of her husband's approach. He walked with a sort of shuffle common to Belfast men. She turned in his direction, then back to the wall. Her back was to him when he arrived. "Nora," he said quietly. She looked round. His dark curly beard grew more luxuriant every week. His blue eyes gleamed intensely under heavy black eyebrows. He smiled, his red fresh lips curling; he had a direct, piercing look that revealed a man of little doubt. His teeth betrayed his working-class origins—they were yellowing, soft, not well cared for, with gaps in them. He approached her and sat in the chair on the opposite side of the little table. The warder who was standing behind them walked off to the top of the hut, where he got back on the high platform enabling him to oversee the prisoners and their visitors. Johnny always surprised her by how well he looked. He hadn't allowed the carbohydrate-based diet of the camp to make him fat; he exercised every day, played sports actively, so his body had lost none of its compact firmness. He was broad-shouldered, taut, physically alert.

This morning he seemed preoccupied.

"What are they saying outside?" he asked. "The rumors in here would drive you mad."

"You know more than I do, Johnny."

He leaned toward her in an impatient gesture. "For god's sake, woman, what are you doing all week?" he replied brusquely. It upset Nora. She'd imagined the ceasefire negotiations would have put him in a good mood.

"You know I don't hang around with those people, John. I don't get to hear much in the bookstore."

He sighed and sat back in the chair. He looked at her. "What's the mood like these days in the Falls?"

"Confused. Nobody knows what's going on, what with all this ceasefire talk . . . . Everybody's hoping for an amnesty." Nora looked at him and smiled, searching for a hopeful response that would bolster her own expectations. But he seemed lost in thought. Finally she asked him if he was feeling okay. He shook his head indifferently. The prison officer passed them. Johnny followed him with a contemptuous look, then leaned again toward his wife. He rested his elbows on the table and smiled a full, rich smile that reassured her. She reached across to kiss him.

"Seamus is back," he whispered, his lips flicking over her cheek. "Tell him . . . ," but he stopped and kissed her hard on the neck. A prison officer looked down at him.

"Okay, Costello, this is not a love nest, you know," he said harshly. "No nibbling."

Johnny grinned up at the officer who proceeded on his round. "Nosey fuckin' bastards," he muttered.

Seamus must have been Seamus Devine, Nora thought, a member of her husband's unit in the IRA. It was believed he was the member of the gang who escaped during the bank raid, presumably with the money. He'd been on the run since then in the Irish Republic. She wasn't surprised that he had returned; part of the truce arrangements allowed wanted men to come back into Northern Ireland again without fear of arrest.

"Is the house being watched?" he asked her when the officer had gone.

"We haven't been raided in a long time."

Johnny leaned closer to her again. "Find Seamus. Tell him 'the Monk's Stone,' " he said in a precise, portentous undertone as he turned to see that the guard had noticed nothing.

Nora looked at him puzzled. She had hoped by now the perpetual conspiracies of the IRA would be at an end. But she knew better than to press John for more. Words were dangerous and had to be used sparingly. She felt the visit was an anticlimax. She was dispirited and smiled weakly when he complimented her on how good she looked. She'd hoped to hear more of the truce—Johnny was still a key man in the IRA within the prison. But he brushed off further reference to it.

He seemed more relaxed now that he'd gotten his message across and began to talk about his prison activities. His Irish classes—he was learning the language—were coming along fine. He was reading a lot of Irish history and keeping busy making models. As one of the top IRA men in the prison, he also spent a lot of time sorting out the organization's problems with the prison administration. When he enthused about what he was doing, his wife felt oddly envious—he led so active a life.

"How's the house?" he asked.

"It'll need patching up for the winter. There's a lot to be done this year," she replied wearily. "It would be nice if this Christmas . . . ," but she paused, not wanting to bring up the subject of amnesty or the talk of early releases again.

Johnny looked at her with a hint of impatience.

"Is that all you can think about? You women! Did you hear about wee Mackie in Hut 6?"

Nora shook her head. She'd never heard of Mackie.

"Billy McIlroy," John explained. "His wife did the dirty on him," he said curtly. "He's bad—cut up about it. I suppose she just couldn't wait . . ."

Nora remained impassive, barely listening as he talked on. Once rumors about wives started circulating inside, it was hard to stop them —fact became sordid fantasy overnight. The men became obsessed. Everything was exaggerated—rumors, feelings, tensions, desires. They searched scrupulously for the slightest hints as to what was going on, what their wives and girlfriends were thinking and doing outside. She became restless.

"What's the matter?" he asked.

"You don't believe all that about her, do you?"

He didn't answer. She wanted to get away from the pressure of the prison, the obsessions. He stared sullenly at the floor.

Sometimes he looked like a dark little demon, a stranger to women. He always seemed aloof from them, and the existence of the prison walls between him and his wife only emphasized his separateness. Nora became aware of that aloofness only after they married. Before, their sexual encounters on street corners, at the gates of the mills and in the back alleyways were fierce. When married, in their own bed, Johnny shrank from her; he lay self-consciously in the big bed as if it were a foreign country where he was a stranger. On their first night together after their marriage he didn't even take his trousers off, but merely unzipped as if he were still in a back alleyway. The years in prison, the long separation, increased his feeling of strangeness with her. Sometimes she noticed him regarding her with a baffled, almost exasperated look on his face. She belonged to another world—the world of women, the outside world, so different from his that he resented it and resented her at times for being part of it.

Nora changed the subject and talked again about her house, the new houses going up on the other side of the street, the mess the builders made, how it was so mucky going to work in the morning that she had to bring an extra pair of shoes and so on until she saw he was quite bored. He almost looked as if he wanted the visit to end, as though the last five minutes were becoming uncomfortably long and he was beginning to miss his hut and friends. But she saw there was still something on his mind. He was obviously brooding.

"You heard the news about Spider?" he said suddenly, interrupting her.

She said no.

"The tout—dead. This morning's news."

Nora remembered the gossip on the bus coming out about the body found on the outskirts of the city.

"Oh—there was a lot of talk about it on the bus."

"That cheered the lads up." He smiled at her, but Nora showed no signs of sympathizing with him.

"You don't seem interested in anything," he said abruptly. "Don't you talk to anybody out there about things?"

"Not those things. Johnny, you know me by now." She sighed and looked appealingly at him. "I'm sorry. Murder always makes me sick."

"It's not murder to kill a tout. It's—"

"I don't want to argue about it. I didn't come here to talk about killing and corpses." The thought of the dead body slumped in the car made her shudder. She was saddened, disappointed, let down by the visit.

Their eyes met. "You seem tired," he said to her, as if noticing her for the first time. The dark demon changed for a moment into the warm, physical man she had loved for six years or more. He reached out his hands and took hers in a confident grip. Action came so easily to him, without self-consciousness. He squeezed her hands and she bent over the table—that hateful little obstacle all the more despicable because it was so small—and Johnny saw her blouse crinkled around her small, plump breasts. He smelled her, breathing in deeply, smelling her neck and white small throat; he glanced down at her lap where her dark, tight skirt hugged her thighs. She was the thing upon which he acted, and only then was she accessible to him or even interesting. Now action was impossible for him, except for the occasional furtive touch or squeeze; and Nora, deprived of that contact, was withering.

The warder called a halt. They had been getting too close. At any rate, their time was up. He announced the visits at an end. Nora sat back in her chair. She felt so heavy beneath her hips, heavy and sluggish, and unable to face the long journey back to the Falls, her empty bed. She had to go to work this afternoon at the bookshop where she'd had a job for the last few years. It was all part of the whole weary routine. Yet there was no alternative. She went blank for a moment, not wanting to move, not wanting to stay.

"Maybe they're right this time," she said to him as she dragged herself up off the seat. "Maybe the talks will come to something. Maybe it will end." But his eyes betrayed nothing. They chilled her. As he bent over to kiss her he whispered, "Remember what I told you. It's important."

"Come on, Costello, cut out the long farewells. Say good-bye till next time. Let the little lady go home," said one of the prison officers who appeared at their cubicle. Nora looked at the contemptible little man in the uniform who ordered them about. He was Scottish, with a thick Glasgow accent, one of those whom the British brought over especially for prison duty, for which they were paid extra money. The women hated them as mercenaries paid to hold their men, to keep them apart. The prison officers gloated over their power. This one was an ugly little gutter rat with wax-white wrinkled skin. He took Johnny by the elbow and led him away. Johnny looked over his shoulder at his wife walking toward the visitors' exit. The swaying motion of her hips, emphasized by her clothes, baffled him again with muddled feelings of desire, anger, longing, resentment: she belonged to the world outside, to which she was returning. The prison officer sneered, "Give your dirty mind a rest, lad. Let's go." Johnny ignored him and passed through the exit.

Outside, Nora heaved a sigh of relief. She leaned against the still-empty minibus in the car park and turned her face up toward the sky as a sun shower burst overhead. The light raindrops fell refreshingly on her face; she didn't run for shelter. The white clouds were scudding over the blue sky, thickening around where the sun was and temporarily obscuring it. It was a fresh day and her spirits revived. She would be away from this place for another week—outside of it if not free of it. Soon the others returned and she was on the unsteady stool in the bus speeding back to Belfast.

When they pulled up outside the IRA's political offices it was after midday. McGreary took her hand as she got out. "Easy, love," he said affectionately. He had a big, burly, masculine warmth, and Nora felt his pudgy fingers with a kind of vestigial response. He was much taller than she was even in her platform shoes. She straightened herself up beside him and said thanks.

"You couldna been too cozy back there," he nodded in the direction of the stool.

"No, it gets rough, Sean. Like a stagecoach," she replied, smiling up at him. Sometimes she felt the greatest admiration for even the clumsiest, stupidest of men—it was an admiration of their physical presence, not really desire. It could lead to desire, of course, at times.

They were standing near the door to the old pub. She heard someone call her from within. It was too dark inside for her to see clearly. She went into the building and saw Peter O'Neill standing behind what used to be the bar counter, but was now covered with ornaments that had been made in Long Kesh by the prisoners and piles of papers and propaganda leaflets. O'Neill was one of the leading figures in the political organization. He was a small dapper little man with a trim black beard and wide eyes. He always dressed well and carried a rolled umbrella, something of an affectation in the area. He reminded Nora of a salesman.

"Nora, how's Johnny keepin'. Good, I hope?"

"Yes, Peter, thank you; he looks great. He's in good spirits."

Behind him on the wall were posters picturing gaunt young men with unshaven, pale faces peering from behind thick, black steel bars. The slogans proclaimed: "AMNESTY FOR ALL" and "CLOSE IRE-LAND'S GULAG."

"Johnny's a great morale booster for the boys," O'Neill said to her. He referred to the boys—the guerrillas—as if he were one of them. But he wasn't; he was just a spokesman. He liked to imply that he was intimate with the gunmen, but it was only a sort of voyeurism that was found among a few of those who associated with violent men without taking part in the violence itself. He was arrested once, but freed after a few hours. In the hierarchy he was on a pretty low rung, being too far from the real business of the organization—which had to do with guns and bombs—for anyone but the naive and foreign reporters to take very seriously. He was never there when the trigger was pulled, so what did he know? Nora talked with him perfunctorily. He assured her in a half-whisper that the talks were making progress and would lead to big developments. Nora looked down at the counter full of harps and lamps made from lollipop sticks and imitation submachine guns carved patiently from single pieces of wood by prisoners over years of incarceration and felt a kind of despair welling up in her again.

"I hope you're right," she said to him, and turned to leave.

"Why don't you come up to the Social Club sometime? Jack Fagan's always asking for you," he called as she walked out.

"I might."

Fagan was the top man in Belfast now and ran the IRA's big drinking club. He made a fuss of her any time she went to it. He had been a friend of her husband.

As Nora left McGreary came in. "Nice bit of stuff," he said to O'Neill, dropping the keys to the minibus on the counter.

"You can say that again. Poor Johnny—seeing that every week and not being able to touch it."

"I'd touch it if she gave me half a chance," the driver grunted.

"You'd lose your kneecaps, so you would," smirked O'Neill. "The boys wouldn't like that."

"It might be worth it though," McGreary smiled, as the image of Mrs. Costello ran through his head.

"You wouldn't think that when Johnny got out. It'd be a hole in the head for you, son."

"When Johnny got out? When's that, 1995?"

"You never know; he might be out by the end of the year."

"That's what I said to the oul ones this morning on the way out.

If so, she'd better hold on to her knickers, for when he gets home she'll have a sore arse."

"Is that all you think about," O'Neill asked with a sneer on his face, "your fuckin' hole?"

McGreary leaned nonchalantly on the counter. "What about it? Comin' for a drink?"

Nora reached home depressed and tired. She was hoping to have heard something positive from Johnny and had heard nothing. Everyone else's talk of amnesty meant nothing to her. She wanted to hear it from him.

She shared the house with her younger sister Patricia, who worked as a nurse in a nearby hospital. By the telephone in the hallway there was a letter. It was from her old friend Kate Hughes, a teacher living near London. They had been very close as teenagers. Kate had gone to university in England before 1969 and ever since they'd been writing to each other. It was always a relief to get news of the outside world. Kate led something of a Bohemian existence and kept up a constant barrage of invitations to Nora to come over for a holiday and stay with her. Nora toyed with the idea often, especially at times when she was depressed. But something always came up to stop her.

The letter was full of Kate's usual ebullience. Her boyfriend was back again after a temporary split. She was for a while in love with a drummer in some local rock group, but that had fallen through. She was going back to college night classes to take an M.A. The weather was great and they were just off to the local seaside resort, Clacton-on-Sea. When was Nora going to give up on Belfast and live? Then there was a P.S. "I got a letter from Michael Boyd in New York. Remember? He asked for your address or number. Said he was on his way back to Belfast to write a book or something—?—Will call on you soon!"

Nora went into the living room and put the letter on the mantelpiece above the fire. Of course she remembered Michael; Kate was teasing her. Michael and she had also been close friends. He was an awkward, inhibited and rather morose youth when she knew him. They had had an intense adolescent relationship, but nothing had ever come of it. He left for England when she was about sixteen. Nora had heard scraps about him since. He'd gone to university like Kate. Then she heard he was a journalist somewhere. But Nora hadn't paid much attention—her life was on an entirely different course by then.

She sat down for a minute and shook her head in wonderment:

Michael Boyd a journalist in New York! What next? She tried to picture what he looked like. She remembered a tall, stooping figure with a sharp face, a rather sarcastic smile. In those days so much had seemed possible for her; she would graduate from art college, go to London or Paris and study for her research degree or become a teacher at a fancy art school. Nora used to share so many of her aspirations with Michael in those days—days which seemed to have passed in a different world from the one she now lived in. At least Kate and Michael had come closer to realizing some of their adolescent dreams, had made the break with Belfast, led different lives.

She went into the cold little kitchen just off the hallway and opened a tin of stew for her lunch. After dumping it into a pan and lighting the gas she made her way up the stairs to her bedroom to change into her shop dress. The new houses were bigger than the ones she had grown up in as a child; they had the luxury of an indoor toilet, a bathroom, three fairly large bedrooms. But, unlike the older working-class homes of the Falls, they had been hastily built and even more hastily occupied, often by squatters. Because of the "troubles," Catholics from outlying areas had swarmed into the relative safety of the west Belfast ghetto escaping the sectarian attacks of Protestants. As a result houses became scarce, the government lost control of allocation, and people simply took them over as soon as they became inhabitable. Johnny and Nora had squatted in this house in early 1971, just after their marriage. It had never been completed. Johnny's arrest stalled their plans for finishing it up and Nora quickly lost interest in making it a real "home." The windows were not properly fixed; the walls were still only plaster. Draughts blew through the house with every gust of wind from the nearby mountains. They had the last house at the top of the ramshackle street, still puckered with potholes like a First World War battlefield. The Black Mountain seemed near enough for them to reach out and touch. In winter the squalls came whistling over the bleak slopes, shaking the house like the wind in the rigging of a sailing ship. It squeaked and rattled. Nora hated the place; she preferred the older city slums, which, though they lacked amenities, were at least snug.

Her bedroom looked out over the back garden, a weed-infested lot that turned into a quagmire in winter. Because the development, known as the Black Mountain Estate, was so high up, she had an overview of the city. On a good day she could see from her bedroom window as far as the round domes of the Mourne Mountains fifty miles away. They broke over the low waves of the Down hills like the great round backs of whales. Her bedroom was cold, as if it hadn't been used in days. She had a little dressing table built into an alcove in the wall facing her bed. On top of it rested a picture of John, beardless, shortly after they married. The walls were bare except for a print of a Constable painting. He was her favorite painter; when an art student she had come to love his work. Her print showed a lush green English scene, a plough team resting at midday by a small lake. Often she would turn to it to refresh her thoughts, to give her eyes some relief from the bleak, wild Irish countryside around her that seemed sometimes to be so uncivilized and inhospitable. The English landscape is a landscape shaped by the Middle Ages, dense with settled life. But in Ireland feudal civilization never took root; this, along with the barbarities of colonialization, has produced an often desolate landscape. Even near the big industrial cities like Belfast, one has only to lift one's eyes above the level of the street to see the bare hills beyond with their lonely scattering of farms.

Nora stood in front of her husband's photograph and groped around her back for her zipper. She gave it a hard tug, holding in her breath, as the skirt was a tight fit. His face beamed at her; his fleshy, moist mouth was drawn back in an unselfconscious smile. She wriggled out of her skirt, which fell in a soft heap at her feet. For a second she stood there breathing slowly, his eyes fixed on her. Her body beneath her hips felt sluggish and heavy again. She went taut, almost too tense to move. She put one hand over the thick dark matted hair, just visible through her underwear. Her head dropped and she went backward awkwardly on the edge of the bed and started to sob. The ache she felt was too much to bear.

His vivid mouth smiled at her as it had when they first met. He had come into her life quite unexpectedly in the summer of 1969 in the midst of the great upheavals that led to the present war. The Catholic civil rights marches had ended in sectarian rioting as angry Protestants, provoked by the Catholics' demands for equal housing and job opportunity, attacked the protesters. The rioting soon spread to the area of the Falls that abutted a big Protestant ghetto. Mobs of brand-waving Protestants stormed into the streets adjoining the two areas, forcing the Catholics to seek safety in the Falls. They fled as their homes went up in flames behind them. Mill Street, where Nora lived, was in a panic; many people were packing to leave. The police, mostly Protestant, were said to have joined the angry mobs and the Catholics were without protection—almost.

The old forces of the Irish Republican Army, then fractured and in disarray from years of factionalizing over political principles, suddenly rallied, thanks to young men like Johnny Costello. A few of them opened up the arms dumps, where the guns had lain in disuse through the years of IRA quiescence and internal squabbling. They were to become the Provisional IRA, armed and ready to challenge the state. But that night when Johnny Costello went to Mill Street with a bulge in his hip pocket, the Provisionals were still unheard of and the IRA was regarded as a force of old men not to be taken seriously.

Nora was at the corner of the street when a young man, his face blackened with soot and grime, walked up to her. People were making their way up the road with their belongings in handcarts and carrying suitcases. Many women were crying, tugging tired baffled children behind them. Johnny looked at the street and shouted at her through the din and confusion, "Get the barricades up here for god's sake— do ya want yer street burned down around ya? Where are the men?" A few of them were waiting indecisively, wondering whether to go or stay. Nora said to him they had nothing to make a barricade out of. He looked quickly up the street. There was a solitary van driving slowly down the road, zigzagging through the fleeing people. Johnny took out a dirty handkerchief and wrapped it round his face; he asked her to tie it behind. She did so immediately, without thought; he had that effect on people, they followed him easily. Within seconds he was beside the van, his .38 drawn, and with one hand dragging the driver out of his seat.

"Get lost!" he said to the frightened man. "We need your van." He got in and swung it across the top of the street, blocking off the main road. Johnny got out of the van and called the men to him.

"Get on the other side of this thing and push!" he shouted. They followed his orders and within seconds the vehicle tipped over with a crash. Then he organized a vigilante group to take turns manning the makeshift barricade in case the Protestant mobs came any further up the road. Nora watched him intently. His movements were firm, complete, his body lithe; he worked quickly, collecting material to shore up the obstruction. He seemed totally absorbed in his actions. Taking her aside, he told her that the ghetto was organizing against the police and the Protestant mobs. A whirlwind of activity, he paused only occasionally to push back his dark wavy hair, which fell over his low forehead into his eyes.

She saw a lot of him over the next few weeks, a time when excitement was running high. They went to meetings together and Johnny helped organize the district and set up defense committees; soon she realized they were a front for more serious intentions. Arms were being smuggled in—the old First World War rifles, the erratic Thompson submachine guns, which made more noise than anything else, were phased out in favor of armalites and AK-47 high-velocity rifles.

Belfast pulled back from the brink; the expected civil war did not break out. There was a kind of anticlimax, but the Irish Republican Army continued to organize. British troops were on the streets of the Falls for the first time in fifty years. Sent in to replace the broken and discredited police, they soon created antagonism with the local population. The IRA waited and got ready to strike; they knew that after what had happened in August 1969 the people were behind them and would never trust the state or its machinery of law and order again.

While all this was going on Nora had fallen in love, quite impulsively. She had taken part in some of the early student demonstrations during the civil rights phase and had spent a lot of time listening to talk about action. But Johnny had so confidently swept her along his course of action that she was caught up by him, by his world. He simply went forward and took her with him.

Nora intrigued him. Unlike the other women he had known, she was not out to entrap him. She was independent, open, full of desire, which she expressed without fear. Her honesty as much as her beauty made him love her; she seemed like the embodiment of the new defiance.

In those days he looked much as he did in the photograph on her dresser. When she stopped sobbing she picked it up, returned to the bed and lay down with it beside her. Often after their visits she felt defeated like this. Events ran through her mind wildly: the riots, the barricades, his dark, sooty face looking like the face of a street demon, their first lovemaking. It all muddled together to make a collage.

One day, about a month after they'd met, he brought her down to the bottom of Mill Street, where there was a big abandoned mill standing near a wasteground. They squeezed into one of the gateways. She was wearing a miniskirt at the time. His mouth gripped hers with a strength she never forgot; his quick hands ran up her thighs plucking her knickers at first playfully, then more slowly, slipping them down to her knees. His hands seemed separate things—like darting nocturnal animals with minds of their own. He unzipped, and for the first time she felt him, pulsing, hard; he thrust into her and she squealed in pain until pain merged with pleasure and she laughed and cried at once. He pushed her deeper into the dark gateway and thrust hard, pushing her further and further; her legs bent in an ugly, humiliating, awkward arc to allow him to come into her whilst standing up, her knickers at her feet in the dust.

Nora had sworn when younger she would not be made love to in alleyways and gateways. Girls who did were despised. Her sensitive, rebellious nature found the prospect of back-street sex revolting. And in a way it was. But Johnny was a street demon, an embodiment of the ghetto, and a force she could not stop. He possessed her easily and she was swept along with him. They made love frequently in alleyways, back streets, gateways and wastegrounds. The street had possessed her, mastered her; she merged with the spirit of the ghetto.

Now she lay on the bed looking at his picture. The bed was not his element. Marrying him had released her from his power, from the demon of the back streets. When home he slunk around the bedroom self-consciously, unhappily. The one year of married life she had with him was a disappointment, an anticlimax. In bed she unfolded before him, but he did not want to look. Undressed, he moved uncomfortably. He took no time with her, rarely fondling her or exploring her as she wanted. He was a creature of the back streets and only there did he flourish. When he had to go on the run he seemed to come alive again. Once more they met furtively—in his element their encounters were passionate again, but now made hazardous and dangerous, and their current of excitement vivified him.

It was hopeless really. She knew deep down that her marriage might have failed anyway, even if he had not been caught. In fact, his capture might have saved it. Long Kesh kept them together; its walls, wire fences and watchtowers held her more securely than any marriage vows. Now her marriage had entered the public arena of ghetto politics and it was impossible for her to take any steps to break with him. She was trapped. She was the prisoner's wife.

She revived herself and put on her shop dress, soft shoes and shirt. When she went downstairs she had what remained of her badly burnt stew and remembered Johnny's cryptic message. She didn't know what he was talking about but he often played games like that with her. "The Monk's Stone," she repeated to herself. She had no idea where she'd find Seamus Devine.

3

"The British are pulling out of Northern Ireland," said Michael Boyd with a smile that anticipated the skeptical reaction of the editor. Below them on Forty-second Street the traffic flowed through the dark like lava.

Walt Healy, the editor of the New York *Globe,* swung round impatiently in his seat. "You've been listening to too many crackpots in Irish bars, Boyd. The Irish thing is dead. There's no new angle. Protestants and Catholics, who cares? Does anybody down there?" He looked down at the traffic flow thirty floors away.

"There is a new angle. Anyway, I don't go to the Irish bars." Boyd rested against the window ledge. "They're over here trying to get money for the aftermath."

"Who?"

"The Provisionals."

"Aftermath? You mean bloodbath. That's all they want money for. Who did you speak to?"

"Someone who told me he could get me an interview with McCabe."

"McCabe? The guy who got sprung last year in the helicopter? That was a good one."

"The same. He's been talking to the British. There is something here that's worth a trip across the ocean: 'THE LAST OUTPOST OF THE BRITISH EMPIRE FALLS.' That's the new angle."

"Yeah, like the fall of Saigon?"

"You liked what I did on that one."

"Sure—you were safe in Vietnam. Sending you to Ireland would be like sending a member of the Vietcong to cover the withdrawal of the U.S. from South Vietnam. You're prejudiced."

Boyd was used to this reaction. Since he'd been slogging away in New York at trying to get bored, skeptical or downright impatient editors to listen to him when he spoke about Northern Ireland, he had developed an immunity to it.

"And when are they going?"

"I'll have to ask McCabe and them. That's why I want to go."

The editor sunk his chin into his chest. He smiled. "That was a good one," he muttered, looking up at Boyd. "I mean—landing a goddam helicopter in the middle of a prison. All those dumb micks running to close the gates! You say you can get an interview with that guy?"

Late that night Michael Boyd was packing his bags. He had just received the note from Kate Hughes with Nora Costello's phone number and address. Whether or not Healy would give him the assignment, Michael planned to go. He'd other things to do in Belfast; one of them concerned a book he wanted to write. Nora Costello—or Nora Lennon, as she was called when Michael knew her—he hoped would be able to help him. Though Michael had not been in the city of his birth for many years, he'd kept up with what happened there. His cuttings file was proof of that: a thick stack on a shelf in his apartment. Abrupt and prone to making generalizations about many things, he was also given to keeping odd little details that often suddenly fell into place to make sense of an unexpected series of events. He'd kept a file of cuttings that traced the career of Johnny Costello until the present: his string of bank robberies, his spectacular arrest, his attempted escapes. At first it was partly sentimental, for Michael was curious about the fate of people who had been close to him at one time. Nora was one. As teenagers they'd been close friends—with a kind of passion that never expressed itself except in long walks, explorations of old buildings and heated discussions about the nature of the universe, of men and women. In other words, it was love. But then he was too awkward an adolescent even to have acknowledged it.

The years had made all that seem insignificant. Nora was the wife of a local legend. Michael hoped to be able to make use of his old friendship to help get him into the inner circles of the Belfast Provisionals, a tightly knit group that did not normally welcome the attentions of prying reporters. The fact that he was from Belfast would help, of course. But he believed the connection with Nora would be more important, especially concerning the book he was going to do on the IRA. He thought that when the amnesty came through, as his informants confidently told him it would, it would make a nice chapter: a portrait of an IRA leader and his wife . . . "Wife of Terrorist Talks About Love, Death and Living with the Gun"; silly headlines kept running through his head. He smiled and thought perhaps he was beginning to be affected by his trade. He toyed with these and a thousand other ideas as the plane glided across the Atlantic and down toward Dublin Airport.

"So bleak and yet so green," he thought looking out the window at the patchwork of fields below. He glanced over the pages on his lap; they contained a list of points he wanted to bring up in his interviews with McCabe.

He got an appointment with McCabe at a hotel on the south side of Dublin. He had never lived in Dublin so he didn't know it well. At seventeen he'd left Belfast and gone to England to work as a laborer, leaving his father, by then an alcoholic, to fend for himself. The rest of his family had scattered. His mother had died when he was still a boy. England was the only way out. There was work to be had in the northern industrial towns where millions of Irish immigrants lived. His older brother Paul lived in a rooming house in Salford, near Manchester. For six months Michael shared a room with seven other men, including Paul. He worked on a nearby building site. One of the men he remembered was a professional thief and nearly every night came back with a load of new shirts. He was a brilliant burglar, but that was his one weakness: he loved shirts. He stole practically nothing else.

Michael had felt more at home in the smokey towns of northern England than here among the elegant Georgian houses of the Anglo-Irish aristocracy. He walked along the Grand Canal and had to admit it was very pretty. The doors of the houses *were* very impressive. The Provisionals' current chief of staff obviously had a taste for elegant surroundings. The hotel was not far from the canal. Michael was partly disappointed and partly relieved to find it did not at all fit in with its eighteenth-century environment. It was a long, low building made of glass and concrete.

His appointment with McCabe was not until midnight, so he had a room booked in the hotel intending to stay overnight. The next day he would hire a car and head up north. At eleven-thirty he was paged. He left the lounge where he was having a few drinks and found a man by the name of Murphy waiting for him. He was short, balding, with something of a beer belly. He spoke with a thick Belfast accent.

"You're Boyd?" he asked curtly. Michael nodded yes.

"I.D.?" Michael showed him his press card. Murphy paid little attention to it.

"Okay, let's go."

"You don't want more proof?" Michael asked as they left the hotel to walk to Murphy's car. They passed a group of women heavily made up and his companion stared at them. Then he turned to Boyd.

"Well, if you're not Michael Boyd, it's your problem not ours. Get in the car."

They drove for nearly an hour, followed all the time by another car. They reached a little seaside town north of Dublin, where they changed cars. Half an hour later Boyd was introduced to the chief of staff of the Provisional IRA in a farmhouse in the middle of god knows where.

"Mr. Boyd, I hope we didn't take you out of your way." Peadar McCabe looked surprisingly respectable. He was well dressed in a blue suit, his hair combed neatly around his ears. His eyes were alert, his cheek bones high and his face lean, narrowing to a small mouth. His cheeks were rather sunken. But for a man in his late forties he looked young, sprightly, quick-minded. A handsome man about McCabe's age stood beside him near the fireplace. McCabe did not introduce him. He wore a long gray coat and didn't say much at first.

McCabe smoked incessantly. Before Michael could speak he asked, "Was your da the Boyd from Farset Place?"

"That's right, he was—"

"Mickey Boyd, eh? You see we know all about you." He smiled wryly. "What do you want to know about us?" He indicated to Michael that he should sit down by the kitchen table. The bald man who had been his driver left the room. Michael took out his notebook.

"When are the British leaving?"

"The sixty-four-thousand-dollar question, eh, son? You come

straight to the point. Well, Jack?" He turned to his companion, Jack Fagan, who smiled back at him.

"Maybe he should ask *them*," Fagan answered, spitting into the hearth.

"I intend to. What I meant was, when did they tell you they were leaving?"

McCabe lit another cigarette. "We can't say. We got a guarantee for a particular time scale."

"Give me an idea of the time scale."

McCabe looked at the other man, who said, "Six months to a year."

"It's a complicated process," McCabe added. "They just can't climb into the trucks and drive off. We're not too concerned about when they go. It's what's left behind concerns us."

"You mean the kind of administration?"

"We're working that out."

"What about the politicians?"

The two men laughed. "They're fucked," McCabe said. "We delivered the goods. They couldn't. We're the ones who are seeing to it that internment without trial is ending—all the internees will be out by Christmas. Then there'll be an amnesty. What can the politicians do but talk?" His voice was full of curt contempt. "You can quote me on that if you like," he added with a smile.

"What about the Protestants? Have they been consulted?"

McCabe threw his fag end into the hearth. "There's a loose end to be tied up."

"A lot of people got left behind in Saigon, didn't they?" McCabe's companion said, grinning.

Michael ignored him and pressed McCabe, "What kind of guarantees?"

There was silence for a moment. Outside, the bald man looked in through the kitchen window occasionally.

"Is it in writing?" Michael persisted.

"We can't say."

"The last truce—1972—collapsed because the British refused to meet your demands for a declaration of intent to withdraw. You say they've given a guarantee this time. But they still haven't made a public statement?"

"Of course not. It's not supposed to be happening. The truce is not supposed to be happening. That's called diplomacy. A public statement is being worked out now."

"Why this time and not in 1972? The IRA was stronger then."

"Was it? You seem very confident about that, son. We are at our peak now. We've got experience, arms, men. We can keep this thing going for a long, long time and the Brits know it. They're not stupid. They want to go. It's just how and who they leave behind. We've solved that."

"Are they giving the IRA the keys to the city?"

"They're not going to make me a mayor if that's what you mean. Some people might object to that." McCabe smiled, then continued. "Our people in the States gave you a good report; you're the first to get to me, but tell your editor—Healy, or whatever he's called—there's going to be a lot more comin' over before long. If you stick around for a while you'll be witnessing the ending of the empire. Now there's a story for you."

"I'd love to—if you would let me know how long I have to wait."

Murphy came in. "Peadar, Seamus says there's a lot of movement down the road. Could be the police."

"Okay, I'm finished here. Tell him to get the other car ready. Listen son," he said, turning to Michael, "go to Belfast and see for yourself. Jack here's your man. He'll put you in touch."

"Thanks, I intend to. In fact I'm off tomorrow. I've a few friends there myself."

"Is that right? Get you homesick, eh?" McCabe put on a light raincoat. He took a revolver out of its pocket and gave the barrel a spin.

"Anyone I know?" he asked.

"I'm sure. Costello. He's one of yours, is he not?" McCabe looked at him for a second, raising his eyebrow.

"Sure enough. You know him then?"

"Indirectly."

"Well, if I was you, son, I'd go through Jack here. Want anything arranged, ask him. I mean . . . ," he paused and smiled, ". . . Johnny's on the inside, as you know, so Jack here's your man . . . . There's really no other way it can be done. Understand me? Belfast is a tight city. I have to go. Murphy'll bring you back."

Murphy dropped Michael off near the canal and he walked the few yards back to his hotel, passing some of the ugliest prostitutes he'd ever seen.

Nora was glad the summer was ending. The students were returning from their vacations and coming into La Librairie for their course texts.

They were always good crack. One or two whom she had grown to know slightly often amused her with tales of Spain or France. They occasionally pressed her to go out with them for a drink, but she always refused. There was also a middle-aged man whom she nicknamed "Baudelaire" because he affected a French manner when he asked for a volume of French verse or whatever. He was never around during the summer. But she welcomed the sight of his long, straggling gray hair, and shabby overcoat wrapped close around him regardless of the weather, and mincing gait so unlike Belfast. She assumed he was a poet of some kind, for he would spend hours browsing through volumes of symbolist poetry.

Since her last visit to Long Kesh Nora had been busy trying to find Devine. She'd gone to the political headquarters of Sinn Fein and indirectly—as one always does in Belfast—inquired after him. She received a blank response. Peter O'Neill had not seen nor heard of him in a long time. She went to the Divis Flats, a large complex at the bottom of the Falls Road where the Toners lived. They were friends of her husband and of Devine. The Flats were once Devine's area; he had lived there, "organized" the guerrillas and used it as a power base. There, too, she drew a blank.

It was late afternoon and she was busy with an elderly man who came in to buy a book on rose cultivation. They had a good selection —Belfast is known for its rose-growing experts—and Nora was helping him choose. He was the only customer and she was restlessly waiting for him to decide, thinking about going to the IRA drinking club later that evening to see if she could get anywhere with her quest. The customer finally decided and went to the cashier with his book. Nora got out the ladder and began replacing the ones he'd rejected on their shelf high above the counter. She was sitting on top of the ladder when the door bell rang. Nora sighed: another customer. A man stood near the door and gazed up at her. He remembered that expectant, slightly impatient look in her eyes.

It was a wintry afternoon and they were exploring the old Norman castle perched on its bleak granite promontory at Carrickfergus, a few miles up the inlet from Belfast. She was wearing a pencil-straight skirt and black stockings. At first he had been ungenerous in supposing that the black stockings were intended to conceal unattractive legs, but they soon had begun to excite him with thoughts of Bohemian life. Nora Lennon and he had been through the dungeons. When there was a break in the rain they climbed up to the top of the central tower and looked out over the cold, choppy waters of the lough. A gust of wind blew the dark hair around her face. They descended into the bowels of the castle and found an unused tunnel. Nora insisted on going in. It was dark and damp. Thick webs hung from the dripping ceiling. A dank fungus slobbered over the walls. The floor was strewn with stones. Michael told her to be careful; there was no way out. It led nowhere. She waited for him to follow her. Once she stumbled and Michael took her hand. Though it was dark he knew she was looking at him. He could feel her eyes, expectant, impatient. But he turned, seeing nothing but darkness at the end of the tunnel, and suggested they go out.

"Can I help you?"

He did not reply, but came forward to the foot of the ladder. "Can *I* help *you?*" he replied, reaching up his hand.

She looked down at him for an instant, surprised and puzzled, before she realized who he was.

"How have you been?" he smiled up at her.

Flustered by Michael's gentle courtesy, Nora came down the ladder holding his hand.

"I didn't recognize you, Michael—you've changed."

"It's been so many years—half a lifetime when you think about it. Pat told me you were here." He looked across at the cashier and smiled. "This is a shop I used to frequent in the old days. It's still the same." He looked around him at the old wooden shelves full of books and the big grandfather clock ticking away in one corner.

"How long are you going to be back for?" She was still thrown off balance, nervous at suddenly seeing this man from a past that was only a fossil in her memory.

"Until I do the story I came to do."

"You're a writer—you always said you'd be—"

"Well, a reporter."

"I only hope you write something nice about us for a change," said the cashier interrupting them. "This poor wee town gets too much bad publicity if you ask me." Michael nodded his head and looked gravely at her in hope of reassuring the lady that he would be eminently serious about his subject. Nora smiled and then winced obliquely at Michael, walking him toward the door.

"What story?"

"The usual."

But when they reached the door, out of earshot, he whispered, "The British withdrawal—what else?"

"I wish," she whispered. "How's New York treating you?"

"The greatest city in the world!"

"It certainly seems to have done you no harm." She looked him up and down. "What do you think of this place now?"

"You know me—I never thought much of it. But you'll have to ask me that question in a week. I'm still only readjusting to it."

"How's John?" he asked after a second's awkward silence.

"How did you know about him?" Nora seemed a bit surprised.

"I read the papers. I've kept track of things over the years."

She opened the door for him.

"Actually—I'd very much like to talk to you. What time do you finish here?"

"Six."

"Can you meet me in the Gown at about seven? The one near the university? I've to see some civil servant or another first, but I'll be finished by then. Okay?"

"Okay, but only briefly. I've to—"

"Good, I'll see you then," he said quickly. "After eleven years you must have a lot to tell me."

Before she could explain that she was intending to visit the club that night he vanished into the beginnings of the rush-hour crowd.

An hour later Nora walked into the slanting evening sunlight. All the old Victorian buildings in the city center were alive with starlings. They flocked on the ledges by the Palladian columns of the confidently massive structures that housed department stores. A few couples enjoying the evening sun lounged on the smooth lawns before the City Hall, a grotesquely ornate building surrounded by the statues of Victorian burghers. She headed south toward the university area, away from the city center. A British army convoy rolled past her in the direction of the Falls Road. The soldiers slouched in the backs of the trucks, at ease here where they felt safe. One of the soldiers winked at her. He was a teenager, probably from Liverpool or Manchester, little different from the youth who might be waiting for him up the road a bit, his armalite at the ready. Nora smiled back at him spontaneously. The convoy disappeared round a corner, heading for the ghetto streets.

What did she have to tell Michael after all these years? She regretted her restricted, inhibited existence. She felt slightly ashamed of herself and wondered if he would think less of her because of her failure to go on to other things. London, New York . . . they were just pictures to her, names with associations, places where things happened that she read about. Once her imagination had absorbed them eagerly, hope-fully, even expectantly, as places where her destiny would bring her. But now it shrank from them as reminders of failed aspirations, adoles-cent foolishness. She tried not to think about them, to compare previ-ous hopes with present problems.

Nora walked quickly and soon found herself in the middle-class university area, only half a mile from the ring of steel security gates that sealed off the city center, and about the same distance from the Falls —but its warren of side streets might have belonged to a different city. She walked along an avenue of elm trees, where handsome old houses with large bay windows bulged opulently onto the sidewalk. The front gardens had palm trees and white wrought-iron garden seats, and there were greenhouses in the back. It was cozy, secure, prosperous still, though only in a faded sort of way.

Queen's University was nearby—a masterpiece of academic Tudor architecture. Its old red brick was faded. The sun glinted off its dia-mond-paned windows in the high central tower with its buttresses and battlements. A light breeze was blowing and the big leaves of garden palm trees flounced luxuriantly. Nora paused at a corner, looking for the Gown. She would have one drink with Michael and then scurry off home to get ready for her visit to the IRA club. She only hoped none of her student customers were in the bar. It was around here that Johnny was caught. The bank was off one of the avenues near the university, but she couldn't remember which—she'd blocked it out of her memory. He'd imagined it would be a pushover, it was so quiet here. No soldiers, no checkpoints—and yet they were waiting. The police had questioned her for hours about the area, thinking she might know where the money was. Sometimes she wished she did. But she'd finally convinced them she knew nothing. Her husband never talked about what had happened.

She tried to remember Michael as she knew him. It wasn't difficult. Though for many years he had been removed from her life by the force of other events, he once made a deep impression on her at an age when she was susceptible, eagerly so. What brought them together was their passionate rejection of their culture, religion, of the narrow assump-tions about life by which they were raised. She was stimulated by him, a youth with whom she could share her deepest doubts and hopes. He was different from the others: sensitive, awkward, rebellious, curious. And Nora scorned the convention of having a "boyfriend" to go to the movies with, or dances, or the whole ritual of furtive gropes in darkened cinemas. She responded eagerly to Michael's dismissive sarcasm.

Soon they had formed a little conspiracy against going to mass on Sundays. Instead, they went up the road to the Falls Park and sat for an hour or more in a shelter pondering the nonexistence of God. Soon Nora inducted Kate into the conspiracy and she joined them in their cold Sunday vigils. But Michael and she formed a special, intense bond —the more intense because it remained so fervently platonic—which Kate grew to resent. Kate was never quite serious enough about the problems of the universe that Michael and Nora felt pressing on them so urgently.

Nora paused near the bar, nervous, full of memories, memories that brought regrets she didn't want to feel just then. She didn't want anything to exacerbate her present isolation.

The Gown, like nearly every bar in Belfast, was ringed by linked concrete-filled barrels. The obstacles were meant to stop would-be car bombers from parking too near the premises. As a double measure there was a wire-net fence in front of the bar; it sloped downward to the pavement. The door was securely locked and to gain entrance one had to ring a bell. A guard peered through the door and scrutinized prospective customers before letting them into the hallway, where they were searched. The bar was nearly empty. A few young men and women sat around one of the tables and Nora glanced at them quickly to see if she recognized anyone. She didn't. The women were dressed in long, flowery skirts and were drinking pints. She felt a bit self-conscious in her unstudentlike close-fitting skirt. She went to the bar and ordered a vodka and orange. It was strange being alone in a public bar—she would never have done this in the local bars of the Falls. It would be a scandal if a woman went into the pub alone, especially if she was married with a husband inside serving time. But here no one paid attention to her. She sat at the bar and looked for a clock. There was a mirror behind the bar and she glanced into it. She was shocked by her appearance; she looked so pale. Since her last visit to John she'd been more anxious than usual; she kept thinking of the amnesty, so much so that her sleep was disrupted. If only someone would come out in the open. The rumors, the talk, the conspiracies only made her more insecure, anxious, tense. She drank quickly and snapped open her handbag. No one was looking so she daubed on a little extra eye shadow.

As she was looking in the mirror she saw Michael Boyd standing directly behind her.

"Michael," she said, swinging round on the stool. She extended her hand. He took it warmly.

"It's good to see you," he said. His eyes were bright with recognition. "You haven't changed much." He noticed her skin was cold, her hands felt thin. Nervously she acknowledged his compliment and let go of his hand.

"Let's go sit by the wall there, in that snug," he said. He ordered another vodka for Nora and a beer for himself and ushered her over to the partitioned-off area where there was a little table and two chairs.

"I'm sorry I couldn't talk much at the shop—it's just that the cashier's a bit of a gossip, so she is." The barman brought the drinks. Michael wished her health and happiness.

"Thanks be to Jesus for Irish beer. That's one thing I do miss in America." He smiled at her, smacking his lips. "How've you been keepin'?"

"Oh," she shrugged casually, "okay, I suppose."

"Any kids?"

She shook her head. "You've heard of British birth control? Long Kesh."

"He's been in three years now, right?"

"Yes, how did you know?"

"As I told you in the shop, I've been following what's been going on here—from a safe distance."

"So you haven't given up on us yet?"

"Well—I don't know about that. I want to write a book about it. I'm always curious about what goes on here."

"I'm afraid you're not talking to the right person. You probably know more than I do."

"All I've heard since I got back is the ceasefire and the British withdrawal. It seems everyone's expecting it to happen."

"It would be great if it were true. There'd be an amnesty. Johnny would get out."

"That's what I heard."

Nora looked up at him expectantly, with eagerness in her eyes. They were wide and brown and deep.

"The IRA seem pretty definite," he went on.

"The politicos up at Sinn Fein always seem definite," she said with mild contempt.

"No—not them. The leadership—between you and me and the wall here. They told me that they'd been given guarantees by the British government." He paused and took a swig. "Do you know McCabe?"

"I met him once years ago—when he was still in Belfast. He knows John well."

"Well, *he* sounds convinced. Anyway, that's politics; there'll be time for that later. I've a lot of catching up to do—I want to know what you've been doing all these years."

Nora smiled ironically and said, "That's politics too. I've been tied down to this place completely because of politics."

"Just so long as you haven't given up going to the park on Sundays."

She laughed a little. "No—now I just stay in bed." She relaxed a little, charmed by the memory.

"Are you politically involved?" he asked.

"I used to be—during the civil rights days, but once the violence started I sort of lost my bearings. I can't say what I am now—I just know I wish the British would go home."

"For personal reasons?"

"No, more than that. But at the minute it's the main thing. Funny, I went along okay for the last three years and sort of got used to being alone. But once the truce started and all the talk about amnesty, I began to fret."

"The sudden prospect of happiness makes your unhappiness more unbearable."

"I suppose so."

This put her in mind of her plans for the evening. She explained she had to be off, but he insisted on getting her another drink.

"Look, I've a car. I'll drop you off wherever it is you're going."

But she refused. "It's awkward for me, Michael. Everyone's watching you and who you're with. It might sound silly but—"

"I understand. I remember what it's like."

She looked up from her drink. He was thinking about how he had scandalized her father once. Mr. Lennon was very perturbed by the fact that his daughter was seen with the son of Mr. Boyd, a known atheist and reputed to be a reader of James Joyce, that purveyor of filth and sacrilege from Dublin. Michael's father was an alcoholic Catholic renegade, once indirectly referred to from the pulpit by the parish priest. He did read Joyce; when he was drunk his "selections" from *Ulysses* were vociferously rendered before bemused and sleepy children and could be heard streets away. And as far as the local clergy were concerned, Joyce was just one rung up on the ladder of damnation from Martin Luther and just below Oscar Wilde, Karl Marx and Charles Darwin.

"It's even worse now than it was when we were young and defiant," she said.

He waited for her to explain, but when she didn't he said, "You mean you've to live up to the image of Mother Ireland?"

She finished her drink quickly. "Something like that." She rose to go. "I'm sorry I have to run off like this. I'd like to talk more."

"I want you to help me," he said, going with her to the door. "You could introduce me to a family, for instance, a republican family. I've been away so long I'm completely out of touch with people here. All my family are in England. My friends . . . well, I never really had many apart from you and Kate. I'd like to do an interview for the book. It would help if you'd take me around the Falls and point me in the right direction."

She smiled at him. "I know a few people—families of some of John's friends who you could talk to."

Michael scribbled his hotel telephone number and address on a piece of paper and gave it to her. "As soon as possible; I have a tight schedule."

She took it and shook his extended hand.

"Okay. It was good seeing you again."

"It's a shame you couldn't stay longer."

Nora apologized again and promised they'd make a night of it before he went back.

He watched her disappear down the avenue. He was disappointed, but not surprised. She was tense, slightly hunched over, nervous in her walk. Yet, the intensity of his feelings for her was still there. It was more than just an adolescent crush—what he felt for her was real sympathy and it had lasted down the years. Now it seemed heightened by the fact that it was never really expressed, except indirectly. When he had seen her that afternoon looking down at him from the ladder it was as if he had never been away. Years before he'd cherished her intimacy with a pride that his companions reserved for boasting of their first sexual conquest. But his remained unspoken. With Nora he had conquered the contempt of women, their hostility toward men, the puritan misogyny of the city, by simply being with her. The pleasurable fruits of that conquest had never left him. What he could take for granted now about women was then only achieved in opposition to the whole moral being of the ghetto. When she brought him into her confidence it was like discovering the earth was not flat after all, but round, with a whole new world of women to be explored! The infinite possibilities of friendship! Not only mother, wife or whore—and he eagerly reached out to grasp the possibilities, not knowing where they might lead.

But something had ended that day of their trip to Carrickfergus Castle, in that disused tunnel. He never forgot that afternoon, the sense of having failed her never left him. He had been caught unprepared for the greatest possibility of all.

It was ironic, he thought, that Nora, who had opened up this new world to him, was now forced to be such a model for the old morality. He watched after her until she was a dark shape under the shadows of the trees and he could discern her no longer.

The white Ford came to a halt at the side of the narrow road. The driver rolled the window down, letting the sweet smell of the pine trees into the car. The pines clustered thick up the slopes of the hills through which the lonely border road ran. The passenger in the back seat smoked and said nothing. After a few minutes he looked at his watch.

"We're early," he said. The man in the front seat beside the driver rested his elbow against the door and peered out his window. The trees rustled gently in the wind. Big black crows cawed above in the treetops. The man in the back seat rolled his window down, sticking one elbow out, and relaxed.

Peadar McCabe and Jack Fagan had made this journey once before, months ago when they were initiating the first talks with the British government—the talks that led to the truce. It had been a wet winter's afternoon on that occasion; the tree-thick slopes were capped with clouds, which slipped slowly down the hillsides until they'd reached the roadway, blanketing everything in a muffled, muted, damp atmosphere. The helicopter had almost missed them. They were delayed for hours. But now they expected no hitches; it was clear and bright, even uncomfortably warm.

Both McCabe and Fagan, his right-hand man from Belfast, were well dressed in business suits. McCabe carried a silver-lined black attaché case. His long legs needed a stretch after the ride; he told his driver he was going for a walk. He stretched himself by the car and looked back down the road. Another car was parked a few hundred yards away. He waved to it. He watched its driver get out and rest against the hood. Then he looked up toward the crows, wondering how beaks that thick and heavy could ever be held up. His driver stuck his head out the window. "See anything?"

McCabe said no.

"I thought I heard something," said the driver, listening.

McCabe walked to the trees and looked into the forest. There was a little path that led to a relatively flat, open piece of ground with some small boulders strewn over it. He stared at the patch and then at the trees around it. It hadn't changed. He turned and walked slowly up the road toward the metal spikes that the British army had placed just inside the Northern Ireland side of the border with the Irish Republic. All the minor roads that crisscross that twisting, vulnerable line on the map were spiked years before to try to stop the guerrillas from moving quantities of weapons across and using the back roads as quick escape routes. McCabe shook his head at the uselessness of the endeavor and smiled. The spikes were painted yellow, which had peeled over the years. The road wound on past them away into the hills beyond.

There was a noise in the distance. The crows heard it first. McCabe looked up. The helicopter was approaching. He walked quickly back to the car.

"I think that's them," he said. Fagan got out while McCabe waved to the car at the back of them. Four men got out and took up positions along the roadside. They were carrying rifles and submachine guns. McCabe patted the bulge on the inside of his jacket reassuringly.

The helicopter dropped slowly downward, landing on the open patch of ground. The IRA men watched behind the trees. After a few minutes two army officers got out and walked toward the path that ran to the roadside. McCabe was waiting there, Fagan behind him. Both officers were unarmed. McCabe's driver waited by the car, out of sight.

"McCabe?" one of the officers asked. McCabe nodded.

"You know the routine," McCabe said, taking out a cloth hood. The officer took it from him and placed it over his companion's head. Fagan led the hooded soldier to the driver, who took him down the road where the other IRA car was parked. If the two IRA leaders were not returned within six hours he would be shot. That was the routine. Within minutes the helicopter lifted off again, carrying Fagan and the IRA chief northward toward Belfast.

Beneath them stretched the bleak hills of South Armagh. White specks of lonely farmhouses stood out against the green patchwork of small fields spattered with gray outcropping granites. The British called it "Bandit Country," recognizing that it was completely controlled by the IRA guerrillas. The officer looked down at the hostile countryside and said nothing. McCabe was chain-smoking behind him. The chief of staff of the IRA was looking directly at the back of his head. The officer shifted uneasily as a most uncomfortable sensation ran down his spine.

Noel Andrews, the British minister of state for Northern Ireland, was standing in the old ministerial conference room in Stormont Castle near the big bay window. He was looking out over the castle's lawns toward the old stables in the distance, relics of another age—a time when the Protestant Unionist upper classes and landed gentry ruled this last remaining corner of the British Empire. Stormont Castle was where the Unionist cabinet used to meet. The British had abolished the local Unionist parliament in 1972. Since then the task of running this troublesome spot was delegated to a British government minister. Andrews, as a member of the Labour government, had had the job for several years already. Every week the conference room was used to hold security meetings. The officer commanding the British forces, the chief constable of the Northern Ireland police, along with civil servants, army and police officers, would gather to discuss the war and ways of dealing with it. More recently the meetings had become truce monitoring sessions. But this meeting would be somewhat different. There would be no army or police officers: just a representative of the British government and the IRA.

The British–IRA talks had been going on for a while now, usually in a mansion some distance away from Stormont Castle. But Andrews had decided this time on a more dramatic gesture. He would bring the top guerrilla leader right here, to the seat of power, away from the informality of the cozy library in the other place. He was worried. He had heard rumors about discontent within the IRA. There was a murder in the Falls—the first since the talks started. It was time to make a deep impression, to make it clear what was at stake and to ensure that the leadership realized they had to fulfill their part of the deal. They were, after all, dealing with Her Majesty's government. These surroundings should convey that. He was running these thoughts through his mind when McCabe and Fagan were brought in.

"Smooth flight, I hope," he smiled, peering over his glasses. He walked to the head of the long, polished table in the center of the room. He spoke with something of a Liverpool accent. Among the leadership of the British Labour Party it was quite fashionable to have a trace of one's working-class origins still in one's speech. And Andrews was proud of his: the son of a truck driver, his first job had been as his father's helper. When tipsy he would often wax nostalgic about the good old days by the Liverpool docks. He felt his working-class background gave him an advantage when dealing with the hard men of the IRA.

McCabe put his case on the table and sat down without being asked, Fagan beside him. Directly in front of them was a large fireplace over which hung an enormous oil painting. Shepherds and shepherdesses lounged under leafy trees. Beneath it was a bust of Lord Craigavon, the first prime minister of Northern Ireland—a man fiercely opposed to the Irish nationalist claims for independence and a virulent anti-Catholic. McCabe looked at the bulging eyes of the bust, the bags of skin under them, the huge protruding forehead, and smiled.

Andrews noticed. He looked at the bust, "Ugly, wasn't he?"

He asked them if they would like a whiskey—"Bushmills of course." The crystal decanter was in the middle of the table, draped with a little silver chain. They refused.

"I must say," he went on, "you two look as if you came here to sell insurance." There was more than a hint of sarcasm.

"We did," McCabe replied, looking him straight in the eye. He clicked open the briefcase and took out a list of names of prisoners being held without trial whom the movement wanted released, and another sheet of paper enumerating alleged truce violations by the police and the British army. Fagan drummed on the table with his fingers.

Andrews came straight to the point. "Your policy is not that reliable these days. At least for Mr. . . . . er . . . Quigley. I believe he was known as 'Spider.' "

"We don't insure touts," McCabe replied curtly. "That was not part of the deal, Mr. Andrews. But a public declaration of intent to withdraw was."

Noel Andrews stood opposite them. "That is a delicate matter, which is being worked out. Your part of the arrangement is to keep the peace, keep your hotheads from embarrassing us any further. Mr. Craigavon's descendents are very much alive—and very much interested in why the British army is not so active around the Falls these days. Just the other day there was a flap in Westminster when one of them demanded to know why wanted IRA men were seen walking around Belfast. And why your political wing is allowed to run its own offices. You see we have *our* hands full."

McCabe looked at Fagan, who nodded. "The Quigley murder is being taken care of. It's under investigation."

"And the state of your organization in prison? There've been rumors—"

"We are negotiating now with the sentenced prisoners."

"And Costello? I mean, what I'm driving at is that you're not much use to us unless you can give us certain guarantees—one of which is that you actually speak for the people you claim to speak for."

There was a short pause. "There is a little confusion, but it's being cleared up," rejoined McCabe assuredly. He pushed a sheet of paper across the table toward Andrews. It glided swiftly over the smooth surface. It was a list of alleged violations of the truce arrangements. And it was followed by another.

"That's a restatement of our amnesty demands. We want it soon. That'll solve the confusion in the prison for you."

Andrews sighed as he cast his eye over the sheets. "All this is under discussion. Her Majesty's government wants a peaceful solution, to accommodate the differing traditions here. But you must understand the difficulties involved. Public opinion is a volatile element that we have always to be aware of." He spoke as if he were addressing an obtuse class in elementary political science. "Your chaps have to be kept under control or these delicate arrangements cannot last. That is the basis of the agreement."

McCabe clamped his briefcase shut. He reached across the table and took the decanter by the neck, pouring himself a glass and another for his companion.

"You'll be sorry to leave all this behind when you go, eh, Mr. Andrews?" he said with a slightly malicious smile on his lips as they savored the whiskey.

4

*d*etective Sergeant Roger Mackal, now head of the Intelligence Unit of the antiterrorist "A" Squad, would miss Bill Quigley. For years he'd been Mackal's eyes and ears in the republican ghetto. He'd never exactly grown to like him—being an informer made Quigley more useful than admired—but some of the files on the shelves in the squad room of the police station would have been a lot thinner if it had not been for him. His killing had come as a shock to Mackal, and to the authorities. It was the first murder committed in the Falls area since the start of the truce. Shortly before his death he'd called Mackal and asked for a meeting.

"Did he tell you anything?" asked Superintendent Norman Black, the overall commander of the squad. Mackal was peering through the peephole in the corner window, which was heavily wired and boarded up. The dark street opposite led to a large park; its trees formed a black, jagged mass on the horizon. He turned around.

"Nothing. But he sounded excited. I arranged to meet him at the usual place. A day after he rang he was dead."

"The British are on my back about it, Roger."

"Why should they care?"

"Their truce, they don't want it messed up."

"Then why don't they ask their friends in the IRA—they meet them once a week for drinks."

"They have."

"And I suppose the IRA know nothing about it?" Mackal smiled sarcastically at his superior.

"How did you guess?"

Mackal walked across to the poster on the far wall. It had mug shots of the ten most wanted men in Northern Ireland. But typed in red underneath them was the instruction: "NOT TO BE ARRESTED UNLESS SEEN ACTUALLY COMMITTING A CRIME." In the middle of the poster was a picture of Seamus Devine, whose rather pudgy face had an insolent look on it, which seemed in Mackal's eyes to be intensified by the instruction.

"At least one of these boys had a very good reason to put Billy out of the way," said Mackal, staring at the poster.

"A lot of people had," Black suggested.

"Most of them didn't know it though," Mackal added.

"Did any of them?"

Mackal pursed his lips. His eyes darted from face to face. "Perhaps," he replied. He went over to the files and ran his eyes down the names until he came to the one marked "Costello." The superintendent got up, yawning.

"It's getting late. I'm going home, Roger. Don't take this too much to heart."

But Mackal was preoccupied and had already begun thumbing through the Costello papers; it had been Quigley's information which had led to the arrest of the leader of the "moneybags" unit and three of his colleagues. Two men had slipped through Mackal's net that morning—one was Devine. The other, Patrick Murray, was shot to death a few hours later driving through an army checkpoint. He hadn't a penny of the fifty thousand missing pounds from the interrupted bank robbery on him. It had vanished, like Seamus Devine, into the quiet gardens and avenues of the surrounding area and then, Mackal presumed, into the coffers of the IRA. That was over three years ago, almost ancient history now. The file had lain untouched. Costello was inside, the "moneybags" battalion broken up, and Mackal promoted to detective sergeant. But Quigley's murder prompted the detective to revisit the past and refresh his memory. He noticed when he took down the file that Black had gone.

Mackal was a Belfast Protestant of working-class stock, with the build of a shipyard worker—sturdy, thickset, with broad wrists and thick forearms. His only vanity was a small moustache, the brown hairs of which were neatly trimmed. His eyes had a wry, distant look indicative of a skeptical, elusive nature. He still spoke with a slight hesitancy that was a trace of a childhood stammer. He was deeply suspicious of the British in a way one only can be of people who are supposed to be one's friends. Catholics, who always expected the British to do their worst, never had that problem. It puzzled him why they would bother over a mere tout like Quigley, truce or no truce.

This file was Mackal's prize collection. Putting Johnny Costello behind bars was regarded as a major breakthrough in the fight to put the Provisional IRA out of business. They were optimistic then! There were more Johnny Costellos than anyone ever imagined. Still, ending the activities of the "moneybags" battalion at least temporarily struck at one of the major needs of the IRA—funds with which to buy guns.

Mackal flipped open the lid of the box and took out the first few pages of reports. They contained the earliest information on Costello. It was sloppy, a fact Mackal blamed on the Special Branch—the political crimes squad. The Provisional IRA had caught the Branch napping; during the years before the current emergency they'd grown lazy, their information out of date. Too many hours spent in downtown bars buying drinks for "sources" who had heard nothing new since 1957. That was before the "A" Squad came into being.

There was always a certain amount of animosity between the Branch and the Criminal Investigation Department, of which Mackal was a member. Apart from the fact that the Branchmen earned twice as much overtime as the CID men, they were very elitist about their information, and tended to hoard it—a sort of "information for information's sake" theory. The formation of the "A" Squad put a stop to that. Now information was pooled and organized in a central headquarters run by the CID. The Branch, of course, resented this intrusion on their turf—occasionally Mackal found them holding back or not being as cooperative as they might.

He skipped through all the early reports of Costello seen at barricades, or riots, or whatever; the Branch had not believed in the Provisional IRA's existence. All along they were saying it was just a bunch of wild kids with rocks and old men with rosary beads. Until the first armalite opened up, that is. But by then it was too late.

Those were bad days for the police, confronted by a guerrilla army that they had been told didn't exist. The British army's intervention demoralized the force. The ghettos were impassable. Information was drying up. In one desperate action the Special Branch was given charge of drawing up a list of hundreds of people to be interned without trial. It proved to be a pathetic effort—half of those on the list were old IRA men from the 1940s and 1950s, long inactive. It was really that failure that sparked the origins of the "A" Squad.

Mackal came across the report on Quigley's first contact. When he was a constable stationed in the Upper Falls area Mackal knew him, long before the troubles started. Then it was a quiet, almost rural district. It was mostly rows of little cottages, a few streets around a brickworks and farms. Quigley was then the manager of a local pigeon club, which had its own license for a little bar at the back of the club's premises. Relations with the police were then so good that the occasional constable was known to pop into the back of the club for a drink. The Catholics, though, never accepted the police as *their* police, even then. But in those days Mackal could at least have helped an old lady across the Falls Road without fear of getting his hand bitten off.

He remembered Quigley was something of a social climber. He wanted his kids to go to university, wanted them to be middle class. He was very annoyed when the housing developers moved into the area. Behind them came the poor Catholics from the old Victorian slums of the city center to occupy the big new housing estates. Then Mackal was transferred and forgot all about Billy Quigley, until a few years ago when his voice spoke to him over the confidential phone that the police use to gather information.

Quigley had information about a series of bank raids. He named names. It was Mackal's first break against the "moneybags" gang. Two of them were picked up and interned. Quigley came back with more, this time the date and place of the next bank job the gang was going to pull. According to him it was to be a south Belfast bank, near the university. A quiet spot, hardly patrolled because it was far enough away from the main ghetto areas and the city center, which the IRA were then attempting to flatten with car bombs.

The morning of the planned robbery was bright and sunny. Mackal had sat in the front garden of a big house opposite the bank. He was comfortable in a deck chair reading the newspapers; he even had dark glasses on. Beside him two gardeners mowed the long flat lawn that ran down to the road. They were both members of the Second Parachute Regiment. Just around the corner, sitting in a parked car, were three other CID men, and down the street a bit, toward the university, another two soldiers in plain clothes sat by the upstairs window of a house, covering the street. It was such a nice morning that Mackal almost felt as if he could doze off.

Shortly after nine, one of the CID men stationed in the parked car came onto the lawn from the back of the house and told him that two Cortinas had been hijacked that morning in the Upper Falls. The Cortina was a favorite IRA car; it was low, fast, and had four doors, permitting everyone to make a quick entrance and exit. Mackal told him to call and have them send another squad of Paras along. Eventually, Mackal had to make the call himself because the army was complaining of being short of men. There had been a series of bombings and shootings in central Belfast and nearly all their soldiers were in the city. The "moneybags" robberies always coincided with some other major IRA operation. He managed to get a foot patrol sent over. Shortly after they stationed themselves behind the hedgerows, the two Cortinas pulled up outside the bank and a group of men jumped out.

A few minutes after they entered the bank Mackal had a loudspeaker in his hands. For him, this was the most terrifying part of the procedure; then, strangely, he was blessed with an extraordinary fluency. His call to come out hands in the air was answered by a fusillade of high-velocity fire, which tore up chunks of the neat lawn. The police and army did not return fire in case they hit the bank staff or customers inside.

The guerrillas' reply made him more annoyed than frightened, and he began to stammer during his next broadcast.

"Come back when you've learned to talk!" someone shouted from inside the bank. There was another blast of gunfire, which chopped up a bed of roses. The Paras were getting itchy fingers, being a regiment that is not used to being shot at without shooting back.

Mackal supposed the undercover soldiers down the street were watching the rear of the bank. They were, but they were not watching the roof. The bank was housed in an old building with Gothic-style turrets and castellated edges, which provided easy cover. While the gunmen inside were holding the security forces at bay, two of the gang clambered onto the roof and dropped down on one side of the bank, cutting through a garden that took them into a quiet street a few blocks from the university. They left with the money.

Costello surrendered, having made sure his friends had escaped safely. There was a fuss immediately afterward, mainly about the two who escaped. Mackal pointed out that he had asked for two patrols to help him seal off the area and instead was given a six-man foot patrol

under the charge of a sergeant. He was told that the security situation
in the city had stretched the army's resources to the limit. So he
shrugged his shoulders and said nothing. He couldn't complain; as well
as getting Johnny Costello, he got a promotion and was given overall
command of the Intelligence Unit of the "A" Squad.

He fingered through the accounts of the raid and the wad of police
interviews with the gang. Costello's interrogation report was very thin.
It contained no names. But Devine was easily enough identified going
into the bank. Murray was shot dead not far from the scene of the
robbery, and as he was suspected of being a member of Costello's unit,
it was almost certain he was the other escapee. As for the money,
Mackal assumed it was dumped then, somehow or other picked up and
distributed through the usual channels, eventually ending up in the
pocket of a gun dealer in Mexico or New York.

Mackal cast his eye over the newspaper clippings about the event:
"WESTERN-STYLE SHOOTOUT IN BELFAST BANK." At the
bottom of one report was a little paragraph belonging to another story:
"YOUNG WOMAN TARRED AND FEATHERED." He didn't
read on, but put the clippings back in the box.

He had seen Quigley a few weeks later at the crossroads where they
usually met. Mackal gave him ten pounds. But Quigley was preoccupied. Devine's escape frightened him.

"He's a smart bastard," he said to Mackal. "He'll want to know how
it happened. I might go to England for a while."

"Devine's gone, Billy," he said, trying to reassure him. "He'll be in
Dublin by now if he has any sense. Anyway, no one knows. Don't get
paranoid." Mackal remembered thinking Quigley was mad. He
couldn't be doing it for the money. How could anyone risk his life for
ten pounds? It must have been a kind of snobbery and resentment—
he hated the IRA, despising them as lower class thugs.

"Just take it easy, don't be getting everyone on the Falls Road free
drink for a while, okay? Any hint or sign that anything's wrong, we'll
get you out of here with the speed of light."

There was no hint of trouble, Devine was not seen around his old
haunts again, and Mackal soon found himself with other jobs to do.
Quigley didn't contribute much after that. He went back to running
the bar in the pigeon club, listening, hiding his contempt for the people
around him.

Mackal got up and walked over to the one window in the room. He
looked out through the peephole. It was hard to get used to the

comparative silence outside—there hadn't been even one potshot at the station for weeks. The large park was very bleak and windswept. If he stared at it long enough the dark mass of its tall trees started to move and form strange shapes. He could hear a few drunks stagger past the huge corrugated steel fence that protected the police station from the armies of the ghetto. It had ceased to look like a police station long ago and now resembled a fortress, more effectively cut off from the maze of streets around it than by any moat or jungle. The steel mesh at the top of the corrugated wall towered over the building, slanting inward at the top like a shell to protect the station roof from missiles; steel-linked concrete-filled barrels, acting as a first line of defense against car bombers, ringed the steel fence. The traffic passed this forbidding structure apprehensively, its pace checked by the yellow-painted ramps—specially constructed bumps in the road that reduced the vehicles to a slow, guilty crawl and allowed scrutiny by the guards stationed in the watchtower.

"God, it's not like it used to be," he thought to himself, peering through the wiring. In the courtyard of the station he could hear the sound of English voices, squaddies getting ready for their night patrol. Since 1969 the police shared their facilities with the army; at the moment the Upper Falls Station was occupied by a unit of the King's Own Light Infantry. Mackal walked across the room, past the shelf of murder files—most of them unsolved—to the coat rack. He was going out with the patrol to have a look around. Devine was on his mind, and he had an idea where he might show up sooner or later.

Mackal clambered into the back of the Armored Personnel Carrier, crouching on one of the narrow benches in the cavelike interior. There were no lights inside. The soldiers, faces blackened, sat bent over. Mackal was last in. He nodded to Lieutenant Beardsley, who sat up front near the driver.

"Welcome aboard," the officer said, still easily recognizable in spite of his blackened face. Mackal looked around him noticing the almost lighthearted atmosphere.

"I suppose you lot are off up the Falls to the nearest IRA club for a drink?"

"You shouldn't believe all you read in the newspapers, Sergeant. It's business as usual as far as we're concerned."

"Glad to hear that, Lieutenant. That means if we see Seamus Devine I can arrest him, right?"

The officer did not reply. The gates swung open and they rolled into the street.

The APC bumped over the yellow ramp heading up the Falls Road. Mackal narrowed his eyes to look through the slit just above his shoulder.

"You know," said the policeman turning to one of the squaddies beside him, "the people in this area are so fierce that it takes half a British regiment to enable one policeman to deliver a summons for a parking violation? They eat cops alive here, son. Did you know that?"

The young soldier looked at his comrades bemusedly. These mad Irish were obviously all the same to him.

"I just hope for your sake they don't find out I'm in here. Could be the end of the truce. And then where'd you be?"

"I'd like to be bloody home in bed," the young man replied. They were passing rows and rows of red-brick houses with little front gardens; the windows shone as yellow squares of light, except where the silver glow of a television screen lit up the glass. The local dogs were all barking and came chasing after the patrol in packs.

"More bloody hounds in this place than children," Beardsley exclaimed.

"Hungry, too, by the look of them," added Mackal. "You're lucky they don't throw stones as well as the childer—or used to—but maybe even that's being negotiated."

"Really, Sergeant, you do have a bee in your bonnet. As I told you, it's business as usual."

Mackal leaned against the back door and said nothing. The bootblack on Beardsley's face did nothing to disguise the officer's fresh naivety.

They circled the main housing estate perfunctorily, stopping occasionally to check out "suspect" vehicles. Later they cruised in one of the newer developments on the lower slopes of the nearby mountain. The Armoured Personnel Carrier (APC) revved up its engine as it climbed the steep street. They all lurched slightly toward the rear of the vehicle. The roar of the engine scared off dogs, who were mostly strays and cowardly. Mackal peered through the slit. There was nobody around. "It's early yet," he said to himself. Soon they were at the top of Black Mountain Gardens. Nora Costello's house stood at the corner on their immediate right. As they turned to go down the street the front door of her house opened and two women walked out.

"There's the good woman herself, with her wee sister," said Mackal as they passed them slowly. The women looked across at the carrier briefly, the younger one with obvious scorn.

"They're off to the Wee House down the road."

The lieutenant turned to him. "You know the Wee House; it's an IRA drinking club. She goes to it every Saturday night to see her da. They'll probably hold a going-away party for you there, Lieutenant."

The lieutenant did not reply, but asked the policeman if he wanted them to stop at the foot of the street. It would be wise to alleviate the policeman's doubts as to the genuineness of the army's commitment to doing its job. Mackal said yes. The APC turned the corner and pulled to a halt. They opened the rear door and the eight soldiers climbed out. They quickly fanned out across the street, taking up positions inside the garden gates on either side.

"Better stay inside, old boy. The police are not exactly popular around here," Beardsley teased.

"Sure enough," the cop replied, "I wouldn't want to be the cause of trouble for your boys, would I?" He knew Nora would remember him —his face was probably imprinted on her memory forever.

When the women turned the corner the officer stepped out from the darkness of one of the gardens. "Sorry to inconvenience you ladies, but just a routine check." They halted and looked around. He asked them politely to open their handbags. Two soldiers also appeared and stood on either side of them. Nora noticed across the street the others in the patrol; two faced down the street toward the main road, their self-loading rifles raised and pointing in that direction. A soldier immediately behind them, just at the corner, pointed his up Black Mountain Gardens. It was a routine formation. Patricia sighed impatiently. She hated the British and openly showed it at the slightest opportunity. Nora was too preoccupied and handed over her bag automatically. He looked at Patricia's first and shone his torch inside; the usual jumble of feminine utensils. Then he came to Nora's.

"No top secrets, I hope," he offered in an awkward attempt at a joke. His beam of light picked up a small picture wallet, a paperback book and a change purse. Wedged beside it was a folded piece of paper. Nora and he both saw it at the same moment. She was annoyed at herself for leaving the address in her bag; it made her angry to give them even the most innocuous information. He picked it up, and putting his torch under one arm, quickly unfolded it. He shone the torch on it. The scrawl read: "Michael Boyd, College Arms, 22331." He smiled at her and put it back in her bag. Nodding in a gentlemanly fashion he said, "Sorry for the inconvenience. Do have a pleasant evening."

The two women turned and walked away, and Patricia muttered, loud enough to make sure she'd be heard, "I wonder why they're trying so hard to be nice to the natives these days. Must be scared of something. It doesn't come naturally to them, does it?"

The officer walked across the street to the APC and opened the rear door. Detective Sergeant Mackal pushed his cloth cap from his eyes and asked, "Nothin', I suppose?"

"Mrs. Costello is a rather attractive filly. I wonder what she's been doing since you put hubby away for the rest of his life? Damned waste, if you ask me."

"I did ask you, but not about that."

"Oh," Beardsley replied with a grin. "No, innocent as the day she was born. Unless the name Boyd means something to you. 'Michael Boyd, College Arms, 22331.'"

"Eh?" the policeman asked, getting irritated with the soldier.

"That's what the note said on the piece of paper she had. A name and some sort of number, telephone, I suppose. Perhaps the little lady is getting rather restive after . . . how long has it been?"

Mackal was not amused by Beardsley's insinuation. He felt he knew Nora Costello as well as he did his own daughter. Ever since the day of her husband's arrest he'd felt quite sorry for her. She was obviously a bright girl. Her record showed she'd been to art college and could easily have gone to university like his own daughter Alice had it not been for her involvement with that bank robber. They had kept a close watch on her at first, but turned up nothing. She wasn't involved. She worked hard and kept faith. That he admired. Her sister was a wee rascal though—he wouldn't be surprised if she was a paid-up member of the IRA.

The name Boyd meant nothing to him however.

5

"There is absolutely no truth in the withdrawal rumor, Mr. Boyd. Her Majesty's government can assure you of that." Noel Andrews smiled benignly at the reporter, who was scribbling in his notebook. Boyd glanced at his watch. He was getting nowhere (he was not surprised) and had to meet Nora at six-thirty. She had arranged to introduce him to a republican family. It was a long drive back from Stormont to Belfast.

"And I'd like once and for all to dispel the idea of 'talks.' " Andrews accented "talks" with contempt. "Her Majesty's government does not 'talk' to murderers. I fear you Americans have got the wrong end of the stick—"

"But, Minister, surely the existence of the legalized IRA political offices throughout—"

Andrews laughed. "Now, Mr. Boyd," he interjected, tapping his desk, "don't you think it's better having them running their little political, or whatever they choose to call it, offices than having them running around the back streets throwing stones and worse—"

"Can I quote you on that?"

"This is a delicate matter," he began. He was no longer smiling. "Words can kill in this country; what I expressed to you was my personal reading of the situation. Her Majesty's government has decided to allow the political aspirations of one section of the community a legal expression—so long, of course, as they remain within the bounds of the law. I think we all would agree with that, no?"

"Why has there been no attack on the British army in the last few months?"

"That, I fear, is a security matter. I suggest you speak to the army's press relations chap—I'm sure he'd be delighted to give you his full cooperation. We all realize how important it is for Americans to get a clear idea of what is going on here, which I fear they don't always have. Things tend to get distorted by the time they reach the other side of the ocean. I'm sure you agree there is a difference between talking about British withdrawal in a bar in Boston and then coming over here to see what is actually going on."

"It's what is not actually going on that puzzles me, Minister. No house searches, no widespread arrest operations, no shootouts; men being released from internment; the talk of amnesty. That all adds up to a—"

"Ahem—I see you are bent on this story, Mr. Boyd. But you can quote me on this: Her Majesty's government is pursuing its goal of a peaceful political solution. We've always said that when Labour came to power internment without trial would be phased out. And that's what is happening. As for those other things you mention, the General Officer Commanding is the man to talk to. I would not presume to speak on his behalf."

Michael dutifully took the quote and supplied his own skeptical exclamation marks. He looked at his watch again, then thanked Andrews and excused himself.

At six-thirty Michael was looking up at the grimey, rather grim statue of Queen Victoria that stood imperiously before the front entrance to City Hall. She bore the ball and scepter of authority; the inscription on her plinth read: "From My Heart I Thank My Beloved People. May God Bless Them." Her imperturbable gaze met the traffic that circled the building before turning up the long avenue opposite —the heart of downtown Belfast. On the lawns around her and the other statues of the Belfast burghers a few girls with their skirts rolled up were endeavoring to catch the evening rays of sun. Most were just sitting on the grass gossiping, relaxing after work in the nearby offices. They seemed unaware of the dour solid citizens who stood around them, represented now in bird-stained marble: factory owners, mill owners, shipbuilders, railway moguls, functionaries of the nineteenth-century British Empire, men of worth. Several of them were carved with their mayoral chains of office proudly displayed upon stout chests of rock. Beneath their pedestals the pigeons wandered, searching for the leftover lunch crumbs, equally oblivious of the austere figures above them. The young couples stretched lazily, the girls showing more leg than those men of marble would ever have imagined possible.

Michael walked over the lawns, having read all the inscriptions and taken a few photographs of the pigeons, girls and statues in their incongruous proximity. He waited at the front entrance, which was sealed off by a heavy wrought-iron chain. He looked in the direction of the avenue. A British army foot patrol passed; the leading soldier, a sergeant, glanced at his camera. The army did not like being photographed and Michael tried to smile reassuringly at him. They went by, edging their way around the railings, the last man in the patrol walking backward. They glanced over the low hedges behind the railings at the young women on the lawn; the women returned their glances, indifferently for the most part. Only the sergeant, a man in his early forties, was confident enough to pay them any overt attention. He winked and nodded at the two girls nearest the railing.

"I 'ope that grass is not too wet," he called, grinning. The two girls, resting on their elbows, looked at each other then back at the patrol. They were slightly embarrassed, but still confident enough to return the glances of the soldiers, who, as they edged past, guns in hand, seemed to Michael to become suddenly self-conscious of their situation. Here they were in the middle of a town that in many ways looked just like their own home towns, geared for war, whilst the women lazed at their ease on the lawn watching them. The last soldier, walking backward, did not even look at the young women; he was too afraid that they might not take what he was doing seriously at all. The soldiers deeply resented what they saw as the smug normality of the civilian life into which they had been so incongruously dropped and to which at times they became so vulnerable.

As Nora approached the City Hall she saw Michael leaning against the statue of Queen Victoria. He was watching the foot patrol and the girls on the lawn. He seemed relaxed, his tall frame propped insolently against the imperious marble monument. His fringe of fair hair fell over his forehead and when he swept it back with a casual gesture she noticed that at the same time his camera rose swiftly to his eye. The two gestures followed each other so swiftly that they appeared to be conflated. His back was to her. As she was about to call to him he suddenly dropped on one knee, shooting quickly with his camera. His back pleased her. It seemed very masculine, lean yet broad, and somehow reassuring in its suggested strength. She did not want to disturb him so waited until he stood up and saw her.

"I hope I haven't kept you waiting," she said. He smiled at her, his camera already swinging innocently at his side. Photography had long been a hobby, and he was happy about his last shot.

"Glad you got here—no, I've been kept busy. I just got a nice shot of a head with the metal helmet floating above a well-clipped garden hedge and a pretty girl stretched beneath it. Odd, don't you think?"

She looked in the direction of the foot patrol.

"They don't seem odd to me anymore. I wish they did."

They walked away from the City Hall and the downtown area toward the Catholic enclave. Nora was shy with him at first. But Michael was eager to ask about Belfast, Northern Ireland and her life with John. So gradually she allowed her curiosity to express itself. She asked how he had gotten to New York.

"By accident," he answered and became suddenly shy himself.

She waited for him to continue. When he didn't she said, "It's a long way from the north of England—that's where you went when you left here, isn't it?"

"Aye, I worked my way round the factory towns of the north for a while. Then I saw what was happening to Paul, my brother, remember? He was bright, but he ended up a drunk, a frustrated working-class intellectual who drank too much. I didn't want that to happen to me. I worked during the day and went to night school in Salford, near Manchester. Eventually I got accepted to university."

"Did you become a poet? That was your ambition, just like mine was to be an artist."

"Quite the opposite, Nora," he said, smiling at her wryly. "I ended up editing the university students' rag!"

"And then?" she prodded him.

"And then—I met up with Kate."

"Were you in love with her?"

"Well . . . we had an affair."

Nora was slightly ill at ease all of a sudden. The word *affair* threw her into an alien cultural world, so far from her own.

"I was in love with someone else," he said, realizing she'd become ill at ease.

"Oh?" she asked matter of factly, feeling perhaps her curiosity had taken her far enough.

"Aye—an English woman. The colonel's daughter, in fact. She grew up in an army barracks and was a dedicated pacifist." He paused, seeing she was a bit discomfited as well as embarrassed by her own reaction.

"Well, that's how I got to New York, anyway."

"With the colonel's daughter?" she asked, with a mere touch of sarcasm.

"No, but because of her. She left me and I left London, where we'd been living. I was working there as a reporter, but I was in need of a change. This American woman suggested I try my luck in the New World."

"Another girlfriend?" she asked. She felt hopelessly provincial and out of her depth.

"Yes, but that ended too. I stayed in America though." He shrugged his shoulders indifferently. "Who knows; our beginnings never know our ends, do they?"

"I suppose they don't," she answered politely.

They came to the ring of security gates separating the commercial area of the city from the ghettos. To leave, they had to go through an iron-toothed turnstile of which there were several at each exit point.

"Hey," Michael said as he passed through the creaking contraption, "it's like leaving a New York subway station. Of course, you don't have to pay a token to get in in the first place, do you?"

"No, but *you* don't have to be searched before you can get a train, so you don't. I'd rather pay any day," she replied, nodding in the direction of a group of soldiers who were standing guard inside a corrugated iron hut through which people had to pass before entering the commercial district. They were screened and searched on the way through.

They passed a small concrete bunker. It had a narrow slit that faced in the direction of the Falls Road, a few hundred yards away. Michael noticed a pair of eyes peering through the slit and following him.

"Doesn't it get to you, being watched and searched like this all the time?"

Nora shrugged. "You get used to it." She did not tell him about the search on Saturday night, nor how the soldier had read his note. They were walking through Castle Street, a bustling little thoroughfare where the People's Taxis, the republican-run London cabs that had replaced the buses, had their terminus. It was also a marketplace and the sidewalks were occupied by little stalls where vegetables, fruit and cheap ornaments were sold. Most of them were closed by now; a few men were still packing up for the night, covering the stalls with tarpaulins. There were queues of people waiting for the taxis—rows and rows of black London cabs. The buses were too often the victims of the riots to be a reliable service anymore. They headed along the Divis Street toward an enormous block of flats that rose out of the surrounding rubble of wasteground, the rectangular shape of its central tower alien to the spires and chimney stacks of the cityscape.

The Toners lived in the complex, and Nora and Michael were going to visit them. The Divis Flats were thrown up hastily in the early sixties to house Catholics displaced by slum clearance. Its central tower was ringed by smaller blocks. Between them stretched two courtyards, one of which was supposed to have been an "adventure playground" for the children. It was littered with rocks and junk, and in the center was a pile of burnt wood and refuse—the remains of the bonfires lit late on every August eighth to commemorate the anniversary of internment. As they walked, every few minutes Michael would swiftly and suddenly turn aside, stop and take a photograph of something, or somebody, that caught his eye. First it was an old man covering his stall with a tarpaulin; then it was a slogan on a gable wall; then he took one of a group of children playing among the ashes of the dead bonfire. The children playing in the rubble swarmed around him when they saw his camera.

"Hey, mister, take my picture, wud ya?" they yelled. They tugged at him like frisky little monkeys. One of them shouted, "Are you a Yank?" They immediately assumed anyone with a camera was American. One of them shouted, "Take us back to Hollywood with ya, mister —ah, go on." He stopped every so often and obliged them with a picture. They shouted in delight.

"You should be at home gettin' your tea," Nora said to them when it seemed to be getting too much to handle. But one little girl persisted. She was skinny, dirty-kneed, with large eyes and glasses that imbued her face with the mournful wisdom of an owl. She followed the two, tugging at Michael's short jacket until he stopped to pay attention to her.

"Mister, mister," she pleaded. He looked down.

"When you goin' back to America?"

"Soon," he answered.

"Cud ya put me in your suitcase?" she pleaded.

"No, but I'll take your picture. Smile."

She smiled quickly and he clicked.

"Now go off with you and have your tea; I'm sure your ma's wondering where you are."

The little girl turned and ran, skipping over the rocks of the wasteground, shouting, "He tuk me picture, he tuk me picture!"

Up above them, leaning out of windows, women were talking and watching them as they passed. Groups of men lounged outside the only bar in the complex. It was built into the ground floor and access to it was down a little flight of steps. Michael was uncomfortable, aware that he was an intruder. He tried to appear as if this was his ghetto—he had, after all, grown up only a short distance away. But it was no use; he felt as if he might as well have been in Harlem. Even Nora was uneasy as they passed the men outside the pub. She suggested to him softly that he put the camera away.

They passed through a narrow alleyway into the second courtyard. Like the first, it was covered with junk and stones. He looked up at the gaunt walls of the flats. There were clotheslines strung out from the windows and tied to tall poles erected in the courtyard. Heavy wet sheets flapped on the lines, scattering tiny drops of water on them as they passed beneath. Every available space on the walls was plastered with republican posters, most of them the "Trust Us" series. They covered over the other pro-Provisional IRA graffiti, which was painted everywhere.

Michael stopped before one of the posters and looked at it. "What's this about?" he asked Nora. "Why all the 'Trust Us' stuff? Trust them to do what?"

"It's the IRA. They started putting up those posters all over the place a few weeks ago. I suppose it's got something to do with talks with the Brits."

Michael noticed that several of them had been torn down. He fingered one of the torn posters; under it was an older one proclaiming: " '74—YEAR OF VICTORY!" He smiled.

"Victory? I wonder what that amounts to."

"A British withdrawal."

"Then what?" he asked, turning to her.

She looked up at him without answering. "Then Johnny comes home," she answered after a moment's silence.

"The British say no, of course. I met Andrews today. No. No. No. To everything." But he spoke automatically, his attention centered on her eager face, her wide eyes that were shy yet full of curiosity. Every time she looked up at him like that he was thrown back. He marveled at how her nature could be so tentative yet eager at the same time.

They made their way into a stairwell and up a seemingly endless series of concrete steps. Though it had been an exceptionally warm day the concrete stairwell was cold and dank. It stank of piss and animal dirt.

"Dare I ask what happened to the lifts?"

"Booby-trapped. It killed a soldier a few years ago. They fixed the doors shut and attached a bomb to them. When the Brits tried to force them open. . . . They've never been repaired.

They reached the fifth floor and walked along the balcony until Nora stopped outside a yellow door.

Mrs. Toner was waiting for them. Within minutes she'd put a pot of tea on the boil and several slices of thick white bread to toast under the grill. She was a short, thin woman with a well-lined but handsome face. When she spoke it was as if she were addressing an otherworldly being with whom she was in customary communication—a habit picked up from years of living with a husband who never listened to her. But he was dead now, leaving her in her mid-fifties with eight children. By the time Michael sat down in her bright little kitchen he'd heard about Kathleen, Sean, Kevin, Gerry, Joseph, Deirdre, Annie and wee Mickey.

"Kathleen's married with five of her own. Sean's doing life for murder of a soldier—and that wee fella wudn't hurt a fly, honest. And wee Kevin—sure he'd give ya the shirt off his back—he's doin' ten for membership and carrying explosives. Gerry was interned for three years, but God love 'im he's out now. Joseph is still at college, thank God. He got all the brains. Deirdre should be home any minute, she works in a shoe shop. And then there's Annie and wee Mickey at school. They're a pair of wee rips, honestly. You could write a whole book about their adventures. Sure the childer have no chance at all in this place."

She turned and looked out the window to the bleak courtyard below. She shook her head.

"Throwing stones at the soldiers all day. That's the only recreation they have. It would put years on ya. You're as well out of it," she said, looking round at Michael.

After tea and toast they went into the living room. On one wall a picture of the Sacred Heart hung beside a photograph of President

Kennedy. And beside that was a photograph of Pope John XXIII. Another wall was decorated by a cloth portrait of the Irish revolutionary leader James Connolly, executed by the British in 1916. The portrait was stitched in green, white and gold, the colors of the Irish Republic, with an emblem of the Starry Plough, the symbol of Connolly's socialist movement, across the top. When Mrs. Toner saw Michael examining it she told him it was made by Sean in prison. She proudly pointed to a model harp her son Gerry had made when he was interned. It was inscribed: "For My Mother. Ireland Unfree Shall Never Be At Peace." Her other jailed son, Kevin, had made a lamp stand from lollipop sticks. It was in her bedroom and she brought Michael in to admire it.

They talked about the truce.

"I don't care what they're talking about. It got wee Gerry out of jail. That's fine with me. And I'm sure Nora would agree. That wee girl hasn't had a proper home in three years so she hasn't. Sure that's no life for a young woman, is it? I think they should talk till Christmas if it means the men'll be out. We've suffered enough."

"Is Gerry here?" Nora asked.

"No, love. He's away somewheres to see his friends."

"I was wonderin' had he seen Seamus at all."

"Seamus Devine?"

"Aye."

"He hasn't been round in a long time. But I'll remind Gerry to tell him you're lookin' for him."

"Is Gerry expecting to see him?"

"Ach, you never know who you're going to see in this place. Wee Tommy O'Brien was round th'other night and you wudn'a recognized . . ."

"I hope that was interesting for you," Nora asked as they left the building.

"Aye, certainly. Belfast women amaze me," Michael answered. "They've such a capacity for life. Mrs. Toner's bursting with energy and enthusiasm in spite of everything. Why is it the women seem so vivacious and the men so defeated? The men seem to lead separate lives—"

"They'll do," said Nora without looking at him. Michael realized he'd been tactless.

"It's obvious who they support," he said, changing the subject, nodding in the direction of the Flats, now behind them. They were standing on a little rise overlooking the middle of the Lower Falls.

"It's been like that since the police killed wee Patrick Rooney," she said quietly, standing alongside of him and looking in front of her.

"That was in 1969," Michael said, "during the riots, right?"

"Aye, the cops peppered the walls of one of the buildings with a Browning machine gun they had mounted on an armored car. They called that "riot control" in them days. One of the bursts went through the wee boy's bedroom wall and took half his head with it."

"And that was the birth of the Provisional IRA," he added, looking at her. She did not reply, the history of those years was in her bones.

"The people here don't forget easily. Why should they?" She was dispassionate. He looked into her face again and saw in her high cheekbones and fine nose, in her large brown eyes, the face of something that is only produced by suffering—a kind of fierce objectivity, a great clarity and strength, which he noticed often in the faces of the women since he had returned.

They stood silent for a moment, looking over the ghetto toward the hills.

"I'd like to ask somebody about those posters," he said, as if talking to himself.

"We could walk up to the Sinn Fein headquarters from here; it's not far. I'm sure Peter O'Neill would be delighted to explain it all to you."

"Peter O'Neill?"

"He's the main spokesman in Belfast. I would have thought you'd met him already."

"I try to stay away from spokesmen. I don't like being sold a line. You may as well talk to a tape recorder. They usually have only the one message. Now this guy Devine sounds more interesting. I like to get as close to the people who make the decisions as possible."

"What decisions?"

"*The* decisions—the important ones. Life or death."

"You think it's that simple?"

"That's what it comes down to, Nora." He paused. "But—I suppose I have to check in with officialdom sooner or later. So why not now? I've already paid my courtesy call on the British spokesman. Let's do go up to the headquarters. Will I find Fagan there?"

"No, he stays in his area; the drinking club is the best place to find him. But he'll probably say the same as O'Neill. They're very close I'm told."

They walked down the rise away from the Flats. The sun was sinking low in the sky, and the slopes of the mountains on the outskirts of the city were darkening to a deeper green.

There were only two old houses left standing in the street beneath the Flats. Michael paused, noticing an old green wrought-iron gaslight. It was incongruously dwarfed by the massive new buildings behind it. He walked over to the lamp.

"This must be one of the few left in operation. I love gas lamps. Remember the girls used to swing around them with their ropes?"

She nodded yes.

"I love the red-brick houses, too. I guess I'm just a child of the Victorian era. When I was growing up I hated these streets, but since I went to live in New York I miss them."

"That's because you forgot what it's like to live in them," she answered sharply, responding to what seemed like the false sentiment of his nostalgia.

"You must admit they were better than that thing!" he said, surprised by her vehemence and feeling caught off guard. He pointed to the complex behind them.

"I don't know. The Flats have baths, indoor toilets, central heating —that's more than the quaint little side streets ever had." She was being perverse with him, and sarcastic. It was a way of keeping him at a distance. But Michael enjoyed sparring with her.

"So—to you I'm a returned Yank hankering for the thatched cottages of Belfast side streets?" His voice was full of mock indignation. "Maybe I should take one of these old broken bricks home to New York as a souvenir." He picked one up and regarded it lovingly. He was now parodying his own former sentiments.

"You wouldn't get it through the customs. Don't you know it's a dangerous weapon?" She smiled at him at last.

"Do me a favor," he said to her suddenly, taken by her smile. "Stand over here, by the lamp." Nora looked at him skeptically.

"Come on," he insisted gently.

"Why?"

"I want to take your picture."

But Nora hung back. "I'm not dressed properly. This dress is too short." She looked down at her knees. "I didn't have time to change after work."

"You look fine, come on. Your knees are perfect the way they are. I was relieved to see them when you took off your black stockings."

She looked at him in surprise. "What?"

"You don't remember. Years ago when we were friends your black stockings were something of a scandal in the neighborhood. They were a sign of Bohemian rebellion. I was very torn. Even though in principle I was all for your right to wear them, in practice I was glad when you didn't.

"Why?"

"Because then I could see what beautiful knees you had."

They were still round and firm and full. She laughed at him.

"Michael, you were always so faithful to me and my little acts of defiance. Yet you were with *them* all along! I'm disappointed." She pouted mockingly at him.

He was leaning against the lamp post with his head nonchalantly cocked to one side, regarding her.

"Don't look at me like that," she said, slightly uncomfortable.

"Like what?"

"Like some sort of thing in a picture, I don't know how."

"I'm looking at you objectively, just the way you look at yourself, that's all. I'm composing."

Without further argument he took her by the shoulder and walked her to the lamp post. "Just stand there," he said.

She did not resist him. Nervously, she leaned against the hard, cold iron. She could not smile, being too self-conscious. "Hurry up!" she said as he stood back. "Is it me or the lamp post you want?" she asked as he circled around her.

"I want you both—you both remind me of Belfast. It'll be nice to have back in New York."

"Oh," she replied, as with a swift gesture he clicked. He'd taken her; she'd the uncomfortable feeling of being possessed.

"I'll make you a copy," he said to her as they crossed the street.

They passed into the warren of half-demolished streets. The district was undergoing redevelopment, and what had been spared during the years of rioting and guerrilla warfare was being leveled by bulldozers. The people lived among the ruins. Nearest the Flats, the destruction was greatest. As Michael and Nora moved further into the ghetto, they found the streets still as they had been over the last hundred years or so, except where a crashing army vehicle had chipped the end off a row of houses or a bomb blast had cratered the street, or a petrol bomb had gone astray and gutted several homes at once. Many of the houses, however, were abandoned and sealed up; there were holes in the walls with circles of white paint drawn around them by the army to mark a likely sniper's nest for foot patrols to take note of as they edged their way along. In reply, the gable walls of many houses were splashed with white paint—this time by the local people to enable the IRA snipers to see the outline of passing soldiers after dark, silhouetted against the bright wall. And everywhere youths and children idled, women leaned in their doorways talking, men stood at corners restlessly. It was as if they were all waiting for something to happen.

A few of the youths whistled at Nora. She was self-possessed and ignored them. Michael looked at the posters in the downstairs windows of the tiny houses: the same beaten face everywhere, the same message of resistance, except where on the walls the new "Trust Us" posters had gone up.

They came to the corner of Farset and Wilson streets. "Home sweet home," he said, looking down toward Farset Place, where he'd grown up. It was a wasteground now of flattened brick.

"During the riots in 1970 the Protestants came over from across the road and burned it down," Nora explained.

"And we used to help them build their bonfires on the twelfth night. That's gratitude for you." Michael remembered the big Protestant holiday on the twelfth of July, the celebration of an ancient victory over the Irish Catholics. "It's well my da is out of it—he'd never have gotten used to this. It would have killed him."

"When did he die?"

"Early 1969. I was in university in England at the time."

"Did you come back for the funeral?"

Michael shook his head. "No, I didn't. Do you remember Maggie? She was my da's fancy woman. A skinny wee woman with a taste for fur coats. God love her, they looked like fur to her, anyway. He took up with her when my ma died. Anyway, she found him in the kitchen on the floor. She buried him. My brother Jimmy was the only one of the family who came back for the funeral."

"That's awful," she almost gasped. "The poor man—if I'd known I'd have gone myself."

"I regret it now. But I was still young enough to swear never to come back here. I hated this place too much."

"I remember," she said softly; it saddened her to be reminded of those things. "So you did. It wasn't just an adolescent obsession then, was it?"

"No, but with time and distance separating you from all that, you grow more objective. But *your* situation is more interesting. You shared my hatred of this place back then—"

"Yes, Michael, but a lot happened between the time you left and—"

"And the time you met your husband."

"It wasn't just John. Oh—I don't know now—but then things seemed to be changing for the better. Belfast seemed worth the effort then. We thought we could make a difference. People were together, rebellious, thinking for themselves. My adolescent preoccupations were trivial in comparison; or so I thought anyway."

"Do you still think so?"

She leant against the corner house, which was gutted and abandoned. "Yes—if this effort, these talks, bring peace." But the words almost died on her lips with lack of conviction. And Michael noticed. They withered before an old vision that his presence had brought back to her: a vision of freedom, of art, of love, of a kind of happiness that she'd hankered after in an intense but vague way when younger. He was standing against the street light looking down the street and for a brief instant she saw that vision in his eyes—it seemed still fresh in him. He walked over to the doorway of the old house and peered in through the rubble-strewn hall. The inside was black, smelling of damp. Wads of wallpaper peeled from the moist, softly crumbling walls.

"Do you remember who lived here?" he asked, coming out of the door again. Nora said she didn't.

"The Neills. They were even more notorious than the Boyds. They were all bastards. I don't think there was ever a man in the family. All girls, no fathers anywhere to be seen. One of them I remember—we called her Ginger because of her red hair. She must have been about my age or younger. I met a sailor once in Liverpool who knew her granny—that's going back a few years. I think they must have serviced the whole of the west coast of England, and Ireland."

"You knew them?"

"Well, I'll confess to having kissed Annie once in the alleyway when I was six. I was sort of forced to do it though by bigger fellas who wanted a laugh. I suppose the Neills were a kind of natural resource in a community where sex was a cruel joke people played on each other after marriage."

"The last laugh was always on the woman," Nora said. When younger she dreaded the fate of the women around her—worn out with years of childbearing, with no control over their lives.

"Aye." He stood back and looked at the house. "What happened to the Neills?"

When Nora looked at the gutter she gave a shudder, as if she saw the ghost of the girl's red hair drifting down the street on the gentle mountain breeze.

"They cut off all her hair," she said sadly, in spite of herself. She seemed in a trance. "That was the day they arrested Johnny." The painful memories of that day came back to haunt her. Michael stepped out of the hallway of the abandoned house.

"Are you okay?" he asked. She looked pale and drawn. She nodded yes. "Let's go on," she whispered.

"Why did they cut off her hair?" he asked, simultaneously realizing the probable reason.

"Oh, I can't remember now, Michael, it was so—"

There was a loud roar of engines. They looked up Farset Street in time to see the ugly, pugnacious snout of a saracen nosing its cumbersome way around the corner about a hundred yards ahead of them. The driver was revving up his engines for a quick spurt down the street, hoping to avoid the expected barrage of bricks and missiles. It rumbled toward them. Michael took Nora by the elbow, moving quickly backward toward the corner house. As the vehicle accelerated there was a loud bang behind it. The splintered metal from a nail bomb spattered the back of the saracen and made it ping.

They ducked into the hallway of the gutted house. Nora crouched down. She knew the drill well by now. Michael stood in front of her with his arms protectively spread over her head. Another nail bomb exploded. Bricks and stones and bottles clanged and bounced off the green iron plate harmlessly. He turned instinctively toward the woman beneath him as the vehicle roared by, pursued by hordes of children and youths. A few bottles crashed and splintered near the doorstep.

Though the saracen had passed, he did not move. Nora was hugging her knees before him.

"It's gone," he whispered. Slowly she began to get up. She was awkward in her short shop dress, so he took her hand. As she rose to full height her breasts brushed lightly against his chest in the narrow confines of the little hallway. She was breathing rapidly. He did not let go of her hand but, holding it, let it hang by his thigh. He could smell her; her warm breath was on his face. He did not want to surrender the intimacy of the small space. Her nipples tingled from the gentle, accidental contact. She had not been so close to a man in years.

"I think it's all clear now," she said, lowering her glance; she did not want to meet his for she felt he was about to kiss her.

"I think so," he replied, not moving. "Nora . . . ," he began, but she moved quickly to the side, avoiding him.

She stepped out and he followed, dispirited and perturbed. They walked in silence toward the top of the street and Sinn Fein headquarters. He did not say anything until they neared the old pub.

"What does Johnny make of this?" he asked, pointing to the "Trust Us" poster on the gable opposite. Nora looked round, as if startled from a daydream.

"Oh, I don't know. We don't often talk politics now."

"Would he support the truce talks?"

"I suppose so; he wants to get out of prison."

"But politically, I mean. Kate wrote me he was a very determined type, even in jail, very uncompromising."

"He is, that's for sure. They can't break him, no matter what. But he's never discussed the talks as such. He'd be angry if he thought they were leading nowhere, or that the organization was giving too much. I know that much about him." Talking about him like this Nora had the peculiar sensation that Johnny was a total stranger to her—a political being, a guerrilla leader she'd only read about in newspapers.

"It must be hard being in jail, having your fate controlled so completely by something beyond your power," Michael mused.

"Aye, it is, but passion keeps him going. He hates the British so much it keeps him going, year after year—"

"And you, do you hate the British enough to keep going like that?"

Nora paused. "It's Johnny's in prison, Michael, not me. I'm free to hate who I want."

"Or love?" he asked quietly.

The question startled her. She did not know quite what to say. She looked away from him.

"That's different, you know that. You know the situation." She spoke softly, as if to herself.

"The situation," he said, undeterred, "is one that runs on hate. It seems to be the basic fuel Belfast runs on at the moment—but it always was like that anyway." He sounded dismissive, almost contemptuous. Nora, already annoyed at him for earlier arousing her smothered desire, and at herself for being pleased by it, rounded on him.

"You're beginning to sound like you did when you were sixteen, going on about love and hate and what Belfast needs and how it really needs love. Why don't you go and stick a flower in that soldier's gun barrel over there, go on! See if that makes any difference to the world. You sound like a bloody hippy! It's really not that easy to love or hate. I've known very few people capable of either!"

Suddenly she was trying to hurt him. Suddenly she resented him. He had come back to Belfast to lecture her, to tell her about love and hate! But even more deeply she resented him because his return had reminded her of the possibilities they had once imagined together. For a second she wanted to denigrate them, dismiss them as adolescent, as trivial, unreal. Yet he stood before her as real proof that they were not: he had left, he had achieved something for himself, while she was still here struggling in the net this city had so tightly cast around her.

He touched her gently on the arm. He knew what she was feeling. "I'm sorry if I sounded glib and patronizing. I hate to see you unhappy . . ." His voice trailed off. Then he paused, not knowing what to say next.

This corner outside the old pub from where the prison bus left depressed her. She was silent. All the mornings of her waiting flashed through her mind; all the women's faces mingled; the beaten, distorted face on the poster behind them loomed over all. Another morning would find her here, and another morning after that: waiting, through the weeks and months and years of mornings full of tired children, cigarette smoke, aging women. She felt utterly wretched.

He wanted to console her, to tell her there and then what she had meant to him. But he didn't. He knew his words would blunder into something they could not quite express. She was at once so strong and so vulnerable. Her vulnerability, her openness, had survived the years of loneliness and sacrifice. He sensed it and it filled him with tenderness for her. When he drew close to her, in spite of herself she still seemed to be waiting for him, expecting him to act in a way he'd failed to before. He could see it in her eyes; he'd seen it years before, but then his desires had been baffled by stronger needs—a need to seek out her strength, to be reassured by her independence, her difference from other women. Then, he could not reconcile that need for her as his strong, independent companion with his recognition that her desires made her as vulnerable as every woman who desires a man. He was simply too young. He had retreated from her revealed vulnerability; confusing it with weakness, he had not been strong enough to accept it.

Aware of his desire, Nora looked at him, puzzled by it. Johnny had desired her so differently. And he was the only man she'd ever had. He had taken her so easily, almost without reflection it seemed; but that's what she had wanted—to be loved physically, directly; even the humiliation of being fucked in a back alleyway was exhilarating because of the intensity of his energy. Yet she could not deny that she desired Michael too, perhaps even more now than before. Her breasts still tingled gently from his touch; her body was responding to a memory of its own, one her mind had long suppressed, a memory of desire, a complex tenderness she'd once felt for him. Johnny was so different. If Michael knew the nature of her first lovemaking with Johnny would he condemn her? Would he feel she had betrayed herself? Would he still desire her? Both men merged in her imagination as she abandoned herself to a fierce image of herself being encompassed in an all-soothing embrace.

Michael felt he could almost touch the tension in her. At that moment she seemed so far beyond his reach, yet in desperate need of it. He looked at her for some signal, some hint of wanted intimacy, the longed-for touch that would help relieve her awful isolation. For the second time that evening he moved close to her, close to her breasts as before in the tiny hallway.

A man called from inside the old pub. It was a discordant sound breaking the fragile crystal of intimacy and desire that had formed again between Nora and Michael. She found herself once more on the sidewalk where she had so often waited, bearing her responsibilities. Peter O'Neill came to the door and called them in. Nora introduced him to Michael and explained his mission in Belfast. O'Neill, always glad to exercise his authority as spokesman for the political wing of the IRA, quickly agreed to a short interview.

They went upstairs into a small back room littered with old newspapers. There were three boney wooden chairs. Michael sat back trying to conceal his boredom as O'Neill announced the policies of the movement. He asked a few perfunctory questions about the ceasefire. O'Neill told him, "We're cutting the ground from under the politicians—I mean the local Catholic politicians. When we end internment, which is what the British have promised as one of the concessions for the truce, they won't have a leg to stand on. The people will recognize that only the IRA had the power to deliver the goods. The grass roots will support us for that."

"Why all the 'Trust Us' posters?"

"The Falls is always full of gossip. Our enemies put out rumors—you know the kind of thing, Nora," he went on, turning to her, "crap about sellouts and god knows what."

Nora did not answer; she felt uneasy, distant. She'd heard all this before. Her mind was elsewhere.

"Then what—after interment's ended—will you fight elections?" Michael asked.

Nora put in, "But there's the sentenced prisoners. They'll have to have an amnesty, won't they?"

"Yes," O'Neill replied quickly, "that's part of the deal."

"All well and good," Michael persisted, "but the point of your campaign was to get the British to leave. Have they said anything about leaving during these talks? Are they going to pack up and go after Long Kesh is shut?" O'Neill looked at him and then at Nora. He smiled in a way meant to intimate he knew much more than he could ever reveal. "That's on the cards," he said.

"And the movement is united behind these moves?"

O'Neill laughed. "You bet. The IRA is a unified force. That's how we have forced our way to the conference table—we couldn't have kept going for all these years without agreement on the basic aims."

Michael asked permission to take a few shots of the headquarters. O'Neill told him to fire away. He then asked if it could be arranged for him to do a story on IRA men training, getting ready for the expected withdrawal.

"Hmmm," O'Neill said, and thought for a second. "That's more tricky. But I'll see what I can do."

Nora had sat half-listening to the conversation, only pricking up her ears when the fate of the Long Kesh prisoners was mentioned. The truce talks seemed far away and unreal as she sat in that bare, depressing little back room. Being there, she found it hard to believe that the movement was actually wringing concessions from the British government. Her attention wandered to a fly buzzing between the newspaper covering the window and the pane itself. She watched the dark dot through the paper. It seemed trapped. She wanted to be alone with Michael again and impatiently waited for the interview to end. Michael was bored, but listened respectfully, glancing at her now and again. Nora wanted to distance herself from the dingy little room and its conspiracies. She sat still, her hands joined on her lap, hoping for a chance to let the crystal of their intimacy grow again. For the moment she abandoned herself to this hope in a kind of daydream, oblivious to its implications or consequences.

Finally, the interview ended. As they were leaving and walking down the dark staircase toward the rear door, O'Neill called from the top of the stairs. "Nora has your address and number, right?"

Michael turned to her; she was just behind him on the next step up. "She has, yes, don't you, Nora?"

Nora said she had.

It was already dark when they left the office.

At the corner of the street Michael asked, "Is he as important as he obviously thinks he is?"

"Who knows? Johnny has no time for him, says he knows nothing but likes to make out he does. But I gave up years ago trying to work out who knows what in the organization," she answered, somewhat indifferently.

"You've been a big help to me," he said to her as they walked slowly up the road. "Come for a drink with me."

"I'd like to, but you know what it's like here, in this area, I mean. Prisoners' wives are not usually seen in pubs with reporters from New York."

"But we've been seen walking around the streets together," he pointed out.

"That's different. Going into a pub would start tongues wagging. I never do that unless I'm with my sister."

"Well then, let's pop into town and go to the Gown or the Europa —it's only five minutes away in a cab. Come on, it's not even nine yet I'll bet."

Nora felt an anticlimax. After the delicate feelings of a while ago the thought of sitting in a bar with him put her off. She would be too paranoid, she knew, to be able to reestablish the fragile intimacy she'd felt before, or even relax enough to enjoy herself. It would all be too deliberate, too self-conscious. So she shook her head and refused. Michael was visibly disappointed. But he did not press her any further.

Then she was sorry she had rejected his suggestion so quickly. She would love his company, but her own feelings were swinging back and forth clumsily, so at times the old sympathy she felt for him seemed lost, only to return again. She was annoyed at herself for her own helpless confusion.

"I have a better idea," he said, seeing her vacillate. "Tomorrow afternoon, after I call in my next thrilling installment to New York, we'll go for a drive. I'll pick you up outside the City Hall. Get sick or something so you don't have to go in to the shop after lunch and we'll take off for the afternoon. I want to see a bit of the coast before I return to the States. Come with me."

She suddenly seemed shy before him. "People will talk."

"People used to talk before—that didn't stop us."

"But I told you, Michael, it's different this time—it's dangerous."

"Dangerous?"

"Yes, I'm no longer Nora Lennon, I'm—"

"Mother Ireland?"

She laughed a little.

"Even Mother Ireland needs a little break once in a while."

But still she shook her head, though the thought of being with him fascinated her. He sighed and said good night, turning down the road toward the city center. She called after him before he'd gone very far and ran to catch up with him.

"You're right, Michael. Mother Ireland would love a drive in the country. But—"

"But what?"

"We'll have to be careful. I hate to seem paranoid."

"But you do. 'Who'll be lookin' at the likes of ya, anyway?' " he teased her. They both laughed, remembering her teenage complaints about her father's dismissive reaction to her eccentric clothes. He succeeded in reassuring her. They arranged to meet at two the following afternoon.

When he'd gone Nora turned and headed up the road toward the People's Taxi stand opposite St. Paul's chapel. Now that she was alone her anxieties returned. The thought of home depressed her. She was going back to her real life—this curious, interesting little intrusion was over, for the time being at least. It left her feeling puzzled, nervous. One moment she felt excited by Michael's interest in her, the next she was reacting by telling herself it was all a foolish distraction that could lead nowhere. Yet now she wanted to hear more about him, what he'd done, where he'd gone, how he lived. She wanted to hear how he had realized those much-discussed possibilities of years ago. Her earlier resistance to being reminded of those hopes had melted away. His desire for her had made her suddenly start experiencing herself in a different light. A man's desire for a woman makes her curious about herself, for she cannot really know herself until she has been desired. Michael's attraction for her still perplexed her, but it made her think about herself—about what had happened to her and what was happening to her.

She found herself standing at the taxi stand opposite the chapel. She stood on the curb, waiting. There was little traffic and the road was quiet. On the side of the chapel was a garden, with a crucifixion scene. The large statues stood out against the dim twilight like pale ghosts. On the cross Jesus writhed in agony, his body curled into a kind of ecstasy of pain, and Mary knelt beneath praying, her face blank, resigned. The images of martyr and mother pervaded life in the Falls. Nora remembered the fascination she felt when as a young girl she passed the statues every day on her way to school. Now she stared at them again as if seeing them for the first time in years. The man's sacrifice is so dramatic, the woman's so mundane. Men die in gun battles, or go to jail after shootouts and bank robberies. And the women go home to an empty house, or one full of children, to cook, clean, resume the dull routine of their daily lives. The kneeling woman who watches the sacrifice of her young man becomes the victim of a more awful sacrifice—that of having given everything. Mary gave Jesus to the world, but Jesus gave only himself away. Men regard their lives as trifles only because they were given them by their women.

Nora, like most women, had a profound instinct for happiness, which was the same perhaps as her woman's power to bring life into the world, and a deep capacity for joy, both of which seemed frustrated and contradicted by the pale writhing Jesus and the kneeling mother, bent in acceptance. She turned her head away from the statues, repelled, depressed suddenly by the idealization of her own sacrifice everywhere she turned.

She felt a void in the pit of her stomach. A few women passed on the other side of the street pushing prams, with tired children crying and trailing behind them. They walked by the sacrificial scene and made the sign of the cross quickly, perfunctorily, exhausted and pregnant, worn down. As an adolescent it seemed to her the worst of fates. But at that moment she envied them their children. Perhaps being a mother would help fill the void she felt within her, or would it only intensify the sacrifice? You cannot share your grief with a child, only your joy. She thought of her own mother and felt instinctively that the presence of a child in her life would make the burden of grief harder to bear, for a child wants only happiness from you and cannot understand your suffering. Nevertheless, she envied them. The women turned the corner with their broods past the chapel grounds and disappeared up a side street.

A taxi stopped. She got in and settled back in the rear seat. The floor was full of cigarette ash and candy papers, and the car reeked of smoke. A youth came in behind her, his head shaven in skinhead fashion, his jeans hoisted in large cuffs above his ankles, his boots square and pugnacious. He sat at the other end of the back seat and began smoking restlessly, glancing occasionally at Nora. She opened her window slightly to let out the smoke. As she did so he looked over at her indifferently. The taxi started with a jolt and Nora gripped the strap.

"Corner of Whiterock Road," he called to the driver. Nora said, "Glenn Road, near the barracks." He stretched his thin legs as far as he could and puffed on his cigarette more aggressively, assuming he was disliked by his fellow passenger. Nora looked out of her window and tried to ignore his crude male hostility. When the taxi stopped to let him out he slammed the door. She felt greatly relieved that he'd gone, and relaxed somewhat. She let go of the strap. It all seemed so hopeless. She was going home to an empty house; a stranger had treated her with undeserved contempt; the brief moment of intimacy with Michael was such a delicate thing that it could not possibly survive in this city. She was on the verge of tears.

The road was quite bare as she left the taxi to walk the rest of the way home. Venus was brilliant and setting behind the rim of the mountain's shadowy mass. A cool night wind slid down from the slopes, lightly brushing her hair from her temples. She paused for a moment to look at the bright piercing evening star.

A little further down the road a car pulled up at the curb. The driver's door opened slowly and a man got out of the seat. He looked around him then walked quickly toward Nora, who was about to make the walk up the hill to her house at the top of the street. She did not hear him until he was directly behind her and only knew he was there when his hand took her by the shoulder. She was so startled for a second that she gasped in a near scream. Turning to his touch, she did not recognize Seamus Devine at first. His face was thinner than when she had last seen him. He had grown a little moustache. It did not suit his soft face. His hair was still thin and swept back from his high, round forehead, which gave him a sharp, intelligent appearance in spite of the roundness of his face. His eyes still had an uncertain, tentative, impatient look, as if he were suspicious of everything.

He said nothing, but took her by the arm and motioned her down the street to his car.

"Where are we going?" she whispered.

"Johnny has a message for me," he said.

In her confusion and fright she'd forgotten about it. "Yes," she replied, trying to remember. They were in his car heading out toward the suburbs and the mountains.

"What did he say?"

" 'The Monk's Stone.' "

" 'The Monk's Stone,' that's it? Nothing more?" He sounded disappointed and slightly annoyed.

"Yes, I'm afraid that's it. What's going on, Seamus?" He did not reply. He was intent on the road before him. The car slowed suddenly. He was peering in his rearview mirror at another car approaching quickly. He slowed down until he was overtaken, then turned off into a narrow laneway that ran between high hedgerows. The gravel crunched under the wheels. They came to a halt outside an old cottage. He sighed and sat back in his seat.

"Lovers' Lane," he smiled sarcastically.

"Seamus, what's this all about? I haven't seen you in years and you sneak up behind me and all but kidnap me for a message you apparently don't even understand. What's goin' on?" She was always impatient with him for some reason, and the years, it seemed, hadn't changed that.

He looked hurt, but did not answer. He looked in front of him at the whitewashed walls of the cottage lit up by his headlights.

"Who was that you were with this evening?" he asked, ignoring her question.

"What's that got to do with it?"

"Nothing. I just thought I'd ask."

Nora was even more impatient. His sudden arrival and abruptness with her interrupted her mood, filled her with anxiety, made her feel there was something being kept from her.

"Okay, you got your message, take me home please," she ordered curtly. "I don't like being followed."

He looked round at her indifferently. "I'm sorry. I had to wait till your friend left. 'The Monk's Stone' was all he said, you're sure?"

"I told you. He seemed to think you'd know what that meant. I don't. Is this another grand conspiracy?"

"This is very important, Nora; are you positive . . . ?" She raised her eyes to the ceiling of the car and closed them in annoyance.

"Does a Monk's Stone mean anything to you?" he asked her.

"No," she replied quickly, "but maybe if you told me what's going on—"

"You're too nosy, Nora."

"I've a right to be, don't you agree?"

But Devine was deep in thought and did not pay attention to her. After a few minutes he backed the car out of the laneway.

"I'm surprised this is still going on," she said. "I'd have thought it would have ended now that the truce has been declared."

"There are a few complications. Hasn't Johnny told you?"

"Told me *what?*"

Devine hesitated, uncertain about whether to go on or not. "We've given up too much already," he muttered after a short pause. He half wanted to hurt her, to disillusion her. The two had never gotten on; he resented her and she him. Now that he felt she was in his power and vulnerable he was tempted to tell her, to throw her into doubt. He succeeded.

"Given up what?" she asked sharply. "Are you trying to tell me that Johnny's not happy with the negotiations?"

He grinned at her. He was pleased that he had rankled her. "I told you you're too nosy."

"Is Johnny behind the negotiations?"

"You're as bad as the rest of the women around here; that's all they think about, the bloody negotiations."

"Can you blame them? I suppose you think it's weak of them to want their men out of jail?" Her tone was impatient, sarcastic.

Devine raised his eyebrows. "You think talking to the Brits will get them out of jail? Wise up. I'm surprised; you're an intelligent woman, you swallowed that crap?" He spoke with such intensity that she felt a complete draining away of confidence. The road was very dark. He accelerated rapidly, jolting her.

"What do you mean, 'crap'?" she asked. But he shook off her question. She sensed that he felt he'd said enough.

"Look, you'll have to get to Johnny tomorrow, it's important. You are our only contact with him now."

"Seamus, I asked you a question." She waited. He did not reply. "I'm not your messenger boy. My visit's already been arranged for—"

"Too bad. Tomorrow."

He drove impatiently along the narrow, deserted road. Within minutes the car pulled up sharply at the foot of her street. She looked at him but he gave no response.

"John will tell me," she said, opening the door.

Devine watched her. His eyes softened for an instant. He seemed about to say something. She paused before closing the door.

"Nora," he began, "it's important for us, it's urgent—tomorrow.

Then you can contact me the next day. Contact me in the Flats, 15B Central Tower, or through Jake at the bar if I'm not there, okay?"

"Is that all?"

He nodded yes. She slammed the door behind her and walked quickly up the long, dark street toward home.

He drove off, turning his car around in the direction from which they had just come. He headed up along the road until he came to one of the more well-to-do areas that still existed on the fringes of the big developments. He turned off and drove through a quiet district of large front gardens and trees, past houses with big garages. When he reached Mourne Crescent he pulled up outside a house with a name on the gate that read "Mourne View." After parking the car in the garage he went to the side door and rapped.

"It's me, Seamus," he whispered, when the door opened a crack. Then the light went on in the kitchen and he went in.

A short, broad-shouldered young man with a few days' growth of stubble on his face closed the door behind him. His hair was long, straggling over his ears. He had a square face with a firm chin and widely spaced liquid blue eyes.

"Hey, Gerry," Devine said to him as he came into the room. Gerry Toner bolted the kitchen door quickly.

"She got the message?" he asked Devine. Devine smiled at his friend.

"I'd give her the message, that's for sure. She's still some beauty."

"Horny bastard!" Toner replied. "Keep your mind on your work."

"Aye, she told me, okay."

"Well, what is it?" Toner asked excitedly.

"The Monk's Stone."

"Is that it?"

"That's it. Does it ring a bell?"

"No," said Toner, puzzled and disappointed. "Where the fuck's that?"

"I don't know, but I told Nora to go see him tomorrow to find out. I told her it's urgent, to contact me as soon as I get back."

Toner switched out the light and they went into the back parlor. A big man sat slumped on one of the easy chairs; his red beard was wet with little drops of beer, a bottle of which he held in his right hand. Jim Byrnes looked up at Devine.

"Okay?" he asked.

"Yep, no problem, except I'm not sure what it means," Devine groaned and flopped down in a chair. "She wiped me out with questions. Give us a beer."

Toner tore one of the bottles from out of the six-pack that sat on a little table in the center of the room and handed it to Devine.

"Where's McAnulty?" Devine asked after he took a long swig. But before anyone could answer he put one finger on his lips and got up. He went over to the little radio that was on top of a corner cabinet and switched it on. No one spoke until he found some loud rock music. He turned up the volume and returned to his seat. It was a habit he'd picked up from years of being on the run. The British had been known to bug houses before.

"Anyway, where is he?"

"He went off earlier to try Fagan again. One last try," Toner answered.

"He's crazy. Fagan's just not on. He's got a cozy setup going for himself, the bastard," Devine retorted contemptuously. "He should catch himself on—Fagan's not about to give all that up, so he isn't."

"But we have to try again," Toner answered with patient emphasis.

"What about the gear?" Byrnes put in, wanting to change the subject. "Gerry told me it was—"

Devine smiled a wide, full smile. "Good stuff—all there. Uzis, Berretas, the lot. We need more like 'em. But we need that fuckin' money to get it. Give me that map." He reached over and took an ordinance survey map of Belfast and began pouring over it. "The Monk's Stone, the Monk's Stone . . . ," he kept repeating as he started to mark off churches in the university area.

They drank. Toner looked down at the pattern of concentric rings on the little carpet. It reminded him of a target board.

"What if Fagan makes a move?" he asked Devine. Devine took a swig, draining the bottle effortlessly and smacking his lips. He reached over to the table and ripped the pack, taking out another bottle.

"Depends on the move. He'd like to get his hands on the money. But he knows we have support. He might just stay out of it and wait till things develop. Once he sees how it's going he won't interfere. He's not an operator."

"I think he will interfere," said Toner. "If he doesn't come over to us he'll make a move. He'll have to. McCabe will see to that."

"It will be the most important decision of his life," said Byrnes, who never said much except what was the crux of any matter.

"It might just be the last one," Devine said. There was a flicker in his eye. The other men looked glumly at each other and at him. Toner got up, irritated by the loud music, and walked to the window.

"Can't we turn that down now?" he asked, looking over at Devine.

"Jesus, it'd take us a month of Sundays to sift through every bloody churchyard on this fucking map. Maybe it isn't even in a church," Devine said impatiently, searching his friends' eyes for any sudden revelations.

Toner drew back the curtains slowly and peered into the darkness outside.

"What's keeping McAnulty?" he asked.

"He shouldn't have gone alone," Devine said. "Fagan can't be trusted."

He got up and switched off the radio. Toner listened by the window, enjoying the sudden silence in the room and the dark stillness outside.

The city seemed unnaturally quiet.

6

"this fellow Boyd is a reporter. Doing a story on the coming British withdrawal," said Detective Constable Reid. Mackal looked at the thin-lipped young policeman and smiled. "Really? I wish he'd tell us about it. Then we would have plenty of time to book our flights out of here." The sergeant slammed the file cabinet shut and took his coat from the rack.

"What's he got to do with Nora Costello?"

Reid shrugged and gave a leering grin. "Three years is a long time, Sergeant."

"Well, Reid, you're the big expert on women." Mackal looked in the direction of Reid's desk where he kept a drawer full of pornographic magazines, managing to hide his annoyance at the remark. "Watch him—have someone watch the hotel. These reporters often get to meet interesting people."

He put on his coat and said he was going home early tonight. "I'd a long drive today. I'm beat."

As he was leaving the squad room the telephone rang. He stopped and looked back. The officer who answered the phone called over to him, "Suspicious car, that's all."

"Where?" Mackal asked, walking back to the desk.

"You're supposed to be going home early, Sergeant."

Mackal took the phone. A woman's voice spoke distractedly into his ear. "It's a suspicious car," she said hurriedly. "There's a big box in the boot of it. It might be a bomb. Please get someone up here quickly, please."

"Where are you, missus?"

He wrote down the location. The woman gave the make of the car, her name and address.

"Okay, thank you for your assistance. There's a patrol on its way."

Then, turning to the other policeman he said, "It's on my way home. Ring regimental HQ and have them send their walking can opener to the corner of Quarry Road and Hamilton Lane. It's a white Austin 1100 and the lady says it's got a big box in it. She lives in number 125 Quarry Road. Mrs. Duffy. I'll take a squad up right away."

"Take it easy, Sergeant," Reid said as Mackal was about to leave. Mackal reminded him of the ceasefire.

"There'll be no ambushes tonight, Reid. We don't have to worry about such things now," he smiled ironically as he left the squad room.

The convoy drove its funnel of light into the darkness, where the road wound and twisted through the still suburbs. Cats scampered crazily, zigzagging across their path; mongrel dogs bounded from behind hedgerows barking at the intruders.

"It should be round the next bend," Mackal said. The vehicle slowed down. As it turned the corner its headlights picked out the white shape of a car.

The back of the white Austin was already open. Peering through the slot in the protected windscreen Lieutenant Beardsley said, "I see we are expected. It's conspicuously open."

A big box was clearly visible in the car's boot. Behind him Mackal heard the Land-Rovers halt and the crunch of military boots on the gravel of the roadway. He looked hard at the box.

"Someone wants to reassure us, sure enough," Mackal muttered. "Still, I'm not budging till that walking can opener has a chance to poke around in there."

There was a roar of engines from the opposite direction. Like little blurred comets, headlights came toward them through the darkness. It was the aid from the regiment's headquarters, bringing the robot bomb-disposal equipment.

"Here's your, ah, can opener, as you call it," said the British lieutenant. He picked up the microphone.

"Target white Austin 1100. Rear. There's a box. Send in the probe."

Mackal always winced slightly at the clipped, precise British accent, which was so irritatingly suited to command. It was an accent that seemed almost embarrassed by the vulgarity of the sounds of language itself and sought to attenuate them.

A few minutes later the large contraption rolled awkwardly round to the back of the car. Its boom was lowered to probe the box. Finding a loose lid, it flicked it off. Through the robot's scope, which was monitored on a terminal component in the back of the saracen, a dark shape was discernible in the box. Lieutenant Beardsley turned to Mackal. "Looks like another corpse, Sergeant. It seems clean. The robot shows nothing much—just a body."

Mackal turned to the officer. "Okay, ask its masters to guide it over the ground toward us. It's conceivable there might be a land mine, isn't it Beardsley, old boy?" he mocked mildly. "I'm harder to replace than that contraption."

Beardsley looked at the detective somewhat impatiently. He was about to reassure Mackal that he thought all the precautions really unnecessary when he saw the look in Mackal's eyes—a wry, skeptical expression that the officer felt obliged to assuage. He relayed Mackal's instruction. Seconds later the robot came toward them. When it reached their vehicle it turned back, only pausing to poke at a brick that lay before it. Mackal watched it rather distastefully.

"Do you think that thing will ever make you redundant around here, Lieutenant? That would be the end of Sandhurst," he said. He pushed down the door handle and swung his legs out, dropping onto the roadway.

He stood by the side of the army vehicle for a moment looking around him. He sniffed something.

"What's up, old chap?" the officer asked, leaning out of the saracen toward him.

"I just smell something familiar."

"Oh?" Beardsley sniffed. "And what's that?"

"Just death, young fella, just death."

He began walking toward the car. He walked quickly and in a straight line. The houses around him were dark. Mackal looked up at the windows, which were nearly all open. It was a warm night. A breeze lifted the curtains and they flapped against the walls outside. He scanned each window as he walked. Nothing but the curtains moved. It was so quiet he could hear the clocks ticking in the bedrooms.

As he got closer to the car he smelt something else. It mingled with the queer odor of death, of inert, lifeless flesh before it has gone off;

it too was a familiar smell. He bent down by the big box: it was the smell of hair oil, and it reminded him of someone.

The body lay heavily on its stomach, the head twisted round to one side. He shone a torch on the face. Grimace of death, blood caked around the mouth, eyes open, staring at nothingness. He knew the face. He remembered the smell. Harry McAnulty, one of the "moneybags" gang, interned for three years, recently released; Mackal shone the beam of light on his head, which was a mass of matted hair and blood. The hair still glistened from the excess of hair oil McAnulty liked to use.

"I recognized the hair oil," Mackal said standing up. The lieutenant beside him stared at the body.

"A head job I believe they call it?"

"That's right, that's the phrase." He directed his beam at Mc-Anulty's temple. "It doesn't take more than one bullet to kill a man."

"You knew him, Sergeant?"

"Aye. I put him away once. Harry McAnulty's his name. Drove a car for the Costello gang. Best getaway man in the business. His friends called him 'Speedy'; he always overdid the Brylcream. Thought he was Elvis."

A few minutes later the sound of the ambulance siren was rousing the people from their sleep. Lights came on all along the row of nearby houses. Inside 125 an old lady called Mrs. Duffy sat wrapped in a bathrobe nervously explaining to Sergeant Mackal what she'd seen.

The next morning on the way to Long Kesh Nora Costello read the account in the local newspaper of the finding of McAnulty's body. She remembered him from the early days when he spent a lot of time with Johnny. They said he was Johnny's driver. The report said that "sources close to the security forces hint at possible disagreements within the guerrilla movement about the current though unacknowledged truce." The chatter of the women around her seemed a world away. Another body, another visit; she felt a nervous sickness in her stomach.

"I didn't expect you today," Johnny said to her, concerned. He was surprised at how pale and drawn she looked. "What's the matter?"

"Did you hear about Harry?" she asked.

"On the radio this morning."

She looked at him intensely, waiting for him to go on. But he didn't. She was about speak when he asked if she had done what he'd requested.

"Yes, just last night. I told him. That's one reason I'm here."

"So?" her husband asked, leaning toward her over the little table.

"He asked me to come this morning because . . ." she broke off, glancing behind her. Then, shaking her head, she whispered impatiently, "He doesn't understand!"

Johnny looked at her, his eyes full of disbelief and annoyance. Slowly he leant back, looking up over the rim of the cubicle toward the platform where a prison officer sat. Then he reached across the table and took her hand gently, affectionately, smiling. "Nora, you must remember the Monk's Stone. I remember you telling me about the trips you and some fella made there before you met me. I always thought it was a bit strange myself going to old graveyards . . ."

Nora was startled by the memory. Michael and she had often explored the old graveyard John was thinking of, searching for an ancient headstone, said to date from the time when a monastery stood on the grounds. She couldn't help smiling a little at the curious irony of all this. John had gotten the name wrong.

"Friar's Bush," she whispered, "that's where we went."

"By the university?"

"Yes."

He looked suddenly relieved.

"I got the place right at least," he sighed, squeezing her hand. "I only hope my friend did," he continued, under his breath.

"It's the only one in the district, John. It's the oldest, and the friar's grave is there—an old headstone."

He nodded. "That's what I told him," he smiled, referring to Murray. "Anyway Nora—we'll soon find out. You'll straighten it out with him as quickly as possible."

"I'm seeing him tomorrow," she replied abstractly. "Why is this suddenly so important?"

He did not want to be bothered with her question, but her gaze would not let him go. Meeting with Devine last night had left her with nagging doubts about what was happening, about the truce, the amnesty, all the things on which her hopes were pinned. Now this sudden need for the money—after all these years. She knew there was something developing and she wanted Johnny to tell her. Instead, he freed his hand from hers and looked away. But she stretched her hand out again toward him, offering it, a pleading gesture. He looked at her.

"It's important for me, for Ireland. Without it our friends will have many problems," he said softly, referring to the stolen money. "You know what I mean."

Now she had to recognize the truth. It was more than just a political dispute: money meant guns, and guns meant more killing, more war. She was silent for a moment, absorbing the shocking implications. She found herself repeating the phrase "But the amnesty, and home, Johnny . . ." Then she looked at him calmly and began, "This means that . . ." But before she could finish he shook his head slowly, reaching his hand up to her mouth.

"No, Johnny," she said, pushing his hand away, "I won't be put off. You have to tell me yourself. I can't go on in this vacuum much longer."

His blue eyes were fixed on her; he blinked as if coming out of a daydream, but said nothing.

"What about Harry?" she whispered. She was clearly distraught. "Is that why he's dead? I can't tell anymore what's . . . Does it mean . . . ?"

"It means they killed him, that's all," he said suddenly, firmly.

"They?"

"Yes—they." He reached across the table and put his arm around her neck, pulling her effortlessly toward him. "Fagan, McCabe, the ones who are behind this sellout," he almost hissed the words into her ear. "They murdered him." Nora sat back, stunned.

"But it's too late, Nora, it's too late."

She looked at him questioningly. "For what?" she said slowly, softly, reluctantly almost, as if one part of her didn't want to know any more.

"The talks, the truce, the whole fucking business—it's too late. I'm sorry. We couldn't go on with it."

"Who's we?"

"Us—the men behind me. Men like Harry—men those lapdogs of the British are murdering to save their skins, their precious little privileges, their new businesses. But it's too late!"

"But, Johnny, how could you—when we were so close to . . . not now . . ."

Their eyes met.

"We?" he repeated.

"You and I!" she answered with growing desperation.

He sighed impatiently and looked around him. He was angry at her now, reluctant to explain any further. Men were being murdered and she was talking about "you and I" as if there was nothing else of importance in the world.

"This is the start of the last big push—we'll win this time—no talks, no concessions—we'll get them out this time for Christ's sake, woman! Listen. Believe me." He reached across and tried to grab her hand, but she pulled it back violently. She could not look at him now.

"I've had faith. I've waited. You're condemning me to a lifetime alone." She spoke dispassionately.

"Nora, don't talk like that. It won't be long, believe me; it has to be this way. All those men must not have died in vain. We can't give up now for nothing!" He spoke through clenched teeth. His eyes seemed hard and glinting.

"It's not for nothing! There's the amnesty, the withdrawal . . ."

Before she'd finished he guffawed contemptuously. "What withdrawal? What amnesty? It's a trick—the British have been promising a withdrawal statement for months. Where is it? What a joke! Where's your amnesty, where? Listen, Nora, McCabe has given up—he wants to believe those things and make people like you believe them. He wants to get political power; he's looking for an excuse to surrender."

"Johnny, no, please, no," she began to sob softly. "I don't care about any of that any more. I'm sick hearing about final pushes and eternal struggles. I'm sick to death of it!" She paused, her eyes dilated, confronting the future with a sudden terror. "I don't have any children, I want to have—"

"You're hysterical! Stop!" He stood up as two watchful prison officers came over. The other women turned to see what was going on. There was a hushed silence in the long hut. Nora felt hands grasping her by the elbow. A strange voice was asking if she was okay.

"What did you do to this poor woman?" she heard someone say. But she could hardly stand. Three years of waiting felt as if they had been telescoped into one instant. In her collapsing universe of grief all time was reduced to this second of despair. It left a dark vacuum at the core of her that at that moment gave out neither the light nor heat of any hope.

Nora lay still, listening to the sounds of children playing in the street outside. The curtains flapped in the strong mountain breeze that was stiffening all morning. She turned and looked at the clock beside her bed. Lunchtime nearly. Over on her dressing table their marriage photograph stood amidst a heap of fresh underclothes. Other clothes lay scattered around the floor. The room was a mess. She gazed at the print of the Constable painting. It seemed to radiate a soothing, subdued green light, a moment of perfect stillness.

Her eyes were washed out. She sat up on the edge of the bed, folded her arms and knees and bent over, resting her head on her knees. She rocked back and forth a little as if in a keen, a silent keen. Outside the children were screaming as the roar of an army vehicle rolled down the street. There was a clatter of rocks and bottles, a screech of brakes, loud cheers. Then the sounds of the vehicle died away and the laughter of the children returned. The incident reminded her of Michael, that moment in the hallway, the tingle of her nipples awakened after years of numbness. Thinking of her appointment with him, she got up and walked to the mirror.

She untied her hair, letting it fall over her shoulders. She loosened her blouse and felt her breasts. Her body seemed a useless thing to her. She wanted to stir it into action, arouse it, make it feel again. It was as if there was a ring of tension at the core of her, the dark, cold core of her, tightening, falling inward toward a central nothingness. She slipped off her blouse, undid the straps of her bra, letting her breasts bend downward gently, buoyantly, and shed her skirt like an old skin. It crumpled silently and softly around her feet. She shed her underwear too until she was staring at her naked image in the mirror. Nora Costello looked at Nora Costello and found her still beautiful. Aroused by the image of her own naked body, she found herself an object of desire—her own object of desire. Her breasts tingled gently, their tips erect, reminding her of a casual touch and beyond that once of a failure to touch. It was the secret memory her body had kept, which her mind had suppressed until then.

She walked to the open window and draped the summery curtain over her smooth skin. She looked out over the back garden. It was wild, untended, overgrown, the soil unturned, undug, heavy, useless. The breeze blew over her diaphanous nakedness, its gentle pressure like a lover's fingers parting softly the hairs around her moist womb mouth.

Belfast was behind them. They drove along the Shore Road that ran down one side of Belfast Lough toward the wilder coastline of County Antrim, where the basalt screes tumbled to the edge of the Atlantic Ocean. Nora had opened her window and was letting the wind blow her hair. It lashed wildly around her face. She smelt the first salty scent of seaweed. She wanted to go faster, farther. After this morning's confrontation she felt a kind of panic grip her. But the farther behind she left Belfast, the more at ease she became. She looked over her shoulder at the grim outline of the city.

"It seems to clog up the mouth of the lough," she said with a tone of distaste.

"Remember Swift's remarks?" Michael asked. "He called that lovely body of water on our right a 'sink.'"

"That's right. Remember the evening we spent looking for his old church around here somewhere? Where he was pastor for a while? Wasn't it near Carrickfergus Castle? Did we ever find it?" She spoke fondly, caressingly, of that past that she now sought desperately to retrieve. It was a relief from the prospect of the future. It was a reminder that then she had a different future.

Michael thought for a moment, finding it hard to concentrate when Nora was so anxious and perturbed.

"I seem to recall finding a ruin that looked like a church. It was full of dead crows. It looked like a pig sty."

Ahead of them the battlements of Carrickfergus Castle stood out above a basalt rock jutting into the water. It was a twelfth-century structure built by the Normans to protect the entrance to the lough. Nora relaxed, enjoying the sensation of leaving the city at least temporarily behind her, of being carried so effortlessly away in a car to nowhere in particular.

Earlier, when she had told Michael about this morning's visit, he tried to make light of it. He pointed out that there was little that John could do in jail; that the talks were going on still as far as he knew; that prisoners were still being released. But it was no use. Nora knew better. She hesitated, not wanting to admit the full extent of her own involvement in the latest intrigues, yet wanting at the same time to share the burden that was thrust upon her. The money from the robbery never got to the IRA leadership. Somehow it remained hidden all this time; now it was to be used to break the truce, and she knew where it was. But she could not tell Michael. She dare not drag him into the whole dangerous mess.

"No, Michael," she said. "Something's been wrong all along. No matter what happens now it won't be settled. Even if Devine and Johnny and their supporters don't succeed in breaking the truce, it might turn out to be true what they said about the British. There hasn't been a statement about the amnesty or withdrawal; there's been nothing but denials. I just can't . . ." She paused, defeated. "I just don't care any more. It's been too long now. Another war won't bring peace any closer. Nothing will." She didn't want to talk about it any longer. It had already exhausted her. She wanted just to sit back and drive off, to watch Belfast get behind her and then see the hills go by, listen to the waves break, smell the sea breezes, forget everything.

But Michael persisted. "The British *have* to deny it, Nora. That's no indication . . ." But when she looked at him the despair in her eyes pleaded with him not to go on with these false hopes, not to try and reassure her any more, and he stopped.

"I'm supposed to be taking your mind off it, I'm sorry."

They drove silently for a while. He looked around at her. She was stretched back in the seat, her eyes closed, her legs crossed. The lovely full curve of her thigh was emphasized by her narrow skirt. She opened her eyes, aware that he was looking at her. His desire distracted her for a second. "I haven't been out here in years," she said softly, her voice full of relief. They were entering the town of Carrickfergus itself.

"Why don't we stop and visit the castle?"

Michael agreed and began searching for a parking space.

There was a small crowd of sightseers around the wooden drawbridge. Michael and Nora went in under the portcullis, looking up at the ceiling of the gatehouse arch, where there was a huge spiked iron contraption that was supposed to be dropped on unwelcome guests. They walked over the first cobblestone courtyard up steps to the battlements facing out over the lough. The water was blue, the sky clear.

Michael was silent. He was taken back to a distant winter's day, remembering the green-gray cold waters, the gray sky, the foggy outline of the city. He leaned against the battlements. A big seagull landed not far away. A group of children ran past, scaring it off again. They walked into the little chapel above the castle's gateway. The narrow windows were covered with stained glass. The sunbeams were refracted into rainbows of color in which swirled clouds of dust. When Nora reached out to cup them in her hands they plunged in primordial eddies. It reminded her of when she was a bored child at Sunday mass and she passed the time watching the swirls of dust in the shafts of light that penetrated the big stained-glass windows until finally the benediction heralded their imminent release. She suggested that they go up the keep, a ninety-foot central tower, one of the oldest parts of the fortress dominating the walls around it.

At the top of the tower the wind was blowing hard. The flag that surmounted it was tugged vigorously tight. Nora leaned over the top, getting giddy at the height, made breathless by the gusting wind. She crouched behind the battlement to regain her composure. She shook the hair from her eyes, combing it through her fingers.

"Michael," she gasped, "that feels good. Try it—stick your head out. Let the wind buffet you for a minute." He peered down at the small figures below in the courtyard. On the green outside by the landward wall there was a brass band playing. The sound was carried away over the lough by the wind. He stared ahead of him, beyond the city toward the Down hills and discerned the humped shapes of the Mourne Mountains.

"I can see those mountains from my bedroom window," she said. He found her standing beside him, her body against the granite battlement. The wind fell suddenly, letting her hair drop in place around her shoulders. He saw she was close to tears. The distant mountains made her think of home—her bedroom, her cold empty bed, this morning's awful confrontation in the prison and the realization of the future that it predicted for her. She turned abruptly away from the view and walked down the steps to the little archway that led to the narrow, winding stairs. He followed her.

The stairway was steep, twisting precariously, stone step after stone step, down to the base of the keep.

"Be careful," he said. She placed one hand on the cold wall for balance. He was close behind her.

"Norman ladies certainly didn't wear tight skirts," she said. The descent made her dizzy and she had to stop for a moment.

"Are you all right?" he asked, bending down toward her. She said she was and began the descent again. Halfway down was a step higher than the rest, near a curve; it was a trick step, meant to trip unwary invaders. As he turned the bend Michael saw it and remembered from many previous visits. He called to her, but she lurched forward off balance. Michael swept his arm around her waist and pulled her back. She fell against him, pressing him to the wall.

"Steady," he whispered. His hands held her. He did not let go. Her waist was narrow, her hip bones broad and powerful; he lingered, unwilling to give her up again. But gently she freed herself, standing a little apart from him. As she did so she gently, involuntarily squeezed his hand.

At the bottom they sat down to rest.

"The last time we were here we found an old tunnel, remember?" she asked. "It was near the base of the tower." She felt like a ghost destined to return to haunt the place of its demise. She got up and walked around the corner to a kind of alcove. The tunnel ran in under the tower down a slight gradient. She called to him; she was standing inside the tunnel now, haunting the spot where years ago their relationship had died.

"It still smells as bad as it did way back then," he said, standing at the entrance leaning against the side of it. He could just about make her out, but she could see him silhouetted against the brightness.

"Be careful, Nora."

She did not answer. Water dripped from the low ceiling. Damp webs brushed his face as he walked in. The walls dimly glistened. She was standing looking down the tunnel toward the darker depths. She felt him brush against her. She was breathing softly.

"It's so cold in here," she whispered, shuddering a little.

Michael's eyes were following her dark shape. It was as if the intervening years had not occurred, as if they had never left this tunnel, this darkness that swallowed them up. All that had happened in between seemed lost in the blackness around them, so that when she called him, "Michael," and reached out her hand, groping through the damp darkness, he found it instinctively and led her through the darkness to him. They faced each other again. There was nothing between them there. In the oblitering darkness her lips parted, her body was touching him as lightly as a web that brushed her face, and she looked up at him.

He had failed her once. Her mute appeal had gone unanswered. She had become as vulnerable as a woman could before him and he had turned away, unable to face it, puzzled, confused, his desire baffled. Now she was vulnerable again, responding to his tenderness, seeking his strength. This was inevitable from the moment he saw her balanced precariously on the top of the ladder in the book shop. And when he held her briefly on the winding staircase he knew his desire could not, would not, be baffled again. Yet at this moment he hesitated. The reassuring obliteration bestowed by the darkness was only an illusion; they would leave it to walk into the brilliant northern light, which would bare everything and bring them back to their torturous responsibilities. But it was only a second's doubt and even before it had passed he was kissing Nora Costello full on the mouth.

She only vaguely remembered the drive back to Belfast. Michael bought her a drink, tried to get her to relax, but she'd clung to him tightly, her body cleaving to his. In the tunnel it seemed as if it had been decided. But as they drew near Belfast she pressed more closely to him, not wanting to face the city with its memories of her married life springing up to confront her. As they did, Nora pressed upon Michael with an instinct that told her he would release her from the fear of the past, the problems of the future; that whatever the fears or the problems that lay ahead because of her decision they would be dispelled by the dread of the alternative: the emptiness that yawned, swallowing up her future.

In the tunnel something was renewed—something there predating John, marriage, the last few years of her life, something to which she always wanted to return. And she had, without ever thinking about being "unfaithful." But back in this hotel it was different. She confronted for the first time the consequences of being unfaithful to her husband. For a long time she thought of John in prison, of what he would think. The pressure of the world she lived in bore down on her heavily. But Michael came to her when he saw her hesitate. He was gentle, calming, and his hands felt so at home as they explored her body that she sensed her doubts ebb, her desperation giving way to a surge of joy.

He knew he could not stop it then. But even as he touched her, as his hands cupped her breasts for the first time and he felt her stomach press upward against him, he needed to caution her somehow.

"I don't want you to be hurt by this," he murmured. "I don't want to . . ."

She rested her head against his chest and hugged him more tightly. She knew what he meant; she knew what risks she was taking only too well; she knew the certainty of condemnation that was staring her in the face.

"Oh, Michael, please love me, that's all—no one will understand but us. But we understand, we always have, before we even knew it—and that's more important now than anything else." She looked up at him, her lips parted a little.

"I know. We have a claim on each other," he whispered, "regardless."

He kissed her parted lips, parted in desire, open in the strange awe she felt for him as a man enfolding her so easily, gently, naturally, firmly. Her body was under his control now and she resigned herself to him with an unspeakable sense of relief. Then there were no doubts possible, not within the protective circle of his embrace, and she was hungering to be naked with him, as if her increasing vulnerability would increase this sweet sensation of security, of being possessed by him. Soon her body was buckling under the fierce intensity of her desire. He led her to the bed.

Naked, she sank in pleasure under him as every thrust drove her deeper, deeper, deeper into herself where she had never been before.

The light of afternoon dimmed to an evening glow. The long twilight behind the hills bathed the city in the valley below in a faint turquoise haze, darkening so slowly that time seemed suspended and then reversed, and dawn would begin again before the day ever ended. Nora lay enfolded in his arms listening to his breathing and the clock ticking. She knew him, she knew him not, she knew him, she knew him not. It rocked gently back and forth in her brain like a pendulum swinging between the known and the unknown. The dark, cold core of her, that tightening ring that seemed at one point to be on the verge of crushing her, was warm with him and moist. Her whole body tingled electrically with warmth radiating from where there was now a glow.

Nora woke early, disturbed by the silence. The avenue outside his hotel was quiet. She lay motionless for a minute, expecting the sound of the mill horn, the sound that disrupted the sleep of the ghetto. But not here among avenues, gardens, lawns, trees; only the leaves rustled and a car door slammed. She turned in the bed where Michael lay sleeping with his back to her. His back was broad, his shoulders wide and light-boned. She touched him gently, afraid to wake him. Her hand ran down his side, gliding lightly over his skin to his hip. The covers were chaotically strewn, exposing him. She felt something around her ankle and looked down under the sheet. Her underwear was wrapped around her ankle like a bracelet. She closed her eyes. He had undressed her with such slow deliberation that she for the first time experienced nakedness with a man as a savored pleasure, the thrill of her own vulnerability so perfect as to be unbearably exciting, yet satisfying in itself. She was not surprised at what happened. She could not recall when she first knew she would make love to Michael. Perhaps, she thought, it was because of what John had done to her that morning yesterday when he so easily condemned her to a longer solitude than she could bear. But then in the castle she realized that it was because something had been left unfulfilled many years ago—it was a part of her that had not been satisfied, not by John's desire nor his powerful lust for her, not by her marriage. No, it was a part of her that only Michael could fulfill.

She rose and padded softly to the window, stooping to pick up her underwear still draped around her left ankle. Pulling the curtains back slightly she peered down into the silent avenue. Her body felt luminous, glowing with pleasure, her loins warm and rich. She wrapped her arms around herself, hugging herself in a gesture of welcome to someone once lost and just returned.

Michael stirred. When he awoke he saw her shape against the window. She was very still, in shadow as she had been in the tunnel. The whole room, the very morning, seemed tranquil. Lazy from satisfaction he lay motionless looking at her. All the time between that winter's afternoon and this summer's morning seemed but a preparation for this moment of repose.

Nora looked around, aware that he was watching her. She stood before him clothed only in shadows, the shafts of sunlight beginning to slant through the part in the curtains, dappled with trembling leaves. She came and lay down beside him again tenderly.

She was startled, almost shocked, when he asked her to return with him to America.

7

*P*eadar McCabe sat at the table drinking. From the corner snug where he and his friends sat separate from the rest he looked out at the big room of the club packed with people. The air was full of cigarette smoke and noise; every table was crowded with pint glasses containing the dregs of beer or Guinness stout. On the stage a local band played a sentimental Irish patriotic song—"Four Green Fields"—but it received only scanty attention from the drinkers.

"Tomorrow," he said, leaning across to Jack Fagan, "tomorrow we lay it on the line. If the Brits want us to run the show we do it our way. If they're gonna go, we have to make sure that's understood." He was confident, a man who knew he was in control, who knew he'd be listened to. The men who were around him nodded.

"It's a pity about Harry . . . but—he was a mad bastard," McCabe added.

Fagan grunted indifferently, "No tears, Peadar. He had to be made an example of—there was no other way—there's too much at stake now. They have to understand we mean business. If they had their way we'd all be in fuckin' jail in no time. The whole thing would be wrecked. Listen, all they know is the gun. Politics means nothing to them. 'Revolution'—that's what they call it! They're not Irishmen, they're fuckin' communists!" Fagan spoke with contempt.

"If the Brits get on our backs about it we'll have to make that plain, Jacky. They'll want to know why the bastard was done. It's up to us to keep the lid on this thing. They don't want a fuckin' Cuba on their doorstep, do they now? We'll make sure they understand that, Jacky. They're not stupid." McCabe sat back. The Cuba line was a good one; he would remember to use it with the Brits next time. His companions shook their heads in agreement.

"What about the money?" Fagan asked after a pause. The empty glasses were crowding over the table top.

"The money? Forget that! Devine probably bought himself a yacht with it years ago. McAnulty said nothing?"

Fagan shook his head. "Not a peep out of him."

No one spoke for a moment. The sentimental clamor from the stage seemed to climax, for a second overpowering the noise from the floor. Most of the men around McCabe were moved by the music—in silence they remembered their dead or imprisoned friends.

The next morning Fagan rose early. He had to pick up McCabe, then drive to the "big house" about twelve miles away by ten o'clock. The meeting would be an important one. Mrs. Fagan was going into town and cajoled her husband for a lift. He said he was pressed for time. He told her he had to meet somebody.

"It's on your way" was her only reply.

He fidgeted impatiently as he waited for his wife to ready herself. He sat down to reread the account of McAnulty's death in yesterday's newspaper. Finally she was ready.

The wind ruffled his dark wavy hair as he walked down the garden path to the car. It had turned cold; there was a touch of autumn in the air. His wife had to run to keep up with him.

He drove impatiently through the morning traffic.

"Not many Brits on the road these days," Mrs. Fagan observed. "I remember the time when there was a checkpoint at every corner, remember, Jacky?"

He smiled a little to himself. "Aye, there's been some changes."

They passed the big club that Fagan ran. He thought of last night's meeting with satisfaction. Next door to it was a cooperative butchers' shop, also run by the organization. Not far from it on the opposite side of the road was a garage, also part of the new economic network under the IRA's control, which had been spreading rapidly through the ghetto. There was little traffic apart from the People's Taxis, the black cabs controlled by them as well; but these were plentiful. Bars, stores, cabs, garages—the economic life of the ghetto was now in their hands. He surveyed the road and all its commerce with satisfaction.

Fagan's eyes moved constantly from the rearview mirror to the road ahead. A black taxi was behind them. An army saracen pulled out of a side street and Fagan slowed up. The taxi pulled up behind him. Before he could pick up speed it swung round his car and sped off in front.

"Madman'll get himself killed," he muttered as the taxi disappeared around the wide bend ahead.

"There should be more control over who gets licenses," his wife said, looking at him for approval. He ignored her remark. She noticed he was slightly on edge.

"Did you not sleep well last night, Jacky?" she asked.

"I'm okay," he replied curtly, "just in a hurry thanks to you."

"I'm sorry, Jacky. If I'd known it was so important I'd have gone on my own. Who are ya meetin'?"

"A friend."

He pulled up at a red light. His eyes scanned the sidewalk. His fingers drummed on the dashboard; he glanced up at the light, waiting for it to change. A youth passed in front of the car. A stray dog ambled in a leisurely manner across the road, pausing to sniff at his front tire. It jumped apprehensively as he started the car with a jerk.

"You *are* in a rush," he wife said, glancing at him anxiously.

Mrs. Fagan saw the hardware store just past the next traffic lights. "Jacky, pull up there for just one second. We need a washer for the sink," she said quickly.

"Christ almighty, Eileen, I'm running late as it is!"

"It'll take one second, so it will. Come on. It'll save me the extra stop on the way back home."

He stopped hard against the curb. She got out and ran to the shop. Fagan sighed impatiently and looked at his watch. He was in good time, but he was tense. Through his rearview mirror he saw another black taxi slow down as it approached. He watched it accelerate past him and turn a corner not far from where he was parked. He was startled to hear his name being called.

"Jacky—have you change of a fiver?" his wife was asking, her head sticking out of the shop doorway. He cursed under his breath and dug his hand deep into his pocket. As he pulled out some bills he spilled coins on the floor of the car. He handed some loose change to Mrs.

Fagan as she poked her head in the window, then opened the car door and got out. He bent down to pick up the coins.

Round the next corner the black taxi had come to a halt. A young man wearing a blue windbreaker got out and walked back toward Fagan's car. Both his hands were in his pockets and he walked briskly. When Fagan came into view he quickened his pace until he was almost running.

Jack Fagan was picking up his last coin when once more he heard his name being called. He looked up. The young man in the blue windbreaker was standing a few feet from him pointing a .357 Magnum. Fagan raised both hands, opening them, letting the money fall. Before it hit the ground he was staggered back by a bullet that caught him in the throat. Another tore off bone and blood and cloth from the top of his shoulder. He lay suffocating, ashen, his eyes rolling. The young man stood over him and grinned nervously. Then he returned to the taxi, which quickly drove off down the Falls Road, turning off into the myriad side streets of the ghetto. As the cab pulled away the killer could hear the familiar sounds of a woman screaming as she bent over her fallen husband watching in horror the life drain out of him into the gutter.

Later that morning Nora Costello was sitting in the back room of the bookshop sipping tea. It was her midmorning break and as usual she was reading the morning papers as she sipped her hot tea. She found it hard to concentrate, however. Last night's pleasures, joys, the sheer relief, were pulsing through her. With the newspaper on her lap she sank back in her chair and closed her eyes. She smiled broadly to herself. It was hard to suppress a laugh. Since leaving Michael's hotel, she had not let herself be troubled by thoughts of consequences. She would deal with Patricia and the rest of the world later. Right now the feeling of relief was too powerful and pleasurable to be destroyed by a troubled conscience.

The cashier came in. "There's someone wants to see you, Nora," she said.

"Oh, dear, is this Patricia, or Michael, or what?" she thought. "Michael wouldn't be so rash, would he; and with any luck Patricia . . ." But it was neither. As she came back into the front of the shop she saw that two men were standing near the door waiting for her. Outside was a group of British soldiers. A small crowd was gathering around them.

"Nora Costello?" one of the men asked.

"Yes."

"We are detaining you for questioning under Section 12 of the Prevention of Terrorism Act. Get your coat."

"But—"

"Come on. You've got seven days to talk about it."

The cashier looked blankly at Nora as she turned to get her coat from the back. "I hope it's nothing serious," she said to the detectives when Nora was in the back room.

One of them looked around the shop. "You never know, do you?" he said.

At a downtown police station she was given her twelve-page arrest form, which stated she had been arrested under Section 12 of the Prevention of Terrorism Act (1974), allowing the police to hold and question her for seven days without charge. She was then brought to the holding center.

She lay on the bed trying to block the noise of the whirring fan out of her ears. It was constant. She couldn't get comfortable because the bed was covered with a kind of plastic sheet that made her perspire. The light bulb burned steadily, hour after hour. Above there were no windows, so she could not tell whether it was day or night. She lost track of time. She guessed she'd been held for over twelve hours already, so it would be night outside. Occasionally a woman constable would peer in through a peephole in the door to check on her.

She was just beginning to doze when the door opened and two women police officers came in. She was taken along a dim corridor that seemed endless, downstairs into a basement area, along another corridor painted in a gray, dull color. At the end of the corridor was a little room. Inside two men sat at a table with papers strewn over it.

"Mrs. Costello," said Norman Black when she arrived, "please sit down." He pushed a chair toward her.

"What do you want with me?" she asked.

"We want a lot. This is a colleague of mine—Special Branch. We're expecting a third any minute." The door opened and Detective Constable Patrick Reid came in. He sat down by the two other officers. He was carrying a folder.

"Yes, Mrs. Costello, we want a lot, and we think there's a lot you can give us." Black spoke with heavy emphasis, leaning toward her. Reid grinned. The Special Branch man was silent.

"Now, Mrs. Costello," Black went on, "this young man has a few things he'd like to show you, haven't you, Patrick me boy? But first I want to ask you a blunt question. May I?"

"Have I a choice in the matter?"

He chuckled a little. "Now, where's Seamus Devine these days?" He looked at her square in the eyes. Nora puckered her eyebrows and looked back at him without flinching. She remained silent.

"Look, Nora—may I call you by your first name? I feel familiar with you. Anyway, Nora, a lot of people are very angry. Some people have been murdered recently, you know, and we've been told to find out who did it. And why. And some people would like to know where Seamus is because they feel he might be able to help them." Black then nodded to Reid, who opened the folder and took out a colored photograph. He pushed it across the table toward Nora. She looked down and winced. It was Jack Fagan's corpse with an ugly red crater in his throat, his eyes in the frozen stare of death. She tried to hide her shock. This must have been very recent. She had heard nothing about it.

"You know him I think? A Mr. Fagan, late of the Upper Falls Road. Not too far from where you live, I'm told. Well, we can't say he was a friend of *ours* exactly, but still, a murder is a murder, right lads?"

Nora turned her face away from the photograph. Suddenly the Special Branch man reached across the table and pushed her face back; his hand gripped her round the back of the neck and bent her head down toward the photograph until her face was almost touching it. "Look, missus! The man said look!" he snapped.

Black watched her eyes. "Where's Seamus Devine, Nora? Do yourself a favor. He's going to cause a lot of people a lot of trouble they don't want. Him and his friends. Now, it's in all our interests for you to cooperate."

"I don't know anything about Devine."

"That's not what we were told. You know what the Falls Road is like—a lot of eyes, a lot of ears, watching, listening. Did he mention anything about buying guns when you met him the other night? Or did he ask you maybe to run away with him and have a good time?" The Special Branch man smirked at this and looked at Reid.

"I'm joking, of course. You're a good little wife, aren't you? Very loyal to John, aren't you?"

Nora looked down at the table. The photograph was still there. She glanced from one of her interrogators to the next.

"I know nothing about Devine or guns. I work in a bookshop. I mind my own business."

Black sighed and stood up. He walked slowly around behind her. She turned to follow him with her eyes.

"How's Michael these days?"

She did not answer, but swung around and stared at the door, her arms folded obstinately over her stomach.

"I said, how's Michael these days?"

"Michael who?"

"You know fine rightly who I mean—now don't play dumb on us. Mr. Boyd. How's his story coming along? Getting all the inside stuff we hope."

Reid began to laugh a little as he looked at his superior. When Nora did not respond Black tapped her lightly on the shoulder.

"You're a very foolish girl. I'm disappointed frankly. You know if this boy Devine has his way things are going to get very, very messy around here again. We know he's a troublemaker. You know he's a troublemaker. Even his former friends know that—the ones still alive, that is. Look at Mr. Fagan there. That's what happens to the former friends of Seamus Devine. That's nasty, so it is. You never know who's next, do you? And things were going so well, too. There was a bit of peace; people were settling down; internment was ending. Even your little hubby might soon have been out. Now wouldn't that have been very nice for you? Any woman who loves her husband would want that, right?"

He hunkered down beside her.

"Well, Nora, do you see my point?"

Back in her cell she tried to sleep, but the noise of the fan and the discomfort of the plastic sheet beneath her prevented it. She got off the bed and tried to tear the sheet off, but couldn't. In the room was a small table and a chair. She sat on the chair, resting her head on the table. Her mind spun dizzily. She felt slightly nauseous. A collage of images flashed past frenetically—John, Michael, the tower, the watch-towers of Long Kesh, the dingy little bus, the lines of women. She dreamt someone was speaking to her and she lifted up her head, but the room was empty. It sounded like her mother's voice. But her mother had been dead for many years.

She knew where Devine was; she even knew where the key to this whole bloody mess—the money—was. Her mind played with an idea, entertained the idea of saying, "Yes, I'll tell you. Only promise me John will be given an amnesty. Yes, I'll tell you . . ." The words swirled and droned on and on through her mind as she lapsed into a nervous sleep.

"Well, Nora, you look as if you've been asleep. I hope you're rested. What did you say the last time about your meeting with Devine?" The voice came from afar. She lifted up her head and began to shake it slowly.

"Let me sleep," she muttered

She felt two hands on her shoulders. Fingers touched her hair. Someone was undoing her braid and letting her hair fall over her shoulders.

"Devine told you about an arms deal, right? Johnny used you as a courier between him and Devine, right?"

Devine, Devine, Devine. The name was repeated again and again, the syllables merging senselessly one with the other as she shook her head. Divine, divine, divine. She began to laugh.

"Look, Patrick here has something else to show you. We've been keeping this as a surprise till now. Nora, are you listening?"

Someone held her by the chin and shook her gently.

"Open those eyes. Here's something you'd like to see. Someone you know."

Her hair was being held, fondled. The fingers felt strange, pudgy, thick, cold on the back of her neck. She reached up her hand and touched another's; opening her eyes she saw the Special Branch man standing behind her like a statue, a round, bald, smiling statue. "Buddha!" she thought, and started to laugh again. "Divine Buddha." She was aching. She started to weep quietly.

"You've got such beautiful hair," he whispered.

"Compose yourself," Black said to Nora, ignoring the Special Branch man. "I want you to compose yourself and open your eyes, Nora," Black commanded. His sharp and thinly authoritative tone brought her back to the present. She sat up and looked around at her interrogators.

"As I said, we have something to show you," Black continued when he was satisfied she was awake enough. "It's on the table."

When she looked down again toward the table there was another picture on it. It was slightly blurry. A woman and a man were arm in arm going up some steps. She looked closely. Beneath it there was another photograph. It too was blurry. This time they were hugging. Kissing. Then the next photograph showed a day-lit scene and the woman was leaving the building. It was Michael's hotel. It was Nora and Michael. It was the night they'd spent together and the morning after.

"That takes you back now, doesn't it, *Missus* Costello," she heard someone say behind her or above her. She did not know.

"And the poor hubby on the inside too, fightin' for his country. Maybe he'd like to know about this. If you like we could send these to Johnny. I'm sure he'd love to have them. What'ya think, Patrick me boy?"

"Oh, I don't know about that now! He mightn't understand. But for a woman three years is a long time. He mightn't understand that."

"Well, he wouldn't be the only one, now, would he? Where she comes from that's not accepted, is it? I mean a woman has her duty, right Patrick?"

"Right. They expect a lot of a woman. They mightn't understand this . . . eh . . . this . . . little episode as much as we do. We're men of the world, eh, Super? I mean we've been around. We've seen a few things. We might even agree to let Mrs. Costello have these pictures. What d'ya think? I think she'd like them. You know, sort o' like to remind her. After three years it's tough, isn't it?"

"Where are they?" she mumbled. Through bleary eyes she saw the table was bare. Her head slumped to one side. Her eyes closed. Blurred figures stood on the stairway of the hotel. One had a beard like John's and was calling to her, beckoning with his finger for her to come forward. Then he seemed to be far away at the distant end of a funnel, a kind of time tube which kept contracting all around her.

"Please let me sleep."

There was silence. Then through the funnel of her ear the whirring came again, spinning into a whirlpool of sound with her turning at its center.

The man who sat at the other side of the table drinking did not talk. His face was ashen, almost yellow. His eyes were motionless. He asked her how Johnny was. He asked her why she didn't come to his club more often. He'd like to see more of her he said. But his lips did not move. His flesh was like cold putty, wrinkled; it had a red hole in it. Nora shuddered and lifted her head from the little table. She thought someone was watching her. For a moment she became aware of the terrible ache all over her. Her head was burning and pounding, the rest of her seeming to follow suit. Incoherent images sped her into a fragile sleep again.

Michael's hand was stroking her again and when she turned her back to him she felt his hands run over her haunches, his fingers softly probing her. She was bent like a bow, a great arc of pleasure that ran like a cord through her. "Michael, Michael, Michael, Michael," she gasped, but the words dissolved into an inarticulate moan. Then there was a flash. A camera clicked and she started to scream. When she opened her eyes a policewoman was bending over her and she was sipping hot tea. She was crying. "What time—please, what time . . . I want to sleep."

"Now, Nora, you see my point—it's just we'd like you to have these photographs my friend took, but we need your cooperation. It's very simple. An address. A place. That's all. Then you're free. Johnny will be home with you and you will be happy for the rest of your life. We're offering you a lot, don't you think? All we want in return is . . ."

"STOP! STOP! STOP!" she screamed. "NO! LEAVE ME ALONE DO YOU HEAR! STOP."

"Take her away for now."

She was falling down a spiral stone staircase that had no bottom. She seemed to be falling into the center of the relentless whirring fan until an arm swung her back again—an arm that gripped her around the waist. Michael was holding her tightly. She shuddered in his grip. It was dark and she was pinned against a damp wall, her underpants were pulled down to her knees, her legs bent. There was a smell of rotting garbage in the alleyway. She was being pushed deeper and deeper into the dark with his every thrust. He lay so heavily on her, like a dead weight pinning her, until her breasts ached and she could hardly breathe. The stink of the alleyway, damp, fetid, clinging, was making her sick. He was saying, "Cunt, you little cunt!" It was a hard, ugly sound, a voice full of contempt. She was afraid to open her eyes to see him. She was afraid to look to see who it was. His bulk, his breath, engulfed her and she sank deeper and deeper into the darkness. It was an alleyway, a tunnel, a chapel, a jail. She became aware of men's eyes watching. Someone was looking at her through the grill of a confessional box; someone was looking at her through the bars of a jail; someone was peeping at her through a hole in the door: men's eyes, grinning, contemptuous. "Cunt, you cunt—don't be a silly cunt!" She was startled and looked up. Black was shaking his head in mock despair. His lips were moving, as in slow motion, his tongue pressed hard against the roof of his mouth, contemptuously.

The same questions came, again and again and again. She looked up and she saw her mother sitting beside her. She was knitting on the steps of their house. Nora was holding the wool taut as her mother wound it up into a ball. Her mother looked up to the blue sky and saw a cumbersome airplane inching across the sky toward the horizon. "That there airplane is going to New York, Nora; think of it! I'd love to go away somewhere. When you're a big girl you can go away." The wool wound on and on, until her hands held nothing and between was merely a vacant space.

"Nora, we've been so patient with you. My friends and I have invested a lot of time in you. You've let us down. Mrs. Costello, listen carefully. We'll give you one more chance. And then, well—we'll have to see what happens then if you won't cooperate. But we can say we did our best, can't we, Patrick?"

"Friar's Bush, Friar's Bush—the Monk's Stone, the Monk's Stone," she thought. The sounds seemed to weave a pattern before her eyes. From the pattern evolved an ancient image, long buried in her memory. It was a dark autumn evening. She was with Michael. He was lean and unkempt. The poor fella never got a decent meal; there wasn't a pick on him. But he didn't seem to notice, or mind. Herself motherless, she wanted desperately to mother him—to reach out to him and care for him. But she didn't. She remained aloof and suffered for him secretly. They were walking past the university, slipping on the slicks of dead leaves. They passed the museum, walking under the bare winter trees round a corner in the road. They were standing under an archway. It was a long time ago. She was wearing her black stockings. He had a coat thrown over his shoulders like a cloak. He was reciting bits of *Hamlet.* In the archway was an old wrought-iron gate. They peered through its bars; thick, rusting bars, always bars, with faces pressed against them. Beyond was an old cemetery, centuries old; the grass was waving in the misty gray wind, the headstones lurched this way and that. Michael pushed the gate a little and it creaked open. They walked in along a crunchy gravel path between the waves of long grass. He lit matches to read the eroded inscriptions on the stones in the ever-darkening gray light. One was merely the stub of a headstone worn almost to the ground: "Here lieth a goodly friar . . ." But the rest was blurred by erosion. When they left they looked up at the arch above the gate. "Friar's Bush Cemetery" the wrought iron read.

Black was staring at her. She knew where the money was. They mustn't even know about it though, at least she didn't recall their asking directly about it, simply about Devine and guns. But she was still saying no and smiling at him when they led her away back to her cell. This time she slept deeply. They let her sleep.

When she awoke Detective Sergeant Mackal was sitting on the

edge of the bed. A woman police constable was near the table on which sat a pot of tea. Nora's eyes focused on his familiar face. At first she thought it was part of her unending nightmare and that somehow she was back in her house in Black Mountain Gardens and they had just raided the house and arrested Johnny. It was the same face as then; the face that she had turned her head up to see standing above her on the staircase. And now it was looking concernedly and perplexedly at her.

"Mrs. Costello, some hot tea here and a slice of bread. The doctor will be along any minute."

"I'm okay," she said. "I don't want a doctor."

"You have to have one before you sign the no-complaints form. You have to have an examination first. Just to make sure you're all right."

"Then will they let me go?"

"Of course. There's nothing for you to be concerned about now." He handed her a cup of tea. There were dark circles under her eyes. Her lips were cracked and dry; her hair dirty and tangled. He walked over to the woman constable and shook his head.

"Did you see any of this?" he asked.

"No, Sergeant. I wasn't present for this."

"Not any of it?"

"No, Sergeant."

"That's against the procedures. Has Black gone mad!"

"Nora," he said, going back to the bedside, "this is important."

"Please don't start again, please," her eyes pleaded with him even as she spoke.

"No, listen, I want to help you—"

"PLEASE, PLEASE!" she screamed at him.

He paused. "Do you want your husband to spend the rest of his life in jail because of a crazy man like Devine?" he shouted at her, flustered by her screaming, her recalcitrance, his own concern. "Nora! If this truce breaks down—"

"I don't care about the truce! I don't care about any bloody guns or Devine! LET ME OUT OF HERE! DO YOU HEAR ME?" The policewoman touched him on the shoulder. He turned to her with a glum look.

"They've made a fine mess of this. I hope they realize it."

Furious and frustrated, he left the room just as the doctor arrived.

"Any complaints?" the doctor asked her.

Nora walked unsteadily through the reception area past the sergeant's desk. Someone was standing at the desk, tapping the floor impatiently with one foot. He turned when he heard her approach.

"Michael!" she cried and stumbled toward him. He held her exhausted face in his hands, examined it carefully, and quickly folded his arms around her, drawing her close to him. She cried softly, still aching.

"You look as if you've been awake for a week," he said, shocked.

"What day is it?" she asked, resting her head on his shoulder.

"Tuesday."

"But that was the day I was arrested."

"That was a week ago," he whispered. "I phoned Andrews, the British minister; I banged on the door of every bloody police station in this bloody town. I threatened them with the power of the New York *Globe,* not that that would do any good! I spent five days until I finally got it out of them. Then I simply arrived and sat tight until they let you go."

Exhausted, Nora leaned against him as he drove back into the city. "I had no idea where I was or what day it was or anything. It was like one long nightmare. How's Pat? She must be frantic." She spoke slowly, wearily, shivering every few minutes.

"She's been going crazy. She calmed down a bit when they finally assured us you were all right and told us where you were being held."

"Michael—something awful's happened."

"About Johnny—what?"

"No . . ." She hesitated. "They know about us." He glanced round at her.

"Know what?"

"About the night I spent with you in the hotel."

"It's none of their fuckin' business."

"Everything's their business—everything they think might be useful to them. They took photographs of me and you when we were going in and when I came out. God knows what else they might have taped." She began to shake; her eyes drooped and she slumped in the seat. He put his arm around her. She looked at him and then in front of her, coming round a little.

"They tried to blackmail me with it. They wanted me to tell them where Devine was. And something about an arms deal. They said if I didn't they would tell Johnny about us. They'd show him the pictures." Her speech was rapid; she was slightly hysterical.

"Did you tell them anything?"

"I don't think so. I hope to Jesus not. But how can I be sure? I might have rambled and said something when I was hysterical from lack of sleep."

He took her hand and squeezed it. "Blackmail is against the law," he said.

She laughed wildly. "What law? The law here allows them to do practically anything they like. They don't care!"

"What about Mackal—Detective Sergeant Mackal? He seemed worried about what was going on. He was the one that finally spoke to me and told me where you were."

"He was the one who arrested John. He might have a conscience, but it doesn't make much difference around here. He'll do what he's told like the rest of them." She closed her eyes. At her request he drove to a coffee shop and she drank cup after cup of tea. She went to the ladies' room and splashed her face with handful after handful of cold water.

"There's somewhere I want you to take me," she whispered when she returned to the table.

"You mean right now?"

"Aye."

"But you should go straight to bed, Nora."

"Not yet; first we have to go somewhere. It's very important. I'll explain in the car."

"What on earth for?" He gave her a puzzled glance, thinking she was hysterical. She just looked at him stubbornly.

"Okay, you're the boss. Let's go."

"Where to?" He turned the ignition.

"Friar's Bush Cemetery."

"Why?"

"That's where the money is from John's last bank raid. It's been there all along and now Johnny wants Devine to get it. He's desperate about it. Do you know how to get there? It's near the university."

"I think so. But do you really think it will still be there?"

Nora thought for a moment, gathering her racing and disordered impressions. She became more confident that she hadn't given anything away. "No, it must still be there—unless the IRA finally got it. What with Fagan dead now and all I don't know what could've happened since last week." She opened the window on her side of the car and leaned out, letting the wind gust through her hair and buffet her face to keep awake. "It's getting cold already," she said. "Autumn's here."

"What do we do if the money is there?" he asked her. She looked across at him, closing the window.

"I don't know." She thought for a moment.

"If it's gone either Devine got it or—"

"If you did talk in your delirium to the police they could be follow-ing us right now." He looked in the rearview mirror. The road was clear of cars. There was only a bus behind them.

"I don't see anyone suspicious," he said. He turned off the main road down a side street.

"Drive to the Falls, Michael. If anyone's following us they won't go into the Falls."

They drove to the Falls and he parked the car on a side street near the Divis Flats. They got out of the car and walked back to the city center, through the security gates, and caught a bus south into the quiet university suburbs.

Half an hour later they stood outside the cemetery, looking through the bars of the rusting gate under the archway. The gate house had been abandoned long ago, its windows bricked up. They looked around them nervously, hesitating.

"You remember, Michael—we came here once, many years ago, on one of those expeditions. We'd been to the museum I think."

"I remember. We were looking for an old headstone. It was sup-posed to be a thousand years old or something. I'd read about it in some old local history book."

"You loved graveyards when you were younger—you were always dragging me off to some obscure plot of ground somewhere."

"I think I was trying to tell you something in my shy, adolescent way."

She smiled at him. He jerked open the gate. Nora walked in after him. The gravel path, overgrown with weeds and grasses, had almost disappeared underfoot. He took her by the hand.

"Which one is it?"

"The Monk's Stone—I suppose it's the friar's headstone."

"How did John know about it?"

"I probably told him about you and me and our little trips to this place. He must have told Murray."

"Then why didn't Devine know too?"

"From what I remember Devine wasn't actually in the bank when the trap was sprung. He'd gone round to the back to make sure the rear was all clear. I suppose in the confusion John told Murray, but Murray didn't have time to get to Seamus. They got separated. Murray was shot dead a few hours later."

They searched as quickly as possible, always on the watch for anyone following them. Both tried to remember where the friar's headstone was located. Michael thought he remembered. "Come here, this way, Nora; I think it's over here." They paused at an old stump. No one was around except themselves. Michael crouched down. He parted the long grass around it.

"Here's the goodly friar," he whispered. "He's very loose." He gripped the headstone with both hands and wiggled it back and forth. Nora watched anxiously, first him then all around, still waiting for the feared ambush. It tilted over finally, coming out of the ground. In the depression it left was a plastic bag full of large pound notes.

"Now what do we do?" he turned to her and asked.

"We take it, quickly, what do you think?" she laughed and bent down to pick it up. It was moist and heavy. Michael replaced the headstone and took the bag from her. He wrapped it as best he could in a copy of the New York *Globe* he'd brought along just in case.

"Healy would love this!" he said as they walked quickly back to the gate. "I think I need a drink."

It seemed obvious by now they weren't being followed.

In the Gown Nora sat sipping a hot whiskey. The rolled-up newspaper lay before them on the upholstered bench between Michael and the wall. Nora was staring at it, her eyes closing involuntarily every few seconds. The excitement had temporarily revived her, but it was wearing off rapidly. Michael was pensive, disturbed.

"You realize," he began after taking a gulp of some of his pint of beer, "that if you give that to Devine you'll be helping finance your husband's stay in jail. I mean it will go for gear, and gear will go to war, and war—"

"I know that. And I know what people would say if they knew about us. They would say I was doing it deliberately to keep him in jail because of you." She smiled a little and searched his eyes.

"My poor Nora, you can't win—either way you're trapped. If you turn it over to the police you're a traitor to your husband, to his friends, to his cause. If you give it to Devine they'll say you're betraying your marriage—that you want to keep Johnny in jail for your own reasons."

"Let them say what they like. I must get it to Devine," she said in a near whisper. She did not look at him; she seemed abstracted, almost asleep. "I can commit adultery, but I can't betray my husband. Not in the most important way—I can't betray what he has given his life for. I just can't."

Michael shook his head emphatically. "No, Nora, you won't take it to Devine."

She looked round at him abruptly.

"I'll take it. It's too dangerous for you. The police won't ever be far away from you for a while yet." He paused. "And the IRA . . . we shouldn't take that risk in case the police did pass the word out about us. Anyway, you're practically asleep on your feet. You can't be walking around with god knows how many stolen pounds in your condition. Just tell me where Seamus is."

"But, Michael . . . ," she began. He put his fingers up to her mouth.

"Tell me where I can find him and let's get this over with as quickly as possible. Don't forget, I'm responsible for getting you into this mess."

Nora thought for a minute about Michael's offer. "Okay, that's a better idea I suppose. But first I'll try and get a message to Seamus before I go home. It'll be safer if he rang you at the hotel and arranged to meet somewhere neutral. If I can't reach him then you'll have to bring it to the Flats. Tonight's the best time; someone's always around then. If he's not in 15B Central Tower go to the bar; you know, the one in the basement. It's safe there. Jake behind the bar knows where he'll be. The area is very tight. It's his old area—he organized it way back. I'll meet you there about ten, after I've slept a bit."

He finished his beer in one go. This is the kind of story Healy would really love, he thought as he left the bar with the newspaper containing the plastic bag under his arm. He saw Nora safely on a bus and walked round to his hotel to secure his package and wait for Devine's phone call.

8

"The British want results, Roger. I had no option." Black paced around his desk glancing occasionally at the detective who sat slumped in a chair by the window.

"Fagan was one of their chief contacts in Belfast. He kept the Belfast organization behind the truce." Mackal looked skeptically at his superior officer.

"Obviously they weren't all behind him."

"That's the point—the administration wants to know who isn't and where they are. Quickly—before it gets out of hand."

"And what did Nora Costello tell you after all that?" Black did not reply at first. He sighed and brushed his thinning hair back with his hand. "We had to try. She might have known . . ." He threw his arms up in a gesture of impatience. "Okay, it was unorthodox."

"Illegal, Superintendent."

"Listen, Sergeant, I've been in this business long enough to know what the law is!" Black snapped at him. "How would you have done it?"

"The killers left the getaway car near the Divis Flats. The Divis Flats is Seamus Devine's old power base—that's his area. Fagan's killers are in *there*. If the Brits . . . the British want them then they'll have to go in and get them," said Mackal slowly, deductively.

"That would mean the end of the ceasefire," Black answered.

Mackal guffawed. "Oh, of course, I forgot. You'll have to get Peadar McCabe's permission first. Isn't that the deal?"

Black did not reply, but returned to his chair. "Look, Roger, this is not our doing. It's the way the government wants it. They want to settle it as peacefully and unobtrusively as possible. A bloody gun battle and riot in the Divis Flats is not the answer. It's just not on."

"Why should we bother to find anything out then since there's nothing for us to do, Superintendent?" Black leaned back in his chair. "It's difficult, Roger, but there's a lot at stake. Whatever we do we have to be careful not to provoke a confrontation." He paused, then smiled and said, "Who knows? These internal disputes have a way of settling themselves."

"Usually by bloody murder and mayhem," Mackal reminded him.

"Murder? Who would miss Seamus Devine? Better that they're shooting each other than us if you ask me."

"Then I don't understand what I'm doing here," Mackal said loudly. "I don't care what the deal is, Norman—we can't resign our authority to a bunch of gunmen. If the British want the IRA to be Belfast's police force then they should let us know so we can all go and look for jobs elsewhere. I know one thing: whatever we're supposed to be doing, torturing Nora Costello is not part of it!"

Black looked at Mackal impatiently. "I'm not here to discuss Nora Costello. I'm here to find out if you know what's going on."

Mackal shook his head slowly, wearily, smiling to himself. "Maybe Quigley did," he muttered.

"Quigley's no use to us now, Sergeant."

"Norman, the people who know most about this are sitting up in Stormont Castle. I think you should ask them. How are we supposed to find out anything if we can't arrest anyone for questioning because of their bloody truce—except women, of course." He laughed cynically.

Black ignored the remark. "Maybe Fagan wasn't killed over the truce. Maybe there was another reason. Maybe his empire was expanding a bit too fast for some—"

"Maybe—maybe—maybe. Maybe not. I know one thing for sure, though: Devine's a purist. Like Costello. Maybe he just got tired of talking to the British . . . *I'm* tired of talking. We can't find out sitting here talking about it, Superintendent." Mackal stood up and leaned across the desk.

"What are you doing, Sergeant?"

"Ringing Lieutenant Beardsley. The Flats are in his command area. He needs a bit of exercise. I know Devine, his old haunts. If nothing else we'll flush him out."

Black sighed hopelessly; his eyes glanced up at the detective, then away to the window. He shook his head. "Put the phone down, Roger. It won't do," he said softly. "I'm sorry, Roger, our hands are tied."

Mackal's head dropped; his chin sank on his chest. "If you'd told me that earlier I'd have gone home," he muttered. "The whole thing —the truce, the talks, these secret deals—it stinks!" he added with distaste. He sat down again as if uncertain what to do next. He was perturbed, confused.

"You didn't tell that to Mrs. Costello," said Black, grinning. "From what I hear you sounded very convincing when you told her she could save the ceasefire by cooperating."

"It was better than torturing her," the sergeant replied quietly.

"What's this touching concern for that little Fenian whore anyway? I'm surprised at an old dog like you!"

Mackal raised his eyes. "I've a daughter myself, Norman. It's as simple as that."

"You're getting sentimental in your old age. The likes of Nora Costello are a dime a dozen in those slums. I wouldn't give this for her!" He snapped his fingers contemptuously. He bent his lean, birdlike form over the table toward the detective. "As far as I'm concerned she gets what she deserves. And I don't want officers under my command shedding tears for the likes of her!"

Mackal was unabashed and returned Black's gaze. His commander was getting rather red in the face.

"You sound as if she's been sentenced already," Mackal said quietly, not taking his steady gaze off Black's face. Black sat back in his chair. He had a cruel streak in him that couldn't resist an opening.

"Sentenced?" he reiterated, drumming his fingers on the desk. "I don't know about that. I mean getting stiffed by some Yank isn't exactly a crime, is it, Sergeant?" He smiled at Mackal, who wasn't in the mood for being teased.

"No, it isn't, Superintendent; but the way things are going around here I'm not so sure anymore."

"Mrs. Costello needn't worry about things around here. It's not the police force she should worry about, Mackal, you know that. It's her own."

"What exactly do you mean, Norman?"

"I mean word has a way of getting around about girls like her, hasn't it. God, sometimes I wonder about you. You know what her own side would do to her if they knew—it would make what we did look like a weeks's stay at a first-rate hotel."

"But no one knows except us and . . . ," he paused for an instant as if slightly embarrassed, "and Boyd."

Norman Black looked at him and could not restrain his skeptical glance—it almost broke into a smile. "It's a small town, Sergeant."

"Exactly how small do you mean?" Mackal spoke quietly, tensely. Something had begun to worry him. At first he had dismissed it as absurd. Yet Black's demeanor and curious reiteration about Nora, as if he were circling around something, bothered him. The superintendent looked at him and then turned his gaze to the window like someone who has a joke, a private joke that he knows he shouldn't share but is finding it hard not to.

"Small enough for the likes of *Mrs.* Costello to get what she deserves," Black said suddenly, with disdainful emphasis. "You might even call it a touch of Black propaganda." His lips wrinkled into a small smile. And then he quickly added, "It wasn't strictly my idea." Mackal for a second said nothing. He stared in disbelief at his commanding officer. Slowly he leaned forward, his mouth shut hard, his eyes fixed stonily on Black.

"Is this what you mean by internal disputes settling themselves? You mean to sit there and tell me that someone—you or someone else in this so-called police force—has leaked word to the Provisional IRA about Nora Costello's relationship—!"

"Relationship!" Black exclaimed. "You wouldn't call that—"

"I don't care what you call it!" the sergeant almost shouted, banging his fists on the desk. "Since when has that been our job, Superintendent?" He raised himself up until he was leaning with both hands on the desk. "My God, Black! You can sit there and tell me that confidential information has gone to a gang of cutthroats? What does that make you? Nothing but a commander of a gaggle of dirty gossips! Police force, that's a laugh, so it is!"

"I don't think that's funny, Sergeant."

Mackal threw back his head and laughed. "Don't you? Well, I'm not surprised. Your sense of humor is a bit different from mine. Tell me one thing—in the name of what was this done and when? Is this another brilliant idea from those bloody fools up in Stormont Castle who've been handing over the running of this city to McCabe's gunmen?"

"Sergeant, you've said enough. There's no need to go on. This is a high-level matter. I warn you not to do or say anything . . ." But before he could finish the detective sergeant had turned and was striding toward the door. He halted suddenly, his hand on the doorknob, and looked back at the angry and embarrassed commander.

"Well, Norman, you are certainly right about something. Belfast is a small town and it's shrinking at a great rate. It's getting too small for me when the likes of McCabe and his boys start to rub shoulders with decent people—but then perhaps 'decent' no longer applies around here, or anywhere else in Belfast for that matter."

Black was about to reply when Mackal opened the door and left, slamming it behind him.

The superintendent fidgeted nervously in his chair. He had underestimated Mackal's sensitivity. He cursed himself for being such a fool as to tell him that a leak had been engineered to assure Nora Costello would be exposed, and thus—so the plans went—her husband and his group discredited.

Mackal sat at his kitchen table drinking a mugful of tea. It was already late afternoon. He was still angry, disturbed by what he'd learned. He wasn't sentimental—quite the opposite; in fact, many thought him bluff and hard and unsparing in ways. He pursued something until the end, that was his manner. He looked into the tiny canyons of the mug running in all directions, stained a deep brown. The mug was badly cracked—it had been his grandfather's. His wife Nancy always pestered him about it. She worried about germs. But she and his daughter Alice were out shopping when he got back so he was able to eschew the precious little cups she had in her china cabinet with impunity.

The hands on the kitchen clock were approaching six P.M. He sat glumly, slumped in his chair, confused, annoyed. He finished off the tea and went into the living room. He stretched himself out on the couch and closed his eyes. The troubles, the war, the police's role in it, had muddled everything. Before, it had been relatively easy being a policeman in Belfast. But so many ordinary, and ordinarily innocent, people had been dragged into the maze of terror and the reaction to it that it was becoming hard for some to tell the difference between the guilty and the not guilty. He would like to be able to discuss this Costello affair with somebody—a woman who would sit down and listen and understand. His wife was a good woman, but a country woman from a strict background. He thought of his daughter Alice. He opened his eyes and looked at her photograph on the table near where he lay. It was her graduation day, Trinity College, Dublin. She was holding her degree; he looked foolish and embarrassed beside her; Nancy stood much more confidently, beaming. Ironically, Nancy had objected strongly at first to her daughter's going to a Catholic city like Dublin for her education, where she would be surrounded by all those Irish Catholics. Alice was tall, broad-featured, with big brown eyes the color of her hair. He smiled proudly at the photograph. She was a beauty!

He remembered raiding Nora Costello's home after the arrest of her husband. One reason he remembered was that he found a big stack of art books in her bedroom—the same kind Alice had read when doing her first degree. Nora reminded him a bit of his daughter—the same color eyes, the same thick hair. He pushed himself up on his elbows. An idea—a temptation—that had been growing in his mind all afternoon since speaking to Black was getting stronger. It was wrong, but, well, what if it were Alice instead of Nora caught in this sordid tangle of intrigue? He had to try to help her. He took a deep breath and tried not to think of all the reasons not to. Besides, something was beginning to take form in his mind.

He knew what Black and the British were after; it just happened to coincide with what McCabe and his boys wanted: they hoped to make a fool of Costello in the eyes of the ghetto, where a man was judged by his wife's conduct. He got off the couch and walked quickly to the coat rack. If he was going to do anything specifically contrary to orders he would have to do it fast, without thinking. It had occurred to him that Seamus Devine might not let it happen. He would probably try to prevent Nora from being used and humiliated. After all, their prestige, and that of their leader, was at stake. Of course, they would have to know first. Though it would be unorthodox and unprofessional, Mackal had a hunch that there was a way that he might be able to intervene on Nora's behalf and get Devine at the same time. He decided to go into town and make a call.

Michael was working feverishly on his latest report, which he had to telephone in the next day. The plastic bag was tucked under his bed. He kept glancing at his watch; he reread the story. It began, "The two-month-long ceasefire between the Provisional IRA and the British army is about to end. Unknown to most people, including, it seems, the British authorities, leading members of the—"

The phone rang. Devine at last, he thought. He picked up the receiver. "Yes?"

"Detective Sergeant Mackal here. I spoke to you earlier at the station when you were trying to trace Nora Costello."

"Yes—I remember—thanks for your help," he blurted. He broke out in a sweat, afraid of what was to follow. I wonder will Healy be able to bail me out of this one, he thought.

"Nora Costello is in danger. This is off the record, son, but listen, I suggest you get her out of Black Mountain Gardens if that's where she is."

"Yes, she went there soon after she left the interrogation center," Boyd said quickly, guiltily, still flustered.

"Well, I suggest you get up there and take her out of the area."

"Why, what's wrong?"

"Look, son, just do as I say. She's going to be in bad trouble . . . I don't know how to say this but . . . I believe the IRA have got some damaging information. Now just do as I say—and don't ring me, okay?"

"Okay, thank you," Michael replied in a bit of a daze. Immediately he rang Nora's house. There was no answer; he let it ring a long time. She could still be asleep. Or with any luck she might have already left for the Flats.

He remembered what Nora had told him about the police threat. He was perplexed, anxious, worried; he paced up and down and stared at the bed. It seemed absurd that what had happened there could have anything to do with what was happening now. But then this is Belfast, he thought. Why should the police suggest that I go up there?

He decided to try to reach Patricia at work. He called directory assistance and asked for the number of the Royal Victoria Hospital. Finally he was able to trace her. Straining to sound as casual as possible, he asked her how Nora was. "She was sleeping like a log when I left for work." What time was that, he asked. "About three." He did not want to alarm her so ended the conversation as casually as it began. "That wasn't much help," he said out loud.

He must go straight to the Flats; that would probably be the best thing. If Nora was not there he would go straight to her house. And if she was not there he would need Devine's help. That would present a very delicate problem of what to tell him without harming Nora. But if the IRA knew, as Mackal said, and if he was too late . . . what then? That didn't bear thinking about.

Michael took the plastic bag from under his bed and put it in a shopping bag.

The hotel was a short distance up the avenue from where Mackal had made the call. In a few minutes he recognized Boyd running down the steps carrying a bag. He hoped that he was right: that Boyd would go to the only people who had an interest in helping the wife of Johnny Costello.

Michael didn't notice the man in the cloth cap and workingman's jerkin leave the telephone kiosk and follow him, carrying a lunch box under an arm. He avoided going through the city center; fifty thousand pounds would be hard to account for. Instead he took another route that led him across a desolate area of abandoned streets and bricked-up houses interspersed with rubble-strewn wastegrounds, the remains of an older Victorian ghetto. He was greatly relieved that there were no army patrols anywhere. It was unusually quiet. As he came closer to the Flats complex the whole area seemed deserted. Only the occasional People's Taxi trundled by. Michael walked quickly into the front court-yard of the Flats, glancing from side to side and hoping he didn't look as anxious as he felt. He stopped at the edge of the "adventure play-ground"—no one was around. It was evening, but there were no street lamps lit so the courtyard was darkening quickly under the shadows of the towering structures that surrounded it. He entered the Central Tower and went to the lift. He pressed the button and waited. A few minutes passed. He heard footsteps coming down the concrete steps of the nearby stairwell. A youth pushed the door open and walked past, pausing to inform him that the lift—like the one in the adjoining block—was busted. He began the weary climb up the dark, dank staircase to the fifteenth floor. There was no answer at 15B, where Nora had told him he might find Devine. He rapped again, more loudly this time. Still no answer. He listened for a minute. The door to the next apartment jerked open. An old woman stuck her head out. "Who do you want?" she rasped.

"Seamus Devine."

"Never heard of him." She slammed the door hard.

On the way down he took the steps three or four at a time.

The bar was at the far side of the courtyard in a basement. Under a passageway he saw some children playing; their mother called them and they vanished. He walked along the pathway that ran round the circumference of the courtyard; all the "Trust Us" posters had been torn down since his last visit. He passed the dark passageway where he'd seen the children playing. The bar was some yards along the pathway. He was relieved to hear sounds coming from it and see its light shining through a small window onto the desolate patch of ground in front. Someone from behind him said, "Mister!" He stopped, frozen with fear, and was about to turn when he was grabbed around the neck and hauled backward toward the passageway. He felt a cold metal barrel sticking in the small of his back.

"What d'ya want, mister?" a youth asked him. Another held him around the neck and pressed the gun into his back. He could not make out any features in the darkness of the passageway. The one in front of him frisked him quickly. They eyed his shopping bag.

"Seamus Devine," Michael replied hoarsely. "I've a package for him.

"Who are ya?"

"A friend of Costello."

One of the youths felt the bag. Then with a sudden tug he pulled it from Michael's grasp and looked inside. He gasped when he saw the contents.

"It's for Devine," Michael said as the other youth peered in. They smiled and handed the bag back to Michael, ushering him forward toward the bar. One of the boys—he could see now that they were in their teens—rapped on the doorway. A slot opened and someone peered out at them; then the bolts were undone.

A group of men were gathered around a corner table in the bar. Otherwise it was empty. The barman looked curiously at Michael. There was a row of pint glasses filled with dark beer sitting on the counter top. One of the youths said, "He sez he's got somethin' for Seamus and he's a friend of Johnny."

"What's your name?" the barman asked.

"Boyd—Michael Boyd. I'm a reporter."

The barman came round from behind the counter and searched through his pockets, taking out his press card. He peered at it. "That's what it says here. Didn't know Johnny had any friends reporters though."

A few of the men who had been sitting drinking came over.

"What you got there?" one asked, pointing at the bag.

"He sez it's for Seamus," one of the youths said.

"I have to give it to Devine himself," Michael said, not sure of who these people were.

"How do you know Costello? He's in jail doing time."

"His wife gave me this to give to Seamus. She's supposed to be here."

The barman turned to one of the youths who'd brought Michael in and told him to fetch Seamus. He left.

"What'll it be, Mr. Boyd?" the barman asked, going behind his counter.

"A pint of Harp," he answered, more relaxed now.

About five minutes later there was a bang on the door. It was Devine. He recognized Boyd immediately. Along with him were the youth and Gerry Toner.

"I'm Seamus Devine," he said, going over to the bar where Boyd was standing now.

"This was under the Monk's Stone," Michael replied, handing Devine the package. Devine looked in the bag and then at Michael, half suspicious, half startled.

"Where did you get this?"

"I told you—under the Monk's Stone."

"And where is that?"

"Friar's Bush Cemetery."

Devine and Toner looked at each other, enlightened at last. Seamus nodded to Michael. "Well, now, Michael, we're very grateful, but you've a bit of explaining to do . . ."

Michael was escorted to the corner table. Gerry Toner and Seamus Devine sat on either side of him.

"Look, Mr. Boyd, we appreciate this," Toner said.

"Nora should be here. I'm worried about her. I've got to go . . ." Devine looked at him quizzically.

"Forget about Nora for a minute—how did you get this?"

"She gave it to me—she found it in the Friar's Bush graveyard near the university there. But listen, I have to get to her." He spoke anxiously and quickly.

"What's the matter?" Toner asked.

"I heard she was in trouble."

"What kind of trouble?" Toner asked, concerned. Michael paused for a second to choose his words.

"I heard the IRA were looking for her—the friends of Jack Fagan."

Toner shook his head and looked at Michael carefully.

"Na—why would they be looking for her? She's not involved with us."

"She is now," Michael reminded him, looking at the money.

"But who else knows that besides us?" Devine asked. He was uneasy and kept looking toward the door, where another two short-haired teenagers clad in heavy boots and broad-cuffed jeans worn above the ankle were leaning against the wall. Michael hesitated. One reason Nora might be in trouble Devine might not appreciate hearing. He looked at his watch. She was supposed to be there a half an hour ago.

"Look," Michael began, "you know she was held by the police for a week. She left in a terrible state. I don't think she told them anything, but maybe they suspect she did, or perhaps . . ." He realized he wasn't sounding too convincing. "We arranged to meet here a half an hour ago. I rang her before I left and got no answer."

"Who told you she's in trouble?" Devine asked.

"I can't divulge my sources," Michael replied half jokingly but obviously nervous.

"You seem to know an awful lot about what's going on around here, Boyd." Devine regarded him suspiciously.

"That's my job," he answered, returning Devine's look. "I know enough to be worried. Leave it at that."

Michael swallowed his beer and turned his gaze toward the door away from Devine's searching, restless, inquisitive eyes.

"Don't worry—nothing'll happen to Nora. We'll see to it," Toner said confidently.

"Relax, give her another five minutes. Women are always late," Devine put in, grinning.

Michael scrutinized the other men in the bar. They were acting as if they were expecting something to happen.

"The road seems empty tonight," Michael said after another gulp of beer.

Devine smiled. "Everyone's off side. There's a war on, don't forget."

"I thought the war was over."

"Well, you can say you were the first reporter to hear that it has just started again."

"Oh—and who's fighting who this time?"

"The army of British imperialism against the . . . ," Devine paused for a sip of beer, "against the revolutionaries of the Irish Republican Army."

"And who are they?"

Devine smiled at Toner and around the room from man to man. "Us," he answered.

After a second's silence Boyd asked, "Aren't you leaving somebody out?"

Devine looked at him with curiosity and suspicion. "Who do you mean, Mr. Boyd?"

"Peadar McCabe and company."

"We left them out a long time ago," Devine answered half reluctantly, still unsure of this unlikely bearer of the long-awaited money. But Boyd seemed trustworthy enough and everything would be public soon anyway.

"Why?" Michael asked, his curiosity overshadowing his concern for Nora for the moment.

Devine looked at Toner. They smiled as if at a private joke.

"I'll tell you," said Seamus. "Fagan wasn't trusted. That's why he never got this money. That's why Johnny saw to it it stayed wherever it was—until now."

Michael looked at him quizzically.

"Johnny had reasons, good ones. When Fagan took over after Johnny went inside things changed. Soon he'd clubs, taxis, shops; next came the talks—then the political respectability. Johnny was right all along—Fagan was soft. Johnny made sure this money stayed in his control till we saw our way clear."

"Clear to where?" Michael pressed him.

"To put it to good use—to use it for what it was intended."

"And McCabe?"

"He agreed with Fagan. He thought that there was a deal to be done. They didn't read the feelings of the movement very accurately. They thought they could sell out—settle things cozylike for themselves. We didn't like that. Our men gave years of their lives—many gave everything—in this struggle for freedom, not for the freedom of the likes of Jack Fagan to run a drinking club or a black taxi service. Not the freedom of Peadar McCabe to have chitchat with the representatives of British imperialism in Ireland."

"And the British withdrawal?" Michael asked.

There was general laughter in the room.

"Aye," said Toner, "the announcement was to be two months ago. Then it was to be at the beginning of August. Then the next thing we were told was that it was to be at the end of August."

"There's going to be no announcement, no withdrawal for a while.

And when it does come it won't be because of any 'talks,' " Devine said quietly but confidently.

"And the amnesty; do you think that was a lie too?"

"They were letting men out of internment camp anyway. The British will get rid of internment truce or no truce—it's too much of an embarrassment to them. But not the sentenced prisoners. There's only one way to get them men out and that's with this." Devine produced an Uzi submachine gun from under his jacket.

"And we have the men to use them," Toner interjected. Boyd looked up at some of the men around him. Toner's assertion seemed accurate enough. It could only mean one thing—open struggle for control of the leadership. And these boys looked able for it.

"And so the dream of freedom becomes another nightmare of feuding and revenge killing," Michael thought to himself. Here it was happening again, right before his eyes. He felt a kind of weariness, knowing what to expect next, another spin in the groove of bloodshed. He couldn't think about it now—it would have to wait. It was Nora he was concerned about—he'd have to get to her soon—pluck her out of all this.

"I have to go," Michael insisted as he got up.

"Sit down a minute," Devine said.

They fell silent again. Devine placed the submachine gun on the table. His agitation would never let him stay still for too long. He tapped Boyd on the shoulder.

"Come 'ere, I want to show you something," he said. He brought Michael to the back door of the bar. Like the front, it was heavily padlocked and barred. He undid the locks and opened it. The inner courtyard of the Flats complex stretched before them, unlit except for the light from inside the bar.

"Look out there," ordered Devine.

Michael saw nothing. But he strained his eyes and began to see shadows moving through the darkness around the walls of the Flats, under the archways in the passageways. Shadowy figures were carrying guns.

"This place is a fortress." Devine shut the door and then went to the front. When he opened the front door the same sight revealed itself in the dim light beyond: armed shadows lurking everywhere.

"Who are you expecting?" Michael asked.

"No one in particular. But just in case the Brits decide to try their hand. They know I'm here."

But Michael had ceased to listen. He was restless, worried about Nora. He kept glancing at his watch. She was very late. It was half past ten already.

"I told you, relax," said Toner. "We'll send a couple of the lads up to her house now to check."

"I'll go with you then," Michael said, relieved that something was finally being done.

"No you won't," Devine said. Just in case, he thought, it's better to keep this guy here till Nora comes to confirm his story. Devine never took chances and was still alive to prove it. He sent two of the youths up to her house with instructions to get back to him as fast as possible.

They sat down and ordered more drinks. The wait was becoming unbearable. Presently there was movement outside on the wasteground and a knock on the door. The guards opened it and a young man came down the stairs out of breath. Devine recognized him; he lived in the Flats. He nodded and the guards let him in.

"There's something I think you oughta know about, Seamus."

Devine did not answer.

"There's a bit of commotion up at Sinn Fein headquarters." He went to the counter and nodded in the direction of the Guinness tap. Devine and Boyd walked over beside him. The newcomer looked at Boyd suspiciously.

"He's okay," Devine reassured him. "What's going on up there? That fuckpot McCabe holding a wake for his friend?"

The young man drank before answering. "They're gonna tar and feather Costello's wife."

Devine glanced at Boyd. "Your information's very good for a reporter. They usually get things wrong."

"I've wasted enough time here," Michael said curtly and walked quickly to the door. He began unbolting it, but Devine's hand was planted firmly on the handle. He shook his head.

"Easy on there. Stay where you are." He turned to the young man at the bar. "Why?"

"I heard the oul ones gossiping at the corner. Peter O'Neill said she was fuckin' around while her man was inside."

"Why should that cunt O'Neill care about Johnny?" Gerry Toner scoffed. "He'd be glad about it."

"Open the door! I want to get up there. O'Neill knows me—he knows I'm a reporter. They wouldn't do that in front of the press."

But Devine looked at him scornfully. "Those bastards would do anything they want to. They don't care about the press." Turning to the young man he asked, "Who's she supposed to be fuckin anyway?"

"Wait a minute," Boyd exclaimed. "You're not going to believe that, are you? Are you going to take Peter O'Neill's word?"

"He's right," Gerry Toner added. "Nora's dead on—she wouldn't mess around like that. The bastards are trying to get at Johnny. They're just usin' her to shame Johnny. I never thought they'd stoop that low."

"They'd do it to their own ma if it suited them," Devine said.

He looked at the reporter with a slight lift of the eyebrows, a questioning glance that Michael met eye to eye.

"I don't intend to let her be humiliated," Michael said emphatically.

But Devine was not impressed. His gaze rested where it was for a second as if he were mulling something over in his mind. "You can't go up there; you might get hurt. This is our fight. It's an attack on our whole movement. Nora is being used to get at us and we'll see to it she's all right."

"The movement's your business. The politics of it doesn't particularly interest me at the moment. Nora does. I'll decide whether I might get hurt or not. Just open the door."

"I said no. Your press card isn't bulletproof. We'll settle this our way."

"Are you kidding?" Michael shouted in frustration. "I suppose you're going to run up the Falls Road with guns blazing?"

Devine ignored the remark and told the barman to look after him.

"The drinks'll be on the house," he said to Michael. "Stay here. We'll bring Nora back. They won't harm her."

Devine went to confer with his friends near the rear entrance. Michael rested against the wall and glanced at the two youthful guards standing nearby at the front door. They smiled at him. If the situation wasn't so serious he would be able to laugh at the irony of it. The barman pushed a pint of Harp over the counter in his direction.

"You're best out of it, son," he advised him in a fatherly way. "You never know what could happen up there."

Michael walked over to get the drink. He was certain Devine suspected the truth about him and Nora.

"It's come to a bad state if that's what they're capable of," the barman was saying, "taking innocent wee girls like that and using them. It's come to a bad state."

Michael heard a whirring sound in the distance. The barman looked up.

"Fuckin' Brits—they fly low sometimes over the Flats just to annoy people."

The sound got louder and louder; the helicopter was dropping down quickly. Devine heard it too and paused in his preparations. He walked toward the front door with his submachine gun swinging nonchalantly by his side. Toner and the rest began pulling guns out from under the seats. They waited. The helicopter seemed close enough now to be attempting a landing.

"Open the door," Devine shouted, jamming a magazine into his gun, "we'll have a welcome for them!"

One of the youths unlocked the door and pulled it open. A brilliant light illuminated the wasteground above which the helicopter was hovering. The searchlight was scanning everywhere. The gunmen had vanished into the passageways. Michael took another swig of his beer. The door yawned before him, the men standing aside against the walls watching.

Devine turned toward his friends at the back. "I think they're gonna land, lads," he began.

Before he'd finished his sentence Michael had reached the open door. He pushed one of the youths violently backward; he fell on a table knocking it over. Devine swung around in time to see Boyd disappearing up the steps into the brilliant circle of the searchlight.

"They'll shoot you, you stupid bastard!" he screamed. But Boyd could not hear him. Seconds later he was on the pathway at the top of the steps, his eyes dazzled and blinded by the searchlight as he raced forward, stumbling, tripping across the wasteground. The noise of the blades above him drowned out every sound and thought. But through it came a voice, "Halt! Halt!" calling metallically from a megaphone. He kept running. A series of rapid booms made him stop. He glanced behind toward the bar. A figure was standing on the steps with a long barrel pointing upward at the machine above Boyd's head. Immediately there was another series of high-velocity booms, which seemed to come from one of the dark archways. The helicopter lifted up rapidly, its beam shining through the windows of the nearby flats, then veering away into the dark sky. Within seconds Michael Boyd found himself on the Falls Road flagging down a black taxi.

9

*t*here was a distant sound of crashing glass, the thud of feet on the staircase. A draft swept in through an open door suddenly, chillingly, and another nightmare began.

Or maybe it was a continuation of the last one; she didn't know. They had guns. Voices were ordering her to dress. She did so without ever properly waking, or so it seemed; a dream fractured by real voices, broken by real light and fanned by cool drafts of real air.

Her room was still dark, with the curtains drawn. They were standing at the door waiting, though they turned away, and she could see the outline of their backs when she was putting on her skirt. They wouldn't look; decencies had to be respected.

Then there was the car waiting outside the door. There was glass in the hallway, splintered, jagged. Within seconds the car was speeding down the street and Nora was slumped in the back half-crying, half-laughing hysterically, while all around her she heard the familiar voices of her own people; not the harsh accents of the Protestant policemen, sometimes middle-class Belfast, sometimes rural, always unfamiliar—but the accent of her street, her friends, her youth. Then she felt suddenly utterly alone, with no succor, no one to turn to for help.

When she came round she was resting against the hearthplace in a dingy back room. Above her burned a naked bulb. Flypaper hung from it, covered in dead flies stuck there like perfectly preserved fossils in amber, and then she closed her eyes again and saw another fireplace —the one at home when she was a girl, the one that would always be stacked up with newspaper, sticks and coal, ready to be lit, ready for the first autumnal chills. The kitchen door to the backyard was always open in summer. In the yard the coal was kept and there was a little shed with a toilet in it. And the flies buzzed in and out, weaving around the length of flypaper that hung from the bulb in their front room. The cat watched as if hypnotized, following them up the windowpanes with his nose, his face tracking them around the bulb. Her father would swat them with a rolled up newspaper; the smudge of the crushed insect would make her squirm. She opened her eyes and stared at the flies' strange ballet around this bulb, dancing round death.

Peter O'Neill was standing by the newspaper-covered window at the other side of the room. Occasionally he bent down to peer through the little hole cut in the paper at the street outside, where a small crowd was gathering.

An hour before, still half-asleep, she had been dragged from her house and bundled into the back of a car. They told her she was to be punished. They brought her here, then left. The doors downstairs were guarded. At first she imagined she was back in the police interrogation center. It seemed like only seconds since she had emerged from that nightmare. Now it began again. She came to consciousness to find herself in more familiar surroundings. Fear sharpened her senses.

O'Neill was shifting uncomfortably, nervously, around the room, not able to look her in the eye, restlessly peering at the world outside through his little hole. Her eyes followed him about the room. He could not meet her gaze full of the contempt that she felt for him and his peephole.

"Are you waiting for someone to come and tell you what to do?" she asked at one point. He stiffened, but did not answer.

Beside her she discovered a stack of the news sheets that O'Neill had printed every week. They were in a big bundle by the fireplace ready to be distributed in the morning. She looked at the front page of the topmost paper. The main story was about Fagan's funeral. There was a closeup of him. The caption read: "Murdered by Pro-British Elements." Another story was headlined: "ANTI-IRA GANGSTERS TRY TO WRECK TRUCE: DEVINE, COSTELLO NAMED AS LEADERS IN PRO-BRITISH PLOT." There was a mug shot of Seamus alongside the story. She turned the page and found another photograph—this time of Johnny. It was very grainy, vague, had obviously been blown up from a much smaller scale. She recalled the occasion when that picture was taken. It was just after internment, in 1971, at the funeral of an IRA man and friend of her husband's who had been killed in one of the many gun battles that had followed the massive swoop on the Catholic ghettos. John had returned to the city in spite of the great risk of arrest just to march in his friend's funeral. She remembered seeing him briefly and furtively afterward in the nearby park. He was distant, preoccupied; he hadn't slept in days; his eyes were sunken, but they burned a cold, blue light. She'd wanted to hug him, make love to him; instead, they'd met like strangers. He was far away. Perhaps that was the first time she felt she'd lost him to something else, even before he was caught and jailed, even before her subsequent despair and loneliness. Now the record of that act of courage and comradeship was being used in an attack on him that was calling him a traitor, a pro-British gangster, a mindless gunman. Poor Johnny, she thought to herself, overcome with tenderness for him; his very consistency had made him vulnerable, had been turned against him. In a fit of rage she ripped the top news sheets off the stack and kicked it over. The thud disturbed O'Neill from his vigil at the peephole. He looked around to see several copies of his newspaper going into shreds in Nora's hands. He rushed over to her and she stood up to hurl a bundle of them at him.

"Tell me this," she screamed. "How can you be a hero one day and the next day be a gangster? What kind of politics is that?"

He stooped to pick up the scattered papers. "You don't understand, Mrs. Costello," he half-muttered.

"Yes I do! I understand that you're using me to humiliate my husband. And I understand what kind of man it takes to want to do that!" She was livid with contempt and hatred. He looked up.

"No one wants to do it. But it has to be done. We're doing Johnny a favor."

"Why are you doing the traitor a favor?" she snapped at him. He scooped up more papers and arranged them in another stack. He was mortified and wished for all the world to be anywhere but here.

"Look, Nora, don't get me wrong. It's nothing personal. It's for the morale of the men inside. You've let them all down by . . ." But he paused, unable to find the words. She glared at him defiantly.

"You knew what was expected of you. You knew what would happen," he mumbled finally.

When he came near her she brushed away from him contemptuously. She walked over to the window and looked through the peephole. A small group of men, women and teenagers was gathering outside at the corner where the lines gathered for the prison van in the mornings. That was the spot where she would be humiliated. The twilight glowed dimly in a clear sky, though it was dark enough for the street lamps to be lit. At this time of year on a clear night everything seemed imbued with a light turquoise haze. She watched the crowd mill around; she heard men joking down by the back door. O'Neill startled her by coming up behind her.

"Get away from me!" she hissed at him. "How could you write such lies about him?"

"He's the leader of a dangerous gang—he doesn't know what he's getting into. He doesn't know where it might lead."

"Do you? Does anybody? How do you know you won't wake up tomorrow morning to find yourself being denounced as a traitor? Once this starts, Peter O'Neill, can you stop it? At least Johnny has principles."

"Have you, Nora—after the way you've behaved? Sneaking off for a dirty night in some hotel with a Yank. What kind of principles is that?" He sneered at her, his moist lips curling in a leer above his short, well-trimmed beard.

"And he doesn't have friendly chats with the Brits or listen to dirty gossip from the enemy police force either, you sniveling coward!" she screamed.

He came toward her, furious. She spat in his face. He reached out to grab her, but then paused.

"Touch me—go on—I dare you—touch me."

He backed off. "I don't like to hit women," he said softly.

She gave a little laugh. "No, but you don't mind if someone else drags them into the gutter to have their hair cut off. You like to watch that!"

He was utterly wretched and defenseless against her. He turned away from her and went to the door. There were footsteps on the stairway. Shaken, he opened the door and looked down into the dark stairway. A group of figures were coming up the stairs.

"They're here. Sit over there." He indicated a rickety chair by the fireplace. He stepped back from the doorway and composed himself as the group approached.

Nora sat by the fireplace, her hands folded on her lap. She did not recognize any of them.

"Where's McCabe?" O'Neill asked the short, bald man who came in first.

"He was tied up elsewhere—maybe later," the bald man answered gruffly, looking at Nora.

"But—he said he'd be here in case—look," O'Neill took the man aside and whispered something in his ear. But the newcomer ignored him and kept looking in Nora's direction. Two young men were standing by the doorway. They glanced furtively at her. One of them lit a cigarette and began to talk quietly to his friend about a soccer match. After a few minutes the bald man left O'Neill and came over to her. He looked down at her and shook his head with a mild gesture of contempt. He was a squat figure with a beer belly and a heavy face.

"How long are you going to keep me here?" she asked him. "My sister will be worried about me when she comes in from work."

"Your sister works nights this week," he answered. "She won't be in till very late."

"The police have kept you well informed," she said turning her face away from him. He came closer to her until he was directly before her, his belly almost touching her face.

"Look, missus, we don't take that kind of crack from anybody—man or woman!"

Nora did not reply, but looked with disgust at the body in front of her and turned in her seat.

"I'll run down and see if everything's all right downstairs," O'Neill said suddenly from across the room. He squeezed past the two at the door. She heard his footsteps descending the unsteady staircase.

"That's always a sign the real business is about to begin," she sneered. The bald man, his head glistening under the naked bulb, looked at her quizzically.

"You're a comedian, eh?" He turned to his two companions. "Hey, lads, she's a joker." Every time he moved he made the flypaper sway. The others smiled a little, but seemed reluctant to join in. They did not say anything.

He went back to the window and got a chair. Then he straddled it in front of Nora.

"Isn't this cozy?" he said. "Now—let's have a chat." Nora ignored him.

"We're doing you a favor, you know that? Look at me when I talk to you!"

"O'Neill said you were doing Johnny a favor. Make up your minds."

Nora could see that he was having a hard time controlling his anger. It was a relief in a way to provoke him.

"Don't pay any attention to what O'Neill says. Listen to me."

She looked at him with contempt and impatience.

"That's better. . . . Now, Mrs. Costello, you know what it's like for the men inside—no wives, no girlfriends; they depend on you a lot. They like to know you're not letting them down. Not taking your knickers off for every Tom, Dick or Harry who comes along . . ." He paused for a second and smiled slyly at her—a look she could only interpret as half-lusting, half-contemptuous. He was close to her now as a priest in a confession box. His voice was soft, insinuating, prying. His eyes had lost their original hard look of dislike and now danced restlessly as if in pleasure at what they saw. But it was a furtive pleasure, almost an appeal to her.

"This Michael now—I suppose he wasn't the first? There's nothing you can do around here without us knowing about it, you should know that by now."

"You and the police!" She almost spat at him.

"I warned you once, you wee whore!" he snarled, raising his hand.

One of the young men at the door shouted over to him, "Come on, Joe—don't take all fuckin' night. Let's get it over with."

He stopped himself and merely glared at Nora, then stood up and walked over to the young guards. One of them opened the door and he went downstairs. Nora rose and walked about the room restlessly.

"I'm sorry, missus," one of her guards said. "Look, we have better things to do. But just stay calm, okay? Here, would ya' like a cigarette?" He seemed perturbed.

"No, thanks."

He lit another one for himself.

"Joe gets a bit carried away like," the other guard almost whispered.

Between puffs on his cigarette the first one said, "We don't like doing this sort of thing."

"But you do it anyway," she said softly, almost sorry for them.

"We're in an army, missus—we obey orders."

"Would you shoot me if you were ordered?"

"Look—I told you—it's not our fault. We've better things to do."

She returned to her chair and sat down. She felt as if she were trapped at the center of some huge maze so that no matter in what direction she turned for help she'd find only someone who shrugged his shoulders indifferently and couldn't or wouldn't tell her any way out.

It was a maze designed to ensure that no one took responsibility for what happened or even for what they did themselves: Those responsible were always somewhere else, around the next corner or the next or the next . . .

The room was ominously still now. The fireplace was full of empty beer cans and cigarette ash. She rested her face in her hands, her elbows on her knees. How lonely it was to be isolated within your own people, surrounded by familiar sights, places, sounds, surrounded by things you knew so well, but which no longer offered any comfort or reassurance. It was much more frightening than being taken away and held in an interrogation center and questioned by police, your enemies. She shivered at the thought of the informer with his friends, now his captors and soon to be his executioners, knowing there was no way out, nowhere left to hide, an alien within his own world.

The flies still executed their convoluted choreography above, inches from death yet seemingly oblivious to it. The smell of cigarette smoke pervaded the room. She remembered being here with Michael. She probably sat on this very chair. Then the room had depressed her, filled her with doubt, despair at there ever being a way out of the mess they were all in. She listened to the crowd outside. There was a lot of bustle. Sometimes she wondered if this was part of the previous nightmare, that somehow her tormentors had merged, had become one cruel, malicious inquisitor determined to denigrate and insult her, her husband and her lover.

For a woman to have her hair shorn and her head shaved was a kind of execution—an execution of her sexuality, the attempted obliteration of her as an object of desire. It was the climax of the city's misogyny, a misogyny she had known and hated all her life. It was a misogyny that made the word *cunt* the ultimate insult, the most degrading word in its vocabulary. She became calm when she thought that this was almost inevitable. She had pretended to be their kind of woman for a long time. She had watched at the foot of the cross in self-abnegation as the eternal sacrifice was being enacted before her. She had attended the writhing agony of man in bondage for his beliefs and said nothing. What she had done was merely what was expected of her. But through the years something else had remained—something that one night with Michael had released and satisfied. But now the city would have its revenge. Yet she knew there and then it would not matter. However much she was to be humiliated and insulted, the fact that they were using her degradation to hurt John fused her love for Michael and her love for her husband into a common bond united by the hostility and hatred of men they both despised. Her love for them suffused her with confidence.

Nora fell into a trance, staring at the fireplace. Time had slowed down, the minutes became agonizingly long. She thought of all the women who had attended the hearths, year after year, keeping the flames burning, nourishing the fire. She imagined flames and sparks in the dead hearth. Her mother used to sit for hours gazing into the fire knowing she was dying, watching the bright flames dance. She would watch the sparks light up the soot that clung like thick fur around the back of the hearth.

"Nora," she would say, "see the little sparks? You can read them. See, there, that's in the shape of an army. When one goes out a man dies. And that's in the shape of a man. That means there's a stranger coming to visit us. And down there I see a procession—all them sparks in a line means a procession with a lot of people in it." The child would stare into the fireplace until her eyes hurt and her mind was mesmerized by the steady steady ticking of the big clock on the mantlepiece above, searching for the procession, the armies, the visiting strangers, a sign of the things to come. But looking into this hearth she could not see the future; rather, among the ash and empty cans was an image of the past.

"It won't be long now, Mrs. Costello." The voice startled her, and she looked up. Joe was back again, agitated, angry. "This'll prove what we've been saying about this gang all along," he went on, addressing the two other men in the room. "Who else but a gangster would marry a whore like that, eh? Whatd'ya think, lads? I think we'll make that clear, don't you?"

There was no reply.

Downstairs Peter O'Neill was wiping a patch of black tar from off the floor in the front room. It had spilt from a big can that was standing near the counter. Two teenage girls in platform shoes and long, heavy, black skirts watched him scrape and scrub. A placard with string threaded through it rested against one of the girls' legs. They were both smoking and chatting quietly to each other.

Joe spat into the hearth and stood behind Nora.

"To be honest," he half-whispered, "we don't like this sort of thing." When she ignored him he walked over to the window and peered through the peephole at the crowd outside.

"Well," said one of the young men, "what's goin' on?"

"McCabe's not around. We'll just have to go ahead. There's a fair enough crowd outside now." He glanced at his watch. "It'll be too late soon."

"Maybe we can just forget about it, Joe," one of the guards said shyly.

Joe shot a determined look at him. "No way, son! Just remember Mrs. Fagan lying in her bed crying her eyes out because her man was gunned down in the street by those cunts . . ." He halted and stared over at Nora. "This'll show the people just what kind o' cunts they are living with—a whore like that!"

One of his companions raised his hands as if to say, "Okay, enough, calm down."

Joe opened the door and called downstairs for the girls to come up. Nora listened to them clumping clumsily up the stairs. The two men, led by Joe, approached her. Joe went to grab her, but she stood up, her back against the hearth.

"Now, Mrs. Costello—take it easy."

"Don't touch me," she spat at him. She reached down and lifted an empty beer bottle from the fireplace. When he reached for her she lunged at him, whacking him on the side of the head with the bottle.

"You little cunt!" he shouted, hitting her in the face and grasping her wrist, dragging her forward. The other men stood back.

"Don't just stand there for fuck's sake!" Joe gasped as Nora wrestled with him, staggering him across the room. They came behind her and held her back by the arms.

"Calm down now. Please," one of them whispered. "Take it easy."

Joe freed himself and felt his temple. There was a slight bump. The girls came in to see Nora being pushed toward them, her face flushed, her arms bent behind her up her back.

"Give us a hand," they were told. "We don't want to be seen beatin' the wee whore—not that she doesn't deserve that and more."

Nora's head was bowed, her hair streaming luxuriantly over her face as she was bundled down the dark stairway to the side door.

A black taxi stopped opposite the Sinn Fein headquarters. "Bit of a crowd there," the driver said as Michael pushed a handful of coins into his hand and jumped out. "Ten pence'll do," the driver shouted, looking at the money. "The rest's a tip," Michael replied without turning around.

Michael made his way through the crowd of women who were watching from the other side of the street.

"She comes from up the road," one woman was saying to her friend who was standing next to her holding a little baby. "I heard she was running round with everything in trousers." The woman with the baby shook her head.

"It's a terrible thing—and her man inside? He was the fella that did all them robberies, wasn't he? It's a shame for him, isn't it, being inside and hearing all this kind o' thing." They noticed the stranger pausing beside them and stopped gossiping.

When he went to the side door one of the guards asked him what he wanted.

"Nora Costello," he replied.

"And who are you?" the man responded.

Michael took out his press card. "A reporter. Now let me in."

"You better go round the front if you want to talk to somebody," Michael was told.

"I said I came for Nora Costello. I didn't come to talk." When he tried to get past, the burly guard blocked his way.

There was a noise from inside the stairway. Nora was being taken down. Michael heard her voice. He pretended to turn to go and then sank his knee into the groin of the guard, who buckled over. Michael took him by the scruff of the neck and hauled him forward, sending him sprawling onto the pavement. Two other men who had been nearby made a grab for him, but he was at the door before they reached him. He pushed it open in time to meet Nora face to face.

"Who the fuck's this?" Joe shouted.

Michael dragged one of the girls into the street and grabbed Nora by the arm. The two young men who were behind her jumped down the stairs. Another came from the rear and gripped him round the neck. They pushed him roughly against the wall.

"Michael!" Nora screamed. "Let him go—leave him alone!"

"Now there's a coincidence," said Joe, breathing heavily and coming over to him. "I'm glad you could make it. This is the cunt, eh, lads?" He dug his fist into Michael's side. Michael felt as if his lung had caved in; his whole body was warped and he was unable to breathe. He slid down the red-brick wall sucking air convulsively.

The crowd grew uneasy; the sudden violence had taken them by surprise.

"That's a wee trick the Brits use," Joe smiled. "They've taught you more than one wee trick," Nora screamed at him.

"Okay, girls, get to work," he said grinning. One of the men brought out the big can full of tar. It lapped thickly over the rim, dripping black globules down the sides of the container onto the pavement. One of the girls gripped Nora round the neck with her arm and wrenched her head back, letting her long hair hang down. The other produced a heavy pair of scissors and took her hair in a bunch in one hand.

By the time Michael had staggered to his feet the first swathe of Nora's hair had glided to the pavement. He watched it swing and fall gently, buffeted on the wind that gathered force in the evening blowing down from the mountains. A few women looked away, embarrassed. But even those who were watching seemed saddened. There was silence. Only the crunch of the scissors could be heard, or the occasional nervous giggle of a teenage girl. The two girls who held Nora worked methodically, quickly, cheerlessly.

Michael found himself pinned against the wall helpless. Though still weakened from the blow to his side he struggled to free himself, without success. He panicked as Nora's hair started to be hacked off.

"How can you let this happen!" he shouted, twisting his head round toward the crowd, only to have it shoved violently back to the wall.

"Nora!" he called.

A shock of discomfort went through the onlookers, but they continued to watch self-consciously.

A van came to a halt a little way up the street. The back doors swung open and a group of men jumped out. They were carrying Uzi submachine guns. There were four of them and as soon as they were all out of the van they spread quickly across the street on both sides. The crowd was too intent on the spectacle before it to notice their swift and silent approach. They came down the street, their guns swinging by their sides. A woman who was standing in her doorway screamed when one of them planted himself beside her and lifted his weapon, pointing it toward the crowd.

Gerry Toner, Seamus Devine, Bobby McCann and Jim Byrnes watched for a second as the crowd became aware of them.

"Okay, Joe, tell the girls to stop and let her go! Now!" Seamus shouted. The people who were nearest Nora backed away, leaving Joe with a clear view of the man who had spoken.

"Stay out of this, Devine!" he screamed back.

"I said *now,* Joe!"

McCann turned his gun in the bald man's direction. The whole crowd began to back off toward the main road. The young men who had acted as Nora's guards froze.

"Joe, do as he says—it's not worth it for fuck's sake," one of them whispered. But the girls didn't wait for Joe's decision. They released their grip on her. Devine never took his eyes off the bald man. He walked over to him. Then he looked at Michael, who was freed immediately.

"You okay?" he asked Nora.

"Aye," she replied softly, looking at the ground where long clumps of her hair lay. She felt the back of her head for her lost hair. It was scattering now on the pavement, being blown into the gutter. Michael bent down and began gathering it up in a handful. He stopped, got up, and drove his fist into Joe's gut. Joe, bent over by the blow, started to retch.

"I've something to read to you," Devine said to Joe as Nora walked, shaken and dazed, over to Michael. "McCabe will probably want you to repeat it word for word so I want you to listen carefully." He took a scrap of paper out of his pocket. The people were watching from across the street and he waved them over. He leaned back against the wall near the street light, his knee raised and his gun resting on it and began to read from the paper in a loud voice.

"The attempt to humiliate Nora Costello," he started rather self-consciously, "by the renegades in the leadership of the republican movement is a propaganda blow aimed at discrediting those who have exposed the sellout policies and the gombeen efforts of that leadership who were trying to once more betray for a few privileges the struggle for freedom. Nora Costello is the wife of John Costello, a man serving a life sentence for his commitment to the fight for independence. This was a cowardly attack on him using his wife, and the people of the Falls must repudiate it and those who would stoop to such tactics once and for all. We call on all rank-and-file members of the Irish Republican Army and all nationalistically minded people to join with us in rejecting the present leadership and its policies inspired for their own profit. Support the Irish freedom struggle! Death to British imperialism!"

He finished and looked around him, somewhat red-faced. The crowd stared silently at him. They too were self-conscious and uneasy. A few women nodded in appreciation. One whispered to her friend beside her, "It's just as well—as long as nobody gets hurt, that's the important thing." They then started to disperse.

Gerry Toner walked into the middle of the road and flagged down a black taxi. He brought Nora and Michael to the cab and told them to go to his mother's place. As the taxi drove off the front door of the headquarters opened; Peter O'Neill slid out almost unnoticed and disappeared round the corner of the next street.

Detective Sergeant Mackal glanced at him from where he was watching and waiting in a narrow alleyway near the corner of the street opposite. He ignored him. His attention was fixed on Seamus Devine. Quickly the detective looked up the road searching for any sign of Lieutenant Beardsley's patrol, which he had called a few minutes before on the little radio concealed in the lunch box. The alleyway stank. There was nothing on the road but the crowds of onlookers and the occasional People's Taxi slowly weaving its way through them. Mackal leaned his shoulder against the wall and sighed impatiently. His hunch had paid off: as soon as he'd seen Boyd go into the Divis Flats he knew Devine would intervene—would have to come out of his little fortress to rescue Nora Costello. And there he was now in all his glory, swinging his gun, making his speech—just like old times again!

The detective had gone as far as a chip shop opposite the Flats complex, not sure what might follow. He waited there for Michael to reemerge. The chips were too greasy as usual but perfect for the butterflies in his stomach. When he heard the shooting he had run into the street only to see Boyd climbing into a taxi. Mackal followed and realized as soon as he saw the crowd outside Sinn Fein headquarters what was going on. So here he was, everything neatly falling into place —except for one thing: he was powerless to do anything! He looked at his watch and opened his box again to call the police station.

"For god's sake!" he whispered, fiddling with the radio impatiently. A woman walked past and he grinned at her. She looked behind her at him suspiciously, but soon became too engrossed by what was going on up ahead to bother. He got through.

"Sam, this is Mackal here. Has Beardsley left yet?"

"Aye," came the crackling reply. "He left a while ago with a patrol."

Mackal noticed a group of men down the street. He closed the box and put it under his arm. He left the alleyway and walked the few yards to a car parked at the corner. It was now or never, he thought. He had been waiting to get this close to Devine for years. Now Devine was getting ready to leave. Mackal noticed the van a little further up the opposite street and one of the gang—it looked like Byrnes—was walking toward it. He knew he could probably get one shot in with his revolver before he was shredded by the Uzis. The way things were going, he thought, he'd have to be careful not to mistakenly hit a future prime minister; then there would be no posthumous award. But instinct took over and he crouched down behind the car and drew his gun. Devine was directly opposite him near the doorway of the Sinn Fein building. Mackal saw him glance up the road then dive into the doorway. There was a clatter of garbage can lids. It was the sweetest sound the policeman had ever heard—it was the Catholic people's way of signaling the approach of an army patrol. From up the road he heard the roar of a heavy engine. People were scattering in all directions.

A few hundred yards up the road a convoy of saracen armored vehicles were speeding toward the corner where the crowd was breaking up. "Brits!" someone had screamed; but it was too late: the saracens screeched to a halt and the troops scrambled out and began spreading across the road. Mackal had spoken to Lieutenant Beardsley on the radio and had warned him to prepare for "real trouble," so his men were ready.

Mackal had his revolver cocked as the soldiers approached. Devine was still at the corner by the headquarters. He knelt down and quickly began to cover McCann and Toner, who were yelling for the remaining people to get out of the way. Byrnes was back at the van and got in.

"Get that thing down here!" Devine shouted to him.

"Don't move, Devine!" the policeman screamed.

Devine got up and swung around in one swift motion, still aiming his gun. He could not see the figure who called to him. The detective was crouched behind his car. He fired. The bullet smashed into the brick wall, sending a red spout of dust shooting out into the air. With a semicircular motion Seamus Devine sprayed the policeman's cover car, shattering the windscreen and tearing metal splinters off the front. Ducking around to the side, Mackal fired again and again. By this time Devine was wedged into the doorway and McCann was firing up the road at the patrol. One soldier fell, his legs shattered by the Uzi. The others dove into doorways and behind cars and opened up.

Devine sprayed the road with repeated sweeps, sending soldiers reeling in agony. One screamed and fell backward clutching his face. Another was torn along the arm and side by the burst.

In the confusion Toner had managed to get to the other side of the street and was crouched in a doorway watching Mackal, effectively pinning him down. The policeman could just see Byrnes bringing the van up. Mackal crawled under the car and took aim at it, knowing the patrol could not have seen it. But before he could fire the ground in front of him erupted in spurting dust and splinters. He rolled over so his head would be protected behind the tire. Mackal's eyes stung and the dust was choking him. When he was able to see again Byrnes was reversing the van down the street with McCann beside him. Mackal fired blindly. There was an ear-shattering series of booms from the British self-loading rifles as they tore chunks off the wall with the posters on it near where Devine was lodged. His eyes were burning from the brick dust. Devine was trapped. From where the detective was lying he could not hit the gunman, and neither could the soldiers. Devine was wedged in the doorway at an impossible angle. But at least they knew where he was. Toner let off another burst in the direction of Mackal's car, forcing him behind the rear wheel this time.

Mackal again fired at the van. Devine made a dash for it up the street, out of sight of the patrol. Mackal fired again and saw Devine stagger and clutch his arm as he clambered into the back of the vehicle.

Beardsley was talking through his radio and when he heard the sound of the van he peered round from the back of the saracen. For an instant his head and shoulders were exposed. There was a dull thud and the lieutenant staggered backward. Mackal looked round, recognizing the high-velocity report of an armalite. Someone had driven a truck across the road further down from where he was, forming a barricade. He just caught a glimpse of a man in a hood ducking behind it; then he saw another, and another. Within seconds they opened up a fusillade, which was ricocheting off the saracens and clipping chunks of brick off the buildings it hit. It looked as if half of the Belfast brigade of the Provisional IRA had arrived at once. There was no answering fire from the army; the soldiers remained concealed behind their vehicles and huddled in the doorways. The few who had been in the open when the armalites began firing were dead.

Mackal edged his way to the front of the car and considered making a dash up the road to the saracen—the cars would prove a flimsy obstacle to the bullets of armalites. When he peered down the road again there was even more commotion than before. This time there were armored vehicles everywhere and the IRA gunmen were hastily departing. But the whole bottom of the road was now cut off. Whether they liked it or not the British were going to have to arrest a lot of IRA men.

Toner had remained unnoticed by the soldiers the whole time he was hidden in the shadows across the street from Mackal. The van had pulled away moments earlier and the driver was anxiously waiting for him a few yards down the side street, undecided whether to drive Seamus off immediately to get help or wait a few more seconds for

Toner to appear. When Mackal's attention was diverted to Beardsley's saracen Toner silently ran over to the waiting van. Within seconds they had swung the vehicle into one of the tiny streets and disappeared into the Falls Road ghetto.

There was an eerie silence broken only by the groans of Lieutenant Beardsley, who lay semiconscious by his radio but aware of a dull ache spreading from his shoulder. Cursing to himself, Mackal got up, and holding his revolver at his side, walked disconsolately toward the silent, shocked soldiers.

"For Jesus' sake!" he said when he saw the gaping red hole in Beardsley's shoulder. He flung his revolver on the road and knelt down beside the dying man.

10

Mrs. Toner woke Nora with a cup of tea. Nora opened her eyes slowly, focusing on the thin little woman by the bedside with the fragrant cup of tea, the light filtering through the closed curtains, the holy picture on the bedroom wall opposite. She hadn't slept well, nor had she the night before.

Nora rubbed the sleep from her eyes and looked blearily at Mrs. Toner.

"It's only half past seven, love; there's no rush around here. Would you like some toast with that?"

"No thanks, this'll wake me up."

Mrs. Toner felt bad about waking her since she was in obvious need of a long lie-in.

"Poor thing," she said, sitting on the edge of the bed, "you look as if you could stay in bed for a week. I wouldn't blame you, after what you've been through."

Nora smiled and took a sip of the strong tea. She knew she could never find any rest in this city again. For the last few days she'd been at the Toners', afraid to go home since her humiliation. The living nightmare of those events flowed into her sleep until dreaming and waking converged in her consciousness to create a restless twilight flux from which neither sleep nor waking provided an escape.

When Mrs. Toner had gone she sat up, resting her cup and saucer on her lap. Each morning when she woke she felt herself in a kind of limbo from which she wanted desperately to escape. She knew she would have to distance herself from the events of the last week or be pulled down into the gray flux forever. She dreamt of drowning, being submerged, suffocating. And in the dreams floated the faces of her interrogators; the waking nightmare of the bare room with the whirring fan; the dirty little back room with the empty hearth and the flypaper that swung above Joe's bald head, and O'Neill peeping through the hole in the newspaper waiting for the crowds to come to watch her public humiliation. The images rose up when she shut her eyes. They confronted her when she opened them.

Michael was getting ready to leave. He had remained with her as much as possible these last few days, but now he was finishing off his final report and packing. He'd spoken to her about going with him, returning to New York. On one hand it seemed an absurd idea. Her whole life had been spent here. She was weak from her recent ordeals: the ghetto had attempted to conquer her once and for all. Perhaps it had claimed its final victory over her. But again and again she forced herself to rally her strength. Then Michael's proposal would seem like a chink of light coming out of a world—a real world that was some-where else, somewhere far away—of which she had no experience. Yet there it was, in the midst of her nightmare, an offer of escape. When she thought about it this way, she felt it was almost inevitable that she should leave. Not to leave would mean that everything that had hap-pened to her would in the end amount to nothing—no change. It was unthinkable now to go back to the years of waiting.

She got out of the bed wearily and went to the window. She pulled back the curtains and looked down on the deserted courtyard several floors below. A flock of pigeons were pecking like automata. Nora noticed an old woman standing near one of the stairwells throwing crumbs at the birds. She sipped the tea and stared at the ritual enacted before her. The old women in her street used to do that every morning before Nora set off for school. They always had aprons full of crumbs ready to give the pigeons "breakfast."

A big seagull landed below and tried to muscle in, scattering a few of the pigeons. The old woman shooed it away vigorously. Nora watched it rise and circle and thought that it might be off across the sea, disgusted by the inhospitable reception, to follow one of the car ferries to England.

Mrs. Toner rapped on the door. "I'm sorry, love, but I forgot if you took sugar. My oul head's goin'." Nora said she didn't, the tea was great, so it was. Mrs. Toner noticed she was watching the old woman below on the edge of the wasteground.

"That's a quare view to wake up to in the morning, isn't it?" Mrs. Toner said sarcastically. "That'll set you up for the day. It would put years on ya, so it would," she went on wearily, gazing down. "We were a lot better off when we had the wee streets to live in instead of being stuck up here. Sure, everybody knew everybody else and we could sit and gossip till our heart's content. But stuck up here—with the bloody seagulls for company!" She paused and peered down at the bleak scene.

"That's oul Mrs. McCourt. She's out there every morning, rain, hail or shine, with her crumbs. The poor oul thing can hardly get down the stairs. She's never been the same since her husband died. Not a bad soul. But she's a bit funny in the head. If you ask me it was because she was moved out of her wee street and got put into this pile o' concrete. That killed oul Mr. McCourt. He took awful bad after they moved. They couldn't get the coffin down the stairs—the lifts were broke. You never know the day, do you?" Mrs. Toner sighed compassionately. "Anyway, I'll let you drink your tea," she said. She scurried off and smiled at Nora as she closed the bedroom door.

Nora looked across the room at the picture of the Blessed Virgin Mary, her beaming face upturned toward heaven, her head covered in a blue mantle. Jesus sat above her in a cloudy seat surrounded by angels, his loincloth flowing over his thighs, his raised hands bearing the scars of suffering and sacrifice. The utter negation on Mary's face filled Nora with revulsion and pity, almost bringing her to the edge of tears. She could no longer endure the sight of it. As she passed the picture of the Blessed Virgin she almost stopped and turned it to the wall. But Mrs. Toner would be deeply offended and would not understand. She slipped off her nightgown and searched through the pile of Deirdre's clothes that had been made available to her. They had both the same figure so the clothes fit her well.

Naked, her body still had a certain luminous feel—it still glowed, radiating a sheer physicality that gave her the deepest satisfaction. She was sorting through Deirdre's underwear and found a nice brief pair that she liked. She put them on and looked at herself in the mirror. Through the nightmare she had been living this was the source of her secret exultation. It was all that remained real to her—her body, the memories of his touch. She undid her shorn hair. It hung in a bunch, ugly, maimed, mangled. Perhaps she would keep it that way for a while, she thought. In spite of it, when she looked at herself naked or nearly naked she was still excited. She was the object of desire to herself in a way she couldn't really understand. She didn't desire herself, but perhaps it was that she defined, inspired desires in others and that aroused her. Only two men had seen her naked and taken the gift of her nakedness, and she loved both. She turned her back to the mirror and looked over her shoulder; her hair ended in a jagged, broken line of hacked strands. Such a contrast to the smooth flowing contours of her back!

She dressed beneath the holy picture, despising the rapt gaze of the Virgin of sacrifice, defying it with her every feeling. It crystallized her temptation to leave Belfast. She had arranged to see Michael later that day. What would she tell him? It would be simple for her to get on the ferry to Liverpool and go down to Kate's house near London. Kate had been asking her to do that for a long time. Then it would give her a chance to think, away from this city and the awful pressures it exerted on her, the penalties it exacted from her. It would give her the time to arrange things with Michael. She could contemplate the possibilities that a future with him afforded. Kate would soothe her, reassure her, support her.

She found Mrs. Toner standing by the kitchen sink. Near her on the stove a big pot of tea was brewing. There was a smell of freshly toasted bread, the cold, fresh scent of a newly opened bottle of milk. The little table was prepared, cups and saucers neatly arranged, the butter dish full, jam beside it. Mrs. Toner was thinking about her sons —Gerry once more on the run, nearly killed a few days before, two others rotting in jail—the violence that lay ahead. She turned to Nora and smiled, glad of an excuse to perform her much-loved ritual of feeding, of homemaking, of welcome, of warmth and love-giving. Nora had toast and more tea and a boiled egg while Mrs. Toner talked and sympathized and regretted what had happened and what might still come about.

Michael was in the bar of his hotel, sitting in a corner booth reading over his last report when Nora came to join him.

"I hope that keeps Healy happy," he said, throwing it on the marble-topped table before him. "I didn't get the helicopter escape into it but I did give a firsthand account of the collapse of the truce."

"Is that what he wanted?"

"He's like most Americans; he loves anecdotes. He's not interested in theories or explanations about the Northern Ireland situation. He wants a little story. So that's what you have to provide. Journalism's rather different over there. It's at a very primitive level, really, the level of parable. The helicopter escape was a good little anecdote—the kind he likes, the kind his paper sells. He really doesn't want to be bothered thinking about anything—especially Northern Ireland."

"At this point I couldn't agree with him more," Nora said and smiled ruefully at Michael. "But why is that?" she asked. Her curiosity was piqued—wasn't everybody in the world puzzling over this place as much as they were, trying to figure it all out?

"Healy shows no capacity for abstract thought," Michael smiled mischievously. "And besides, he's too busy!"

"Is that supposed to be true of Americans in general?" she asked.

"In a certain way it is—they tend to be impatient with explanations, especially as regards anything to do with Europe. After all, that's what most of them left behind and they don't want to waste too much time worrying about it." Nora was very surprised. She had never thought of America that way. She very much would like to go and see it for herself.

"You think the truce is completely over then?" she asked after he ordered a round of drinks.

"McCabe has disappeared. No one can find him. He was the architect of the truce—him and Fagan. But let's not talk about that now."

A waiter set the drinks on the table.

"How's life with Mrs. Toner?"

"Okay."

"You can't stay there forever though, Nora. You have to make up your mind." Michael looked at her intently. "In fact, it's already decided for you by what you've done. You can't stay here, you know that."

She drank up and looked around her at the other customers: well-dressed young men and women, chatting, flirting, relaxed. It didn't seem like Belfast at all but another city in which she felt a stranger. If she left it would be like this wherever she went. Michael noticed her unease.

"New York, Nora. Remember that story you told me about your mother watching the planes and wondering where they were going? You can't end up doing the same thing. Now you can find out yourself."

She sighed and looked at the shiny table top. Her eyes dwelt on its swirling patterns.

"Michael, it's complicated. I'm still married to John. I . . ." Before she could finish he took her by the hand and leaned over to kiss her cheek. She rested her head unselfconsciously on his shoulder and for a moment closed her eyes to see if she could imagine what it would be like if she accepted his invitation. Even the prospect of such a change made her breathless with fear and excitement.

"I want to live with you," he said to her gently, running his finger in a circle round the wet, cold tabletop.

"And John?"

"He's already made his choice long ago; you know that. He's chosen Mother Ireland."

Nora looked up at him sharply, knowing that what he said was true, but hurt by the unsparing concision of his remark. Something of the old bitterness still showed in him. His confident intolerance excited and worried her at the same time. It made him unpredictable in ways John never could be. Michael intrigued her, made her curious. Her love for John was so simple in comparison; he was difficult but never complicated as Michael would be. The thought of leaving John deeply pained her. But the thought of staying horrified and panicked her.

"Must every choice involve a sacrifice?" she asked.

"Obviously," he whispered.

She reached down and gripped his circling finger. It was so slender, like a pianist's or a poet's should be. They sat, silent for a while.

"You haven't spoken to him since—"

"No—I'm going to see him soon. I have to." She had taken his hand and was squeezing it rhythmically and unconsciously.

"What are you going to tell him?"

She did not answer. She took another sip of her drink.

"Kate keeps asking me over to England," she said after a minute. "She wants me to stay with her. That's one alternative."

"But you don't want to live with Kate," he answered irritably. "I thought you'd already made up your mind to come to New York with me." Michael was perturbed that she might be weakening.

"It would give me time to think, Michael. I need time. I need a few weeks alone . . . I'll come, I know I'll come to you, but just be patient."

As she spoke she loosened her grip on him and he began to stroke the back of her hand gently and rhythmically, as in a slow massage. She yearned to cleave to him again, to stop thinking, to be loved by him. She was tired of torturing herself with alternatives. But most of all she wanted to tell him that. She was still unable to, however.

"Enough talk. We've talked enough," Michael said with emphasis as he stood up and started to lead her to the door, still holding her hand. "Let's settle this problem upstairs where it *can* be settled," he whispered, smiling, "in bed."

Nora was a bit shocked at him, but his directness thrilled her. He had read her mind. They left the bar and went up the carpeted staircase along a quiet corridor lined with fading Victorian paintings, past small, well-polished mahogany tables holding vases full of dusty dried flowers to his room. He closed the door softly behind her and walked to the window. He looked down into the avenue and then drew the curtains.

"Living here could make you paranoid," he said, turning to her. She had slipped off her jeans and was unbuttoning her blouse, standing in the shady room near his bed.

"It makes no difference now. I want to make love to you, Michael."

He kissed her neck, ran his hands through her hair, buried his face in it lovingly. She wanted him to pay homage to her sign of shame, to worship it, to love her for it. And he did.

There was a hush when the other women saw her coming. The chatter died away and the children were curbed. Nora took her place, the usual place, resting against the wall of the building near the poster of the prisoner with the battered blood-bloated face. At first there was an embarrassed silence. The other women did not look at her. There were whispers at the front of the group near the edge of the pavement. Then a little boy broke free of his mother and ran back to see his friend. His bag of sweets fell and scattered on the street. Nora bent down to help him pick them up. She looked up to see his mother standing there.

"Thanks, Mrs. Costello," she said quickly. "Don't bother yourself; I'll clear them up for him, the wee tory." She gave him a swat on the bottom. There was another hiatus as the two women gathered the sweets.

"I should throw half of these away—it's not good for them this time of the morning," she muttered. She filled the paper bag and stood up. The two women confronted each other. The mother was in her late thirties, very thin, with a head scarf. Her face had been handsome once, but now it was creased, and the mouth already appeared to be set in an expression of anxiety and harassment, which even when she smiled haunted her face like a ghost. She looked at the small bag of sweets and then at Nora.

"We're awful sorry for your trouble, Mrs. Costello. We don't think it was right for them to do that, you know," she blurted out finally. Another woman heard her and turned.

"That's right, love. It was a shame to do that for them reasons. I think so, don't you, Maggie?" another mother said, asking the friend beside her.

"Aye—they'd no reason. We saw you here every Saturday morning for the last three years or more, that's right. You were always here hail, rain or shine, so you were. It's politics behind it if you ask me."

"And after you being harassed an' all by the RUC. It was a crying shame and a disgrace to the boys."

Nora's hand was resting on the head of the little boy. Without realizing it she was combing her fingers through his hair. She looked from face to face—she was as close to them now as she could ever be. She knew that in one way it was only an illusion, but while it lasted it was a comforting one. She blushed, looking away trying to hide her emotion, and blurted out her thanks. The little boy went to his mother, who gave him a warning look. He understood, and returning to Nora, offered her a sweet. She took one and thanked him. Everyone felt more relaxed. Shortly McGreary arrived. The driver's usual joviality turned quickly to shock and intense embarrassment when he saw Nora. One of the women took Nora by the arm. "Come on, love, get you on in there," she said as she gently pushed Nora into the van. The other women watched McGreary steadily in a way indicating that he was to offer no objections.

Summer was ending. The gusts of mountain winds were colder now. Nora hugged herself under the cloudy sky. She rested against the back door in her usual place, rubbing the fogged-up window clear. The countryside flew past her like a moving picture she was watching alone in an empty cinema. The talk of the women was far away. Already the first autumnal scents were on the wind filtering in through the pervasive smell of cigarette smoke in the van. Everything outside was gray and green. Clouds tumbled over the top of the basaltic mass of the Black Mountain blowing in west from the Atlantic. She looked at the distant glens and gullies that scarred its slopes and which, since her childhood, had been her landscape. To the east the pastoral drumlins still had sunshine brightening their pleasant patchwork of fields. Locked in the little van, perhaps for the last time, she was able to contemplate that contrast—those poles of existence expressed in the landscape between which life hung in Northern Ireland.

When Long Kesh loomed up above the hedgerows it daunted her

again and she was overcome with guilt, regret, terror, at what she had to do. The other women would be here next week, and the week after that, and the one after that, faithful as ever. Nora knew she could not, would not be. She fell into a kind of trance, distant and removed from what was going on around her and from what was to come. The van went over the first ramp into the wide car park just outside the first gates. She imagined these women here next week looking at her place at the back of the van, vacant, the windows fogging up, the gossip. Perhaps if she could somehow glide through this morning trancelike, as if already removed from these responsibilities, from this prison world, from her marriage, her city . . . For in a way she was—she had made her decision. She would leave. She had made a commitment to someone else and to herself. Being here was an awful purgatory, an awful test she had to endure, it seemed, before finally entering into her new life, her new world. She had to do it for her own sake, but more important for John's.

She was staring in a daze at the blank cubicle wall when John came in, his face strikingly pale under his thick dark beard. The sight of her maimed hair startled and sickened him. He took it tenderly but hesitatingly in his hands.

"It'll grow again," she whispered, full of sympathy for him, responding to his vulnerability. He sat down opposite her. His heavy, dark beard sank in his chest; in spite of it being cold his blue shirt was open at the neck. His short, broad figure seemed full of bull-like life. Her words withered in her mouth, scorched by the intensity of the tenderness she still felt for him. He was silent, looking at her. His lips were shut tight and a kind of baffled, hurt and angry look set in his face like that of a wounded child too defiantly proud to show his grief. But she was hurt too, realizing that even if they were alone again together in bed, embracing, making love, she would not be able to express what she felt for him. Even if she did she knew it would pass unrecognized. So much of her had gone unnoticed by his vigorous impetuosity that in the end it had almost crushed the very life out of her.

They were silent for what seemed a long time. They listened to the others chatting in the long hut and to the sound of the autumnal winds rattling outside, to the sounds of the prison officers' footsteps passing by.

"It's over now, Nora," he said suddenly. She looked at him in surprise.

"McCabe and that lot—they lost. We won. Ireland will not be

betrayed. What they did to you finally exposed them for what they were. It will never happen again." She did not talk. She watched him; she watched his clear blue eyes glinting hard, demonically again. He would never change.

He talked on about the future, about the success of this part of the freedom struggle. As he spoke he gained strength and confidence until his boyish enthusiasm and energy were almost infectious and nearly made them both forget that he was talking about these things only to avoid the agonizing questions. Her experience was once more in abeyance. Since hearing about his wife's public humiliation he could not even tolerate the thought that there were any grounds for believing Nora was unfaithful to him, yet he hungered to hear that from her own lips. He wanted to dismiss the whole episode to the realm of abstract politics, a dirty trick played by his rivals—while at the same time his mind was tormented by the possibility that his enemies knew more than he did.

Seeing she was not responding, he was silent. He knew then there was something wrong. But the words wouldn't come off her tongue— her emotions tumbled around inside her in a chaos of tenderness, resentment, anger, sympathy, pity and love. She was afraid that when something did come out it would be a muddled outburst that would make her seem foolish, hysterical, weak, making him resent her even more. She knew time was passing quickly from the pacing of the guards' footsteps, which seemed to her to measure the minutes like the ticking of the clock. Finally she could bear the silence even less than she could his talking about the politics of her attempted humiliation. She had to tell him now that she was leaving Belfast.

"I didn't come here to celebrate the defeat of Peadar McCabe or anything like that—truce or no truce," she said with deliberation.

He looked at her puzzled, as if she were a total stranger to him.

"I don't care about whether what happened to me was of any use in the freedom struggle or not. I just want you to understand me and why I have to leave Belfast. That's all."

"I was wondering how long it'd take before you'd give up," was his reply, harsh and contemptuous. "You never really had it in you, had you?"

"You can reduce it to that if you like."

It hurt her deeply to be dismissed so coldly. She was not prepared for such a rebuke even though she half-expected it. Had all those years meant nothing to him? What she had endured was merely what she was expected to endure, hardly deserving of recognition or thanks.

"I'm going to London to stay with Kate, to get away from this—far away."

"Her!" he exclaimed with disdain.

She fell silent, rebuffed but unmoved.

"How long for?" he asked quietly, with sudden resignation that to her sounded almost like relief.

"I don't know—there's another possibility . . . ," she began and paused, unable to continue.

John sank back in his chair and looked away from her. He did not want to hear. He still saw her as an extension of himself, her ordeal a justification of his actions, nothing more. It pained and confused him to contemplate her in her own sphere, obeying laws of which he had no knowledge. But she persisted, breathing deep down to get the words out.

"It's got to do with someone else, John—another man." He pursed his red lips, regarding her quizzically. The prison officer walked by and shot him a black look. A strong gust of wind shook the hut sending a cold shudder down Nora's spine. He frightened her; when gloom settled on him she feared the dammed-up feelings, the great head of energy that built up inside him would burst out. She felt so cold and alone, isolated in that bare, little space where he sat staring at her.

"Who?" he finally asked.

"Michael Boyd," she whispered.

Johnny smiled scornfully at the sound of his name. "They were right then," he muttered, his eyes turning away from her to the scene behind her, then glancing toward the table—not knowing where to come to rest.

"Were they? Then maybe your friends should have let them finish the job."

"We had a more important job to do!" he snapped.

She felt it was hopeless. "I'm going," she whispered, standing up. The guards looked over at her. Johnny stared at her sullenly. She could not move.

"I don't want to leave you like this," she whispered desperately.

"So I have a choice," he said sarcastically. "I'm sorry I won't be able to see you off at the boat."

"Oh, Johnny," she cried, sitting down again. "Please understand!"

"What good will that do? What difference does it make?"

"It's important to me, because I still love you. I want you to understand that. I need time to think about everything. I have to be away from this place; too much has happened."

"Three years is a long time," he said bitterly. Nora looked at him fiercely, hurt. She was on the verge of tears, fighting desperately not to be devastated by his reaction and angry at her own continued need for his respect.

"Are you on their side?" she hissed. She could no longer hold back the tears. She grabbed his hand and placed it on her shorn hair. "Are you on the side of the people who did that—the kind of people you hate, that you fought against, that you said betrayed everything you believed in—you gave your life for? Do you share their beliefs?"

He tried to withdraw his hand, but she clasped it firmly.

"Look at me," she whispered through the tears. "Look at me, Johnny!" But speech failed her; she couldn't speak. She could only cry softly and look at him through the blur of tears. How could she explain what had happened? How could she express the reasons for what she'd done when he sat before her like an impetuous child whose impetuosity was suddenly baffled? His mouth was clamped shut; his lips a red mark within the darkness of his beard. She sighed deeply. Even her efforts to help him get the money to Devine seemed like an attempt to further her own designs, to keep him in jail instead of something she did out of the deepest respect for him. How could she untangle all that here, now, surrounded by guards and strangers. Then to her surprise his hand began to finger her hair tenderly. He saw confusion in her tear-stained eyes. She let go of his hand; it slipped down her neck and rested on her shoulder; it caressed her. He put his other hand up to her lips as if to say, "Say no more." His lips curled, loosening. His mouth was no longer hard and set, his eyes no longer malevolent. He brushed the tears from her cheeks.

"I asked you to do something and you did it," he said finally. "That's what matters." Seeing her so devastated, he had shifted her behavior to a plane that he could understand. He had decided to dwell on this, knowing that to try to grasp the other was hopeless. Like the honest man he was, he decided it was best left alone; his energy was only directed toward that which he could master, understand, achieve.

"I did it because I love you," she cried with quiet desperation. He saw it in her eyes.

"I know that, Nora," he answered, pulling her gently toward him. They kissed a long deep kiss, across the ugly little table that lay between them—at that moment the only obstacle they were aware of.

The prison officer rang his little bell to signify that there were only five minutes more. Nora felt a kind of panic grip her. She felt intensely loyal to him. It was a primitive feeling, a strange, demanding instinct that reared its head like some wonderful fairy-tale beast to confront her now as time ran out. She had to get his approval, for she still loved him. She knew that his refusal would hurt her deeply and disappoint her, but not finally defeat her. But he stayed silent, gloomy again, his brow wrinkled, his clear eyes baffled. It was unfair for her to have to bear the full responsibility of leaving him, but the world, and Johnny, would not see it that way. For it was he, her husband, who had made the crucial decision and from that all else had flowed. He had been disloyal to their marriage, yet here she was seeking his understanding. Men could reconcile their loyalties or sacrifice some for others with an ease that amazed her.

"I know one thing and that's certain: whatever side the Fagans and McCabes of this world are on I'm on the opposite," he said finally. His eyes fixed on her as she rubbed her tears away with the back of her hand.

"I never misled you, Nora—from the night we met at the barricade you knew what to expect. You knew what I had to do and you knew that I would do it no matter what. I cannot apologize for that."

"I don't want you to. I love you for that."

The jailer's bell rang again. She froze, unable to move.

"I can't say that I understand you when I don't," he said.

She looked up at him, her eyes wide, tear-stained.

"But I admire you, Nora, for everything. Maybe someday I'll understand—and maybe someday you will too. Maybe some day . . ." But he didn't finish. He smiled at her and in his eyes there was no hint of malice or contempt or injured feelings or resentment. They seemed extraordinarily confident. But then they always were.

A guard stood behind her and she became aware of his jarring presence. John stood up to leave. As he passed her she gripped him impulsively around the waist and pulled him close to her. She would never be forgiven by the world for leaving him and if she didn't leave him she would never forgive herself.

His hands ran over her hair as Michael's had done, but with a very different touch. Different hands, different men; John's touch was so diffident, hesitating, shy at showing affection overtly—it brought her whole life with him to mind. Her whole life with him swam before her eyes as she clung to his waist. The officer intervened. John helped her stand up. Gently he separated from her.

"Nora, it's important I know where you are."

Suddenly he was gone.

She did not look round but slumped again into the chair. She stared at the blank wall opposite across the little mean table that for years had been such a petty but overwhelming obstacle. Her ears picked out the sounds of his footsteps until they were drowned by the scraping of chairs and the chatter of last farewells of the others in the hut. The commotion submerged everything. The chair, the table, the cubicle itself seemed frozen in time, time which spun her last three years before her eyes. Her stomach tumbled. She felt queasy. These bits of cheap furniture were her life's static emblems—a life contracted to this table, this chair, a few hurried moments lost among years of waiting.

She stood up and with a violent thrust of her foot pushed the table, knocking over the chair on which Johnny had been sitting. She wanted to smash them into bits, as if by doing so she could destroy the mean deprivation of the world they represented. An officer came running over and ushered her quickly out of the Nissen hut.

She found herself in the open air looking up at the sky. There were patches of blue among the autumn clouds. A flock of wild geese were making a V-shaped journey south over the Down hills. It was surprisingly cold.

11

"And what became of this fellow Mackal?" the British minister for Northern Ireland, Noel Andrews, was asking.

"He's gone on a long holiday to a little island off the North Antrim coast," said Superintendant Black. Andrews was standing beneath the expansive oil painting that hung over the fireplace in the old ministerial conference room in Stormont Castle. There was a bright fire burning in the hearth; its flames cast shadows on the shepherds and shepherdesses who lounged in the rather pathetic pastoral scene above him.

"It could have been handled with somewhat more dexterity, Black." Andrews turned his back to the flames and looked glumly at the officer, who was standing at the opposite side of the long table.

"I know; but Mackal—he's a good pliceman, but he is sometimes dogmatic about his work and—"

"You mean he's something of a zealot. That's the trouble with this country of yours—too many zealots," the minister interrupted him impatiently. Black smiled gently at the irony of a British government minister referring to Northern Ireland that way. After all, it was supposed to be part of the United Kingdom.

"Anyway, Black, we've managed to retrieve something from it all." He looked over his glasses at the superintendent and smiled knowingly.

"We've started the ball rolling again. This time it has to go on, no matter what, understand? The instructions of earlier this year must stand. We have to get them talking again."

"And how? After what's happened—" But Black was once more not allowed to finish.

"Superintendent, you don't know these types as well as I do. They're all just failed politicians. They can be flattered." He paused, and turning again to the flames behind him, he put his foot on the polished brass fender.

"Contact has been made. It's a last effort."

"McCabe?"

Andrews nodded.

"Can he hold it together?"

"We'll see what he can offer."

"And Devine?"

"And Devine, and Costello, and the rest—yes, I know." Andrews thought for a moment, as if searching the dancing flames for an answer.

"Why is it the Irish are so factious?" he sighed. It was getting too hot so he walked to the table.

"They will be dealt with, Superintendent, one way or another, when the time comes."

Peadar McCabe sat back watching the high, stony fields race by. His driver was speeding with grim determination along the narrow, twisting roadway that ran between the bleak hills of Louth and the cold, deep fiord of Carlingford Lough. The fields depressed him; he looked out the window on one side and saw the poor little farms perched insecurely halfway up the mountain slopes and shook his head despairingly. Louth was perhaps the poorest county in the country. The lough divided Northern Ireland from the Irish Republic. On the northern side the mountains of Mourne stood out, domes of granite, round and smooth, giving an impression of extraordinary height, though they were not in fact high. The lough waters lapped against a stony, inhospitable beach covered with seaweed, which steamed in the autumn sunshine.

"I used to come down here for my holidays," McCabe said.

The driver nodded. "Aye, it used to be a great spot for the Belfast people." His driver was a local man from the nearby town of Newry.

"We rented a cottage not far from here. Tell me, do you still have the jaunting cars?" McCabe remembered the open horse-drawn coaches with side seats that used to run along the road they were on. His mind was eager to get back to some more pleasing memories than the events of the last few weeks would allow.

"Na—they're gone," came the matter-of-fact reply.

"Pity," said McCabe, looking at his watch.

The car turned right off the main road. The laneway was steep and stony. McCabe looked back to make sure the other car was still behind them. It was. He hung onto the strap at the side as the car bumped up toward a little cottage just visible between the hedgerows. The IRA's ruling body, the Army Council, would be there by now, waiting for its chief of staff to deliver his account of the recent events and to suggest the guerrillas' future strategy. Its seven members came from all over Ireland—though now mostly from the North, the theater of operations. He would have to reassure them about Belfast; that was the key to the whole thing. He would have to convince them Belfast was still behind him. He had arranged to have the new Belfast Officer Commanding come down to the meeting, a young, bright and articulate fellow called Kelly. He had lost four men to Long Kesh because of that bloody shootout over that wee cunt Nora Costello; he thought of her and it made him angry. The whole thing was a stupid mess. His men should have stayed out of it—let that bastard Devine get what was coming to him. He would insist now that Devine be put on the list. He would have to go, one way or another. The Brits had been in touch again—God, were they scared! McCabe knew now he had them by the balls. After that incident they still came back! Still wanted to talk! It proved he had been right all along. The Brits want to go. We just have to give them the chance, that was the only way. Give them the chance to go. The IRA couldn't go on fighting forever.

He clicked open his case, in which there was a memo from Peter O'Neill setting out all these points. He glanced over it to refresh his memory, but he couldn't concentrate. His mind kept drifting back to Devine, Nora Costello, Jack Fagan, and he clenched his teeth and swore they would pay dearly for what had happened.

With a jolt the car swung around, turning off the lane into an even narrower pathway that ran under some dense overarching hedges to the door of the cottage. It braked and McCabe gave a deep sigh.

Inside the big front room a group of men sat. A wide hearth was banked high with burning peat and gave out a rich-scented smell; occasional puffs of smoke were blown out across the room by wind gusting down the spacious chimney. When Peadar McCabe entered they looked up. Sean Lynch from Derry, a young blond-haired man with a light beard, nodded to him.

"Good to see you, Peadar," he smiled.

A man in his late fifties was sitting near the hearth. Like McCabe, James McGoldrick was from Belfast, an old veteran of the 1950s campaigns, a silent man who had spent half his life in jails. He acknowledged McCabe by raising an index finger to his forehead, then, hunched over, he resumed sucking on his pipe. A Dublin man rose to greet the newcomer. Billy O'Donnell, was an elderly, well-dressed house painter, whose involvement went back to the 1940s. He had thick gray hair brushed back from his ears. He gave Peadar a pat on the shoulder. The other three Army Council members were hunkered together in a corner by the little window talking when McCabe came in: Seamus McKerry, the guerrilla chief from nearby South Armagh, a short, laconic individual in his thirties; a southerner called Joe Curran from Cork; and Brendan Greene, a big ex-paratrooper who ran the North Armagh–South Down area. They all acknowledged McCabe, who smiled in their direction. He was standing by the window near a table. He peeked outside to see his backup car pull up. Then he settled his case on the table and rubbed his hands.

"Bit of a nip in the air up here," he said. He opened the case.

"I've a wee lad—Liam Kelly—coming down from Belfast. He's replacing Jacky Fagan. He'll put youse in the picture about the Belfast situation—the lads are still firm; they're still behind us in spite of the . . . uh . . . misunderstanding of recent days. But I thought he'd better tell you so himself. He's a bright lad. Jack'll be hard to replace, a man of his experience, but Kelly's sharp, keen. You know him, Jimmy."

He turned to McGoldrick, who thought for a second then shook his head pensively.

"I'm not sure I do, Peadar."

"You'll recognize him. Anyway . . . ," he picked up the paper sheets, "this is a summary of the last Brit contact. It proves they're still interested, they still want to talk. It just reinforces what we've been saying all along—they're desperate to go."

"Did they say anything about releasing the lads?" asked McKerry slowly, referring to the men captured during the recent shootout.

"Well, not yet. That's a hard one. They got them redhanded—gear, everything."

"Too bad," said McGoldrick, spitting into the fire. His spittle hissed on the smoldering peat.

"Too fuckin' bad!" Greene said angrily. He looked up from the corner where he was sitting hunched with McKerry and Joe Curran.

"Look, Brendan," McCabe began, "we can't get sidetracked. The Brits are running scared. Why do you think they wanted to talk again after all that happened?"

Greene got up and walked to the table where McCabe's case and papers were. He looked down at them and then at McCabe. The others sat silently for a minute. McCabe looked round at them uneasily. Greene glanced at his watch.

"Look," McCabe started again, going over to the group by the fire, "I'll set up another meeting. The Brits contacted *me;* they want to talk again. They want to pull out. Let's give them the chance." He lifted up O'Neill's memo in his left hand. With a sudden movement Greene plucked it from his grip and cast his eyes over it without speaking. McCabe was startled by the gesture. His eyes narrowed as he scrutinized every face in the room for an answer. They avoided his glance.

"We've someone we'd like you to talk to, Peadar," he said. "Wait here." Greene went to the door and into the hallway. McCabe listened. He heard another door open and voices. They spoke in Belfast accents.

"What's going on?" he said to McGoldrick. McGoldrick merely stared into the flames. When he didn't get an answer he turned to O'Donnell, who smiled nervously and affected a puzzled expression. McCabe turned from him in contempt. He heard the sound of footsteps in the little hallway and then the door to the front room opened.

Greene came in first and stepped back away from the door. He nodded. Seamus Devine and Gerry Toner walked past him into the room. Devine's arm was heavily bandaged up in a sling. Peadar McCabe glared at them.

"You murdering bastards!" he muttered; but Greene looked at him hard.

"Sit down, Peadar!" he barked.

Greene was still holding the paper with the latest truce proposals on it. Slowly he crumpled it in his fists, then flung it into the hearth. Peadar McCabe watched it go up in flames, its burnt scraps crumpling into the fine, soft ash of the peat fire.

He had turned the final corner to find himself at the heart of the murder maze where there was no exit, except one.

As before, the cars were parked by the side of the lonely country road where the thick pine trees ended. As before, the air was heavy with their scent. The crows cawed above in the highest branches. Soon they were wheeling and screeching in the sky at the sound of the descending helicopter. The ground beneath was rock-strewn but clear enough for a landing. The severing blades came to a halt. There was silence; there was no sound in the forest. The crows returned cautiously to their perches. The pilot and the two soldiers beside him listened. They peered down the narrow, twisting, little pathway that ran from the open patch of ground between the thick trees to the roadway where the cars waited. They saw someone moving along the pathway. It was time to get out. The captain looked at his watch.

"Late as usual," he said, and jumped out.

In the dark woods an unseen hand pressed a button. The ground under the helicopter erupted as the five hundred pounds of gelignite exploded, sending chunks of earth and rock and metal spinning into the air in a cloud of thick earth and dust. When the dust settled there was silence again, except for the soft patter of broken earth falling on the pine needles.

The blades of the broken machine were ripped and torn, thrown against the trees. The helicopter was a shattered tangle of metal. There was no sign of any human being anywhere. Except in the woods. Shadowy figures moved between the trees. There was a rustle of footsteps. The men walked briskly away from the woods down the road to the parked car. They took a can of petrol from the boot and poured it inside and over the car, then threw a match on it. It burst into flames. Within seconds Peadar McCabe's vehicle was a blackened hulk. Another car pulled up and the men got in. They drove off quickly into the nearby hills of South Armagh.

The curious crows watched the car vanish into that barren, secretive landscape, the only spectators of the ending of the ceasefire. The pine woods were theirs again.

The remains of McCabe's car were found soon afterward, along with those of the helicopter. And then they found McCabe himself. Like his car, he was discovered in South Armagh, his body bundled into a telephone kiosk. He'd been shot once in the head with a .357 Magnum. Beside his body they also found a suicide note.

12

*P*igeons and seagulls flocked along the quayside following the big grain truck. The grain tip-
pled slowly onto the cobblestones and the birds
pecked eagerly in a soft rain. A curtain of drizzle had descended onto
the Lagan Valley and seemed to seep to the core of everything.

The Liverpool Ferry knocked gently against the side of the wharf;
the wharf groaned under the strain. Children stared in trepidation over
the side of the wharf into the dark waters between it and the boat.
Parents, their suitcases resting on the ground, held them by the hand.

Nora Costello and Michael Boyd walked slowly down the quayside,
scattering the gulls and pigeons. He held a case in each hand. She
carried a light bag and pocketbook slung around her shoulder. Her
trimmed hair was brushed back under a black beret. The soft rain
patted her face, a few drops hung on the strands of her hair that fell
over her forehead. She shook them off every now and then as she
walked. Occasionally she glanced over her shoulder as if expecting
someone behind her.

Already passengers were being searched at the foot of the gangplank
before going up and into the boat. A group of plainclothes police
officers scrutinized everyone. A few British soldiers waited disconsolately nearby, their rifles resting in the bends of their arms. They envied

the people leaving Belfast for England. They watched them go up the gangplank longingly, wishing for home.

Michael put the cases down on the wharf some distance from the policemen and soldiers. Nora looked at the clock tower in nearby High Street.

"We've still plenty of time," she said.

"They'll want to open these I suppose," Michael said, looking at the bulging cases. "That'll take them a while. We'd better get on with it."

But Nora put her hand on his arm to hold him back. "Can we wait a minute—just in case?"

"Just in case what?"

"Pat might show up, or . . ." She sighed, realizing it would be a lonely sendoff. She could not have expected her sister to turn up, much less her father. Her last talk with Pat was very painful. She could hardly bear to think of it. When she got back home to pack she had found her younger sister sulking in the bedroom. Nora began by trying to ignore her. She went into her bedroom to get a few things, only to find her wedding photographs missing. Pat had taken them and she refused to return them.

"You don't deserve these—you've insulted the man enough already!" she screamed from her room. Nora finally convinced her to open the door.

"Please, Pat. I spoke to John. He understands what happened; I tried not to hurt him—I love him."

Pat laughed. "You tried not to hurt him, did you. Well, that was brave of you! Nora, don't you realize what this means to him?" Her eyes flamed with anger, her sharp face seemed like a fury's under her bright red hair. Nora knew it was hopeless and merely asked for her wedding photographs back. Pat almost threw them at her.

"You've disgraced everything and everyone, Nora!" she hissed.

But Nora did not want to fight this final action. Everything she did was automatic, without thought. She knew she must keep going, not look back, stop weighing on the scales of grief the pain she was causing against the misery she would suffer if she stayed. She went back into her bedroom to clear it up. It was then she hesitated. She could not resist one last look over the garden and the mountains beyond the Down hills. She was almost relieved to find that the view had been extinguished, that the round domes of the Mournes were covered in blank gray clouds, invisible to her. Pat did not respond to her farewell. Nora had left the house as quickly as possible to join Michael.

She looked back toward the city draped in misty rain. The big, gray, ribbed gasworks tank stood out above the rooftops; the chimneys of the little houses crouched under it were smoking—the fires were lit in every home, a sure sign that autumn was here. The smoke and drizzle intermingled, wafting across the wet sheen of black slate rooftops.

The wharf groaned again as the ferry drifted gently outward. Michael walked to the edge and peered into the murky waters, oily, black. Nora touched him on the shoulder and he turned to her. Her face was wet with rain, her skin glistening, her eyes clear and fresh.

"Michael," she whispered to him. He took her by the hand and put one arm around her, holding her close to him for a moment. From over his shoulder she could see into the dark waters of the harbor rocking gently back and forth between boat and wharf. The harbor waters merged into those of the lough and into the sea beyond, the cold wintry sea. It was these waters she had gazed at from the tower in Carrickfergus Castle that winter's day many years before when they were young. Then her stomach tumbled at the sight of the faraway waves churned by the winter wind gusting from the mountains. Michael was with her then, but could not offer the reassurance she had needed, the warmth, the touch. He held her securely as she gazed into the waters, cold and inhospitable as they were then, but which would now take her to a new life.

Belfast was behind her now, shrouded in a pall of drizzle—the soaked ghettos, the children trapped resentfully in the small rooms waiting for the rain to end, the wet soldiers edging along the hostile streets, the suspiciously deserted corners, waiting, watching, listening for the next crack. She shuddered and he comforted her.

"We should go," he said softly.

But she pressed against him still. The more she looked at the waters the more the very quayside itself seemed to sway, making her feel slightly sick. The portholes of the boat were lit up; water was gushing from a hole above the water line. The boat's horn gave a sudden harsh, piercing shriek, which shook her, and she clutched him more tightly. Within hours she would be at sea with him far from this, from Belfast, from John lying awake perhaps in his bunk thinking of her. She closed her eyes tightly and tried not to remember.

She heard the sound of English voices, working-class accents of Manchester, Liverpool, London, Sheffield, Birmingham, Leeds—all strange, foreign voices from cities where nothing was known of what she was abandoning.

Michael calmly detached himself and went for the cases. Nora did not move. He stood for a second, a case in each hand, waiting. She raised her eyes toward the city, trying to peer through the mist to the mountains beyond, to see them one last time. But there was nothing beyond the gray mass of the gas tank.

"Nora," he called, walking toward the gangplank.

She turned and followed and did not look back.

It was the end of autumn and the dead leaves lay in deep drifts in the park. The smell of burning leaves filtered through Kate's apartment, hung in the air in every room. She lived a few miles northeast of London in a quiet backwater on the estuary of an old, sluggish river. Nora settled in, had her own room and began to work part-time in the library of a nearby university. In the mornings she would go to the mailbox, then the news agents, and then to the park, where she would walk and read and crunch the dry leaves underfoot. She had written once to John, but had not got a reply. Michael wrote frequently from New York, anxious to know about her visa application, when she was coming. There was nothing from her sister.

The war had been renewed; shortly after her arrival she had read of a helicopter ambush that killed three soldiers, one a high-ranking officer; of sniping attacks in streets; of bombings. She had been startled one morning to find a story about the strange suicide of Peadar McCabe—a "suicide" suspected by the police of being the end result of "internal disputes." So it was going on, endless as ever. All talk of truce and negotiations had faded from the pages of the newspapers. So the women would still be lining up, the van would still be trundling along full of cigarette smoke through the now bare countryside. Nothing would change.

Kate was a great comfort to her and urged her on to strike out for the New World, for New York. Kate admired her for what she had done and their friendship was as fresh and vibrant as ever it had been years ago. But she told her not to read the newspapers so much for news of Belfast. It was best to put it out of mind, to plan for the future. But Nora couldn't resist and read everything she could about home and what was happening there, day after day, death after death, scanning the columns looking for names.

She pressed her application diligently. There was a lot of paperwork. Finally, the visa was granted. The way was clear. She rang Michael in New York and told him. He would help pay her fare out. It only remained for her to get the tickets.

The day after the visa was issued she was walking in the park, having gone through her usual morning routine of checking the mail and going to the news agents. Under her arm was a bundle of papers. She would linger this mild morning among the beech trees and trim lawns and the blue smoke curling up from the burning piles of dry leaves. It reminded her of the Constable print that hung on her bedroom wall back home —this was his landscape, subdued, civilized, cultivated, dense with settled life. The events of the last few months seemed unreal here, where people lived such ordinary, normal lives. The mundane comforts of ordinary life came as a shock to her, a pleasing shock that she relished.

She sat on a bench near a drinking fountain that she liked. It had an old rusty iron drinking cup attached to a metal chain. The fount was full of dead leaves. She'd grown to like the landscape of the park; its quiet regularity, rather melancholy, was comforting. Now she would say good-bye to it. She was booking her flight to New York.

She opened the pages of the first newspaper and scanned the headlines. The old park attendent passed with a stick for spiking leaves. He wished her good morning. They had gotten to know each other over the weeks. She watched him shuffle along the pathway, round the corner and out of sight. She returned to her papers.

On page two, halfway down, she read:

DARING BREAK FROM NORTHERN IRELAND JAIL

Last night twelve men tunnelled their way to freedom from the Long Kesh prison camp near Belfast. Police say that among those who escaped were some of the most wanted men in the province.

She put the paper down. The name at the top of the list was Johnny Costello.